IF
SONS,
THEN
HEIRS

IF
SONS,
THEN
HEIRS

A NOVEL

LORENE CARY

ATRIA BOOKS

NEW YORK   LONDON   TORONTO   SYDNEY

ATRIA BOOKS

A Division of Simon & Schuster, Inc.
1230 Avenue of the Americas
New York, NY 10020

First Atria Books hardcover edition May 2011

ATRIA B O O K S and colophon are trademarks of Simon & Schuster, Inc.

For information about special discounts for bulk purchases,
please contact Simon & Schuster Special Sales at
1-866-506-1949 or business@simonandschuster.com.

The Simon & Schuster Speakers Bureau can bring authors
to your live event. For more information or to book an event,
contact the Simon & Schuster Speakers Bureau at
1-866-248-3049 or visit our website at www.simonspeakers.com.

Designed by Kyoko Watanabe

Manufactured in the United States of America

10   9   8   7   6   5   4   3   2   1

Library of Congress Cataloging-in-Publication Data

Cary, Lorene.
If sons, then heirs : a novel / Lorene Cary.
p.   cm.
1. Absentee mothers—Fiction. 2. Abandoned children—Fiction. 3. Families—Fiction.
I. Title.
PS3553.A78944I38   2011
813'.54—dc22   2010040093

ISBN 978-1-4516-1022-2
ISBN 978-1-4516-1024-6 (ebook)

For Robert Clarke Smith

For you have not received a spirit of slavery leading to fear again, but you have received a spirit of adoption as sons . . . And if sons, then heirs . . .

—ROMANS 8:15, 17

If we know that the past also lies in the present, we understand that we are able to change the past by transforming the present.

—THICH NHAT HANH,
OUR APPOINTMENT WITH LIFE

The NEEDHAM Family

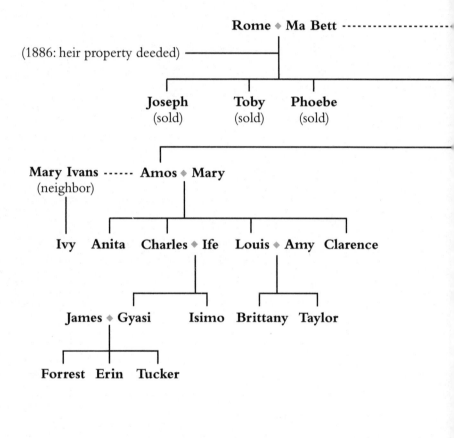

Rome ◆ Ma Bett -------------------

(1886: heir property deeded) ——————

Joseph   Toby   Phoebe
(sold)   (sold)   (sold)

Mary Ivans ------ Amos ◆ Mary
(neighbor)

Ivy   Anita   Charles ◆ Ife   Louis ◆ Amy   Clarence

James ◆ Gyasi   Isimo   Brittany   Taylor

Forrest   Erin   Tucker

Carlton ------ Lillie ----------

Khalil

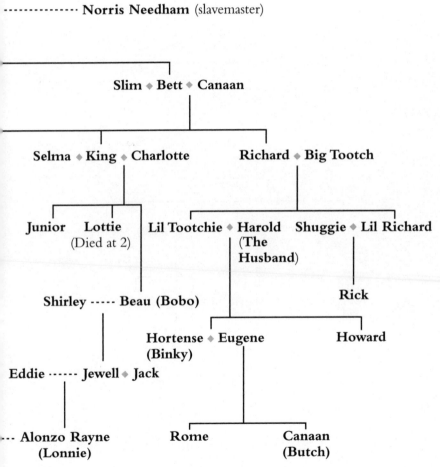

------------ **Norris Needham** (slavemaster)

Slim ◆ **Bett** ◆ **Canaan**

Selma ◆ **King** ◆ **Charlotte**   **Richard** ◆ **Big Tootch**

Junior   **Lottie**   **Lil Tootchie** ◆ **Harold**   **Shuggie** ◆ **Lil Richard**
            (Died at 2)   **(The**
                                     Husband)

                                                              Rick

Shirley ----- **Beau (Bobo)**

                  Hortense ◆ **Eugene**   **Howard**
                  (Binky)

Eddie ------ **Jewell** ◆ **Jack**

--- **Alonzo Rayne**   **Rome**   **Canaan**
    (Lonnie)   **(Butch)**

IF
SONS,
THEN
HEIRS

CHAPTER 1

Jewell Thompson nosed her sedan into the narrow Philadelphia street. She had directions on the seat next to her, and also the letter. In her mind, a voice from the past, her grandmother's, shouted: "We home!" which was ridiculous, since she'd never been on this street, or even in this section of the city, before.

Outside her noisy mind, rows of identical two-story brick houses squatted beside Cobbs Creek Park, muffled by heavy fog and a cold, early-spring, early-Sunday-morning quiet. She had to drive cautiously. No more than four or five inches separated her driver's side from the curb or her passenger's side from the parked cars, whose owners had carefully folded in their side-view mirrors. She slowed nearly to a stop when she saw house numbers that matched the return address on the letter. They were gold and white, painted onto a glossy black brick face. Prim white sills and lintels, like shirt cuffs, shone through the drizzle, and white lines traced the mortar.

When she'd left her house, Jewell had told her husband that

1

she might, depending on the way things looked, knock on the door. Now, presented with the reality of this shiny black cookie jar of a building on the misty working-class West Philadelphia street, she doubted she'd have the courage.

In front of the house grew a large sycamore that had buckled the sidewalk. At the level of the second floor, mottled limbs reached out over the street and twinkled with tiny white Christmas lights. An extension cord connected them to the second-floor window. She couldn't quite see, but it looked as if they'd drilled a hole in the storm-window trim for the cord, so as not to have to leave the window open. Jewell smiled to herself. Clever. She imagined that the lights made the little street feel inviting at night. A parking space under the tree beckoned, but it seemed too close and obvious, so she let her car roll forward one car length to the stop sign. Some bright, false part of herself congratulated her on the trip: *There, done. Now I can go home.*

Instead, she sat motionless at the stop sign. She did not even notice the large red pickup truck behind her, until the driver touched his horn. In her rearview mirror, she could see a man of about thirty, who seemed to fill the cab. He indicated the parking space under the tree, which he could not maneuver into with her car in the way. The truck would have to swing out very wide. Jewell crossed the intersection, put her foot onto the brake, and checked her rearview mirror again. The big, ocher-colored man was unfolding himself from the cab of the truck and stepping into the street. She shifted in her seat to see him better. He looked familiar.

The letter to her was folded in its envelope on the front seat. She'd read its block capital letters so often in the past week, she almost knew it by heart.

Dear Ms. Jewell Thompson,
    I am looking for my mother, formerly Jewell Needham,

the daughter of Bobo Needham, originally from the town of Gunnerson in Beaufort County, SC. Please let me know if you are that lady.

We lived in New York, in Harlem, I think, until I was about 7. Then I was sent to my grandfather Bobo Needham and his stepmother Selma Needham in SC, who also raised him.

Now I am 30 years old. I am doing well, I am a contractor now, and just received my first contract with the city of Philadelphia. I said that I wished I could tell you, and my girlfriend suggested that I write this, and she would try to find an address for me to send it to. I live with my girlfriend and her son. He is about the age I was when I was separated from my mother. That's another reason I'm writing. Watching him grow has made me think about you.

I hope that you will agree to meet. If you are not the right person, please let me know. This could just be one meeting, if you like, it doesn't have to be more.

Here's my information for home or work. Email is best or cell.

Sincerely,
Alonzo Rayne

That was Lonnie in the truck behind Jewell. She knew it.

Jewell remembered her son's deep-set, coffee black-brown eyes, like her grandfather's. A big gap between his front teeth came from her grandfather, too. When Jewell had allowed herself to think of Lonnie as a man, she'd fitted his seven-year-old face into the image in her head of her grandfather King's old sepia-toned photo. Nana Selma had had a mantel built, sans fireplace, just to make a proper display, like an altar, for that photograph.

It had been taken by a black photographer in Columbia, whom Selma referred to as famous. Later, when Jewell learned about African ancestor worship, she thought of that photo. Surely, the hulking farmer in his white shirt and stiff collar had seemed to live with them. Selma spoke to him as she walked by. She asked questions of him in passing, and seemed to receive answers.

King had been a big, pale man burned bronze by the sun. His head and neck and shoulders filled the frame; the wide mouth and jaw were set, as if against the coming misfortune. His deep-set eyes looked straight and unsmilingly from under dark, arched brows into the small room that his father had built and he had improved. Jewell had been afraid of those eyes and their judgment. Now she was similarly afraid of her son's.

His letter had been perfectly cordial, but, surely, he had to remember what she had done, just as she remembered and could never forget, starting with the train.

Jewell had put him onto that southbound train and convinced herself that he'd be riding into a new, wholesome boyhood. "He's much better off." Recalling how far she'd sunk back then, she'd repeated it to herself through the years: "*much better off*." And, until this moment, she'd mostly been able to keep herself from thinking about how very deeply he might hate her.

She stopped the car and watched him in the mirror. It looked as if he were even taller than her father, big and hulking like him, with a walk that rolled his shoulders side to side. On his head he wore a skullcap stretched over thick dreadlocks that reminded her of how unruly his hair had been when he was a boy. He unloaded from the back of the truck two boxes, walked them to the black-and-white house, and rang the bell. A young woman peeked her head out into the drizzle; slim, brown, animated, she waved her hands even as he shook his head no. She had big hair, too, twists or some similar style that poked out in all directions.

She stepped onto the stoop and clearly strained to pick up one box and take it inside. They were open boxes filled with objects Jewell could not identify, except to see that the heavy contents seemed to slide when the young woman tried to pick up the top one.

He called to her. Jewell saw his raised hand make a dismissing movement, which the young woman ignored. Instead, she called into the house. A boy of about seven erupted from the doorway, danced a little moonwalk on the top step, then held the door for her, hands and legs moving in place. With that, she bent deep and hoisted and then carried first one box, then the other. Once the woman finished, the boy banged the door closed and ran shouting into the quiet street. Lonnie—Jewell called him that in her mind—pointed to the truck bed and spoke to the boy. It looked as if he was directing him to carry something else into the house. The boy climbed up onto the bumper and reached in at the same time that Lonnie pulled out another box. Instead of grabbing his own parcel, however, the child vaulted onto Lonnie's back, laughing. Lonnie bent forward slightly to accommodate him, said something to him sideways, then stopped in the middle of the street to regard Jewell's car and the woman inside it, watching *him*. He squinted pointedly through the dim drizzled light at the rearview mirror and opened his big hands in an impatient gesture that communicated: "What are you looking at?" to Jewell.

Flushed and embarrassed, Jewell took off too fast down the one-way street.

The next intersecting street went the wrong way to aim her back toward the expressway. One block more took her to a street that was stoppered with a police barrier around construction. Although she was turned around now and confused, Jewell decided, superstitiously, that her way home was blocked because she was supposed to drive back to Lonnie's house and introduce herself.

Besides, she wanted to see him close up. She wanted to feel again the totally undeserved surge of pride that had filled her as she'd watched him, with his rolling gait and strength, and his relationships, whatever they were, with the young woman with hair as big and wild as his own and the boy who whooped with glee and jumped onto his back. She wondered if he still had his great-grandfather's gap-toothed smile. How could such a person have burst, full-grown, into her life?

———

It was a strange feeling. The driver of the champagne-colored Lexus on the next block was studying him, and so intently that when Alonzo Freeman Rayne looked up and squinted into her rearview mirror, it was as if the driver didn't register the challenge, but only continued to observe. Rayne stared at her hard. At first he thought she was a case of early-morning road rage, pissed off because he'd urged her forward to let him into the parking space in front of the house. But she had not seemed offended: no visible huffing and puffing, no flip of the finger. From what he could see at this distance, she appeared simply to have been watching, head to the side—was he imagining her smiling?—as if he were a movie.

It crossed Rayne's mind that the woman in the car might be his mother responding to the letter he'd sent just three weeks before. His mother had smiled that day on the train when she left, a memory that clicked into his brain like the sound of an accident: not the image of her so much as the fact of the smile. Now it came back to him. And had Khalil not hopped onto his back, Rayne would have walked toward her, to get a better view or, if he didn't like what he saw, to move her along.

From a distance the driver looked white. Did his mother, really? For years he'd assumed that he'd know her when he saw her, but now he knew that he couldn't. He could only conjure bits of feelings about her or moments: he remembered the train, holding on to the fine material of her skirt, and then letting go. He remembered that she smiled at him with such love that in the years after, he could never believe the things his grandfather said about her. And he remembered the loss of her that seared him to his bowels; just the smallest incitement could ignite the rage that had made him want to burn things, burn houses, burn his own house, with himself in it even, in hopes that she'd come, see, smell, hear his cries, and finally, finally, love him.

In his adolescence Rayne had taken up boxing. His grandfather Bobo suggested it, having correctly gauged the depth of the boy's sullenness. And, indeed, Rayne came to life in the Philadelphia gym of a man named Magic, who encouraged him and other young men to feed their hungers with closed fists. Rayne's big, long arms knocked boys down. He would let a boy come at him with a hard chin, lean out and away from his fists, and then he'd come in close and hard with a few uppercuts that the opponent couldn't have expected; then he'd rear back, feint a little, all this fast, so fast that his mind knew it in the body only, and couldn't say it; then rock back on the heels and check for the other guy's fear, see it, hold it in mind, then plant his feet, find the open millisecond, and throw in the hardest punch his opponent had ever taken—each time it was to be a better punch than ever before, the punch he trained for with the heaviest heavy bag Magic had, going at it again and again, past exhaustion, running harder and longer than the other boys, bringing all of it into his shoulder and arm—and slamming it into a young man's chin. One time he actually sheared off a tiny bit of bone; he knocked one boy's tooth out, and drove another's back into his gum, laying open part of his face, shocking him, insulting him, rearranging.

———

One of Lillie's Zen stories told about a man holding on to a branch with a tiger above him and a deep gully below. Rayne usually forgot the whole story, but that image described how he'd felt through much of his adolescence. The sense he had on the train that his mother loved him so perfectly, exclusively, in a way no one else could ever know, had not been confirmed. After all, she did not come get him that September when school began. She did not come back for him at all. But he held on anyway, because there was a tiger above and a gully beneath. Boxing helped him hold on, at least until Bobo went to prison.

Then, the discipline of boxing held him over into adulthood. It sopped up some of the anger that used to slosh into his sunny days and threatened to drown him in plain sight of the whole wide world. By the time Lonnie reached manhood, his own rage was not inevitably the final word, though great quantities of it had been compacted and stored in basement catacombs, not dead but buried alive, like the Irishmen he'd heard about who'd contracted cholera in nineteenth-century Philadelphia. They'd gone into comas, and been buried, only to wake up underground.

Sometimes he felt it stir with Lillie. It was not her fault, but since he'd moved into her house, she could get in there where the monster lived.

"There's a guy came to the hospital to see his little boy," she told him, "and instead of asking the kid how he feels, he just roars at 'im. *Roar!*"

"That's what you should do for Khalil. He'd love it."

"Nah, that's what I'ma do to *you* when you get like that, because can't nobody talk to you."

Roar! It was their shorthand. He'd want to rip the head off something alive, but would go outdoors instead and trot along Cobbs Creek. You could do a lot of miles on Cobbs Creek. He'd wear himself out and come home spent, no need to roar.

Lillie had suggested, the year before, that he write his mother.

At first it seemed to come out of nowhere, and it annoyed him. She told him that if he wrote the letter, she'd help him find an address. He'd told her that he was not trying to dredge anything up.

When you're ready, she'd said.

He hadn't liked the word *ready.*

———

The image of his mother in Rayne's mind was of a flawless twenty-year-old beauty with dark, shiny hair, shining eyes, perfectly bowed red lips, and an expression of perfect contentment. It was from a photo she'd had taken and sent to Selma when they lived in New York. The caption, written in black ink, said: "To Nana Selma, from your rascal in New York—who won't give up!"

Rayne had no personal memory strong enough to trump that stunning picture, which remained as sharp and glossy in his mind as it had in the bottom drawer where his grandfather Bobo kept it out of sight. When he'd first found it at age twelve, Rayne had just about lost the ability to see her face clearly in his mind. The image underneath Bobo's old socks, which Rayne had gone to pilfer, appeared so beautiful that he burst into tears, right there in his grandfather's dusty old bedroom in Selma's otherwise fastidious little farmhouse. Rayne vowed that that would be the last time he cried for her.

Now the image stayed submerged, mostly, down at the bottom of his brain stem, quite perfect, engaged in a vague personal tragedy almost separate from himself. His memories of his mother had been surfacing since the letter, which he wrote the night after Khalil, squatting over a pile of junk just like this one, had ventured to call him Dad.

———

On this raw Sunday morning as he prepared to drive to Gunnerson, South Carolina, the creamy Lexus purred away and did not come back. Rayne decided that the Sunday-morning white lady was probably a real estate agent hoping that the latest foreclosure might be worth more than three dollars and eighty-five cents. Halfway through her two-year nursing program, Lillie had dropped behind in her monthly payments, with only a few years to go to finish off her mother's mortgage. It was why he'd moved in with her. Who knew that six months into it Khalil, who'd been so cool for a year, would squat among the found objects—or Found Lost, as Lillie had scrawled on the back brick wall—and address him, secretly, with penetrating intimacy, as Dad with love that made him want to run?

But after the car drove away and did not circle back, Rayne dismissed the moment, finished unpacking the truck, and went inside quickly to lay out the stuff, say good-bye, and get on the road to his Nana Selma's. He could almost hear her calling "Yoo-hoo!" as he did.

Yoo-hoo. You comin home? Or what?

CHAPTER 2

I t was already past seven. Lillie was filling the cooler with lunch, dinner, and snacks. She was very careful and very intentional about food. As a nursing student and the daughter of a diabetic Filipina mother and an alcoholic black father, she said, she had no choice. She said it regularly as a matter of faith, and Rayne never failed to laugh and counter: "Oh, you had some choices, there, baby. You had choices." To tease her, Rayne said that he was hoping to grab fast food on the drive.

She'd already put a twelve-pack of water bottles and his construction thermos filled with fresh coffee next to his duffel bag by the vestibule. She'd peeled his favorite navel oranges, torn them into sections, and put them into a plastic container for him to eat right away. The house smelled of coffee and oranges, which made him want to sit down in the kitchen and read the paper as he had when they'd first fallen in love and she'd spent the night at his apartment. No morning now was that relaxed. Every day was a push as Lillie powered through a two-year postgrad nursing program at Jefferson University, "while she had the help," she'd once said before apologizing, but that's how it was: he'd cosigned the educational loan, and he was paying the mortgage on the little house her parents had left her. At first Rayne and Lillie said that living together would be "like family," which each of them missed: hers having died young, his, in prison, down South, gone. But, in fact, the easygoing lovers made for watchful, even tense, cohabitants. Everything was hard: nursing school was hard; starting the construction business was hard; sharing the space and their lives tentatively, and figuring out how to handle the boy together; all of it kept them on edge. And Rayne's sense that she was pushing him to be other than he was. Only Lillie's son, Khalil, made the decision to commit, full stop.

Lillie bent over the cooler as Rayne walked the boxes through the house to the backyard, making sure not to let them weep dust along the way. The thin floorboards vibrated. The countertop was crowded with food, and it irritated him that she worked so hard. He really would have been just as happy with fast food.

"Everything all right?" she asked, head down.

"Yeah. I told you that I had to go make sure they'd locked up the little job downtown properly, didn't I?"

Lillie flashed him a tight grin and shrug; he'd left at 5:00 a.m., after she'd obliged him with perfunctory early-morning sex. He'd said something, sure, but she couldn't remember what.

He told her how he'd driven to his shop in North Philly to collect the boxes quickly at 5:20 a.m. and to switch trucks. Then, when he drove by the downtown construction job whose building permit was still pending, he saw that the demo crew he'd hired had "lost" the padlock on the construction door and tied it with an old rope. He'd thought about simply nailing the place shut, but the neighbors there were suspicious. Instead, he drove back to the shop in North Philly for a new padlock, left the new key on his desk with a note, and drove back downtown to secure the building before leaving town for five days. "So now it's seven, and I should be, like, halfway through Maryland."

———————

"Khalil would've been happy with one box," Lillie said as Rayne stomped through with the last of the heavy parcels. Everything in them was made of metal and brick, concrete and wood. There were faucets with glass handles cut in the shapes of long crystals, claw feet without their table legs, a large, rusty knocker forged in the shape of a wolf's head. "Spring vacation is just for the week."

"You know what I really want?" Rayne stopped and shifted the box under his arm. Lillie's glasses were on, and her thick, wild hair was pulled back and tied in a scarf as always when she cooked. The warm kitchen smelled of corn bread. This was as close to home as he could imagine creating; but he did not trust contentment. Neither, Lillie admitted, did she.

"What do you really want?" she asked. She came toward him, pulled the step stool from the corner with her foot, stepped up, and kissed him deeply. A desire flared up and caught them off guard, careful as Lillie usually was when Khalil was nearby.

Rayne held her to him with his free arm. She smelled like oranges and early morning. "I must have been too fast this morning."

"I was sleepy."

"Now you're awake."

"It's seven o'clock."

"Just a quickie."

Lillie surprised him by looking slyly from him to the kitchen door to the yard and back again. "Give him that box." Then she scampered upstairs.

When Rayne stepped into the backyard, a chilly mist carried

the familiar smell of horses. From the box he was carrying, he handed Khalil what he thought was the best find of the lot: a stone-carved gargoyle about a foot and a half high. Khalil made a first inspection, running his palm over the spikes and curves and poking his finger down its throat. Rayne explained that a downspout would run into a pipe in the throat to conduct rainwater, and they could make a small funnel from the house downspout through this gargoyle when they mounted it.

"If your mom says yes. I'll have to angle it so that it hits the drain there by the corner of the house."

"Whoa," Khalil said. He cradled the heavy demon to his wiry body and sank down onto his haunches to inspect it, ignoring the sound that still startled Rayne each time he heard it here in West Philadelphia: the whinny of a horse and the pawing of her hooves on the packed yard.

Across the alley from Lillie, a bizarre, quasi-legal stable, maintained by a leathery urban cowboy in his sixties, took up two house plots on the next street. It featured a dirt yard, alternately dusty, muddy, or frozen throughout the seasons, where one beautiful old chestnut mare sometimes came out for air, or to be saddled, or groomed. The horseman wore a hard brown saddlebag frown and a dusty cocoa-brown cowboy hat and chaps. He ching-chinged through Rite Aid and Pathmark in pointed boots with spurs. He and a dozen and a half comrades called themselves Buffalo Soldiers. They rode singly or in a movie-soundtrack cantering group over the tough green-and-brown bank of Cobbs Creek. On Saturdays they gave rides and dispensed history lessons and tough love to neighborhood boys.

At first Rayne had leaned a ladder against the wall so that Khalil could climb up and look into the tiny corral. Soon enough, the boy began to play on the ladder, straddling one of the middle rungs and the top of the fence, or grabbing a handhold on the sill of the bay window. They began to plan the

Climbing Wall to replace the ladder, with a perch past the second story that would command a view of the barn and the alley. The found objects from Rayne's demo sites would serve as handholds and foot supports. Lillie had not okayed the idea yet, so Rayne had held off building, just as he'd held off stripping the black paint off the front. Until she came around, he told Khalil, they could sort and design the wall, and then redesign and draw plans.

When Rayne brought in his boxes of found objects, he and the boy knelt together in the intimate space under the bay-window overhang, discussing their attributes and possible placements. It was there that Khalil had first called Rayne Dad, so quietly and tentatively that Rayne could not be sure he'd heard properly. And it was in that same space now, crowded with new boxes for Khalil's inspection, where Khalil asked, as lightly and naturally as if Rayne were going to the supermarket: "Can I go?"

Rayne's hand was on the storm door knob, and his mind had already traveled upstairs to where he hoped Lillie was still waiting. Had he heard him?

"To South Carolina?"

Khalil nodded. "Yeah. It's Easter break. I'm off'a school anyway. Ooh—and we could go fishing in that mermaid place, where you said the sea backs up into the river."

Khalil looked up at Rayne, wanting to ask again but afraid to knock over the delicate balance of Rayne's quite real consideration. Khalil gripped the gargoyle's head and dragged his hand over the ears and across the rough neck, as if he were petting a new family dragon.

"Can I?" Khalil asked again, almost a whisper that traveled nearly six feet up to Rayne's ears only.

They'd talked about it that year: the fact that Khalil was just about old enough to join Rayne on a trip south; how good it would be for him to have the experience of earlier generations, to spend time in a rural setting, to know from their own experience that black people hadn't always lived stacked in match-boxes, and that they owned land and barns and silos, that they had rights to water from creeks and streams. Besides, speaking of that land, Rayne planned to talk to Nana Selma about selling it so that he could set her up, down there or closer to him in Philadelphia, in a nice retirement facility. It was not a conversation he looked forward to having with her. Khalil would be the perfect buffer.

"If it's okay with your mother, it's okay with me."

Khalil jumped right up from where he'd been squatting.

"Shh–shh–shh. Yo, Lil. Half a yes can still mean no. Lemme ask her. You stay here. I'ma go ask her. Do not come in till I call you. Hear me?"

"You don't want me to go pack?"

"C'mon, man, don't wreck it. What I tell you? Lemme go talk to your mom, okay? So we get everything straight about when I'm gone. Okay?"

Khalil did not look up, but shook his head happily. He put down the gargoyle, selected a screwdriver from the small, ancient toolbox Rayne had given him, and tried to release a purple glass doorknob from its rusted housing.

"Here," Rayne said, reaching into the corner of the toolbox for a can of WD-40. "Soak it up real good for five minutes and then go back to it. Use that rag over there to hold the knob so you don't drop it when it's greasy.

"Don't come up till somebody tells you, hear?"

———

Upstairs, Rayne stopped in the bathroom to wash his hands. He scrubbed them under the hot water, not only to clean but also to warm them. When he stepped into the bedroom, Lillie closed and locked the door behind him. She had taken off her clothes and glasses and scarf. He breathed in sudden delight. She used to call it the sneak attack, one of his favorite surprises in his apartment after he gave her the key. She'd be waiting for him, nude, sometimes sitting in the living room, wrapped in a blanket. "Do me!"

Now she said, "What took you so long? Look, I turned on the computer. I was about to check e-mail," she said, loosening his belt and pants.

"E-mail get you hot?"

"Depends. You send me anything good?"

"Khalil was talking to me. He had something to ask me."

"Shhh. Stop talkin. Pick me up. Come on. Just like that."

———

They enjoyed each other fast and hard and simply. They laughed and groaned together happily, easy, like before. Rayne called it country sex, suitable for barns and lean-tos, best suited for early morning or late evening, unwashed. When they finished, he sat down with her straddling him on their one bedroom chair.

"Khalil asked me to take 'im. I said yes—if you agreed."

"What do you mean, take 'im?"

"Take him with me today for the week."

"Down South?"

"Yeah, down South. What do you say: five days to study alone?"

"Five days? You sure? It's a lot, baby. The K-boy's a handful when you take him on twenty-four seven. Or even twenty-four five."

"You think I'll leave 'im at the rest area?"

"Hadn't thought of that. Scary."

"I won't. This'll be good for us. So, he's seven. That's how old I was when I went down there to live."

"Oh, so you're gonna take 'im and leave 'im there. Compulsive repetition. You are not convincing me that this is a good idea."

"Nah, baby, Nana Selma ain't in the kid business no more. I guess I want him to see the old place."

"Okay. I can't believe I'm giving you push-back, bad as I need study time. He asked you? He must've been thinkin about it all the time since we talked about it. He hasn't mentioned it to me."

"He's strategic."

"Yep."

"And when I come back, can I get some?" He made a nest in the top of her hair, laid his head in it and surprised himself by dozing. He was back on the farm. As soon as his neck threatened to relax, he woke.

"What are you thinking?" he asked.

"Nothing."

"Yes, you are, you were thinking so loud it woke me up."

"Khalil loves you. If anything happens between us, it'll break his heart. That's what I was thinking. And then I was thinking how I shouldn't say that, because it might sound desperate."

"We said we'd get you through school, baby. Let's do one thing at a time."

"That's what we're doin," she said. "Khalil's busy with his own agenda."

"I get it, baby," Rayne said. "Who you think gets it more than I do? Now, lemme get goin and try to talk this old lady outta that damn trailer in the swamp."

"She could come here, you know. I'm fine with it. I've told you that."

He wrapped his fleece sweater around her naked back, feeling the fineness of her skin against his rough hands. Selma had lived on that same land since she was a girl. "Might take dynamite to blast her off the place."

"Well, maybe you've gotta just tell 'er no."

"Yeah. That's what I tell her. She says I was born to inherit that land, and I tell her I was born so that somebody could say no to her besides King."

"Did he ever say no to her?"

"He never had to. She worshipped him. She was a girl, really, when they married. Like seventeen or eighteen."

"Maybe she's got another twenty years in 'er. You said she was tough . . . Oh, God, I hear Khalil calling," Lillie said. She pulled on her clothes so fast that Rayne felt the breeze of her movement. She motioned for him to pull up his pants. Rayne reached for a handful of her hair before she pulled it through an elastic and retied her scarf. She swatted his hand, then turned with the bright look of a new idea: "Bring back some farm implements or handles or something from down there for the Climbing Wall," Lillie said.

"Whoa. That's perfect. Why didn't I think of that?"

———

When they opened their door, Khalil was standing at the top of the stairs with his backpack.

"Man, didn't I tell you stay downstairs?" Rayne said.

"I was just gettin my stuff. So I'd be ready."

Lillie looked from one to the other, afraid to trust the love her boy had for this man. "I gotta pack his stuff, and that's putting you even later," Lillie said.

"No, see," Khalil said, pointing to the backpack, "I packed!"

"C'mon, baby," Rayne said. "Just some jeans and a couple T-shirts and some drawers."

"I packed. All that stuff I packed already."

"Toothbrush?"

Khalil jumped sideways into the bathroom and grabbed it along with his brush. He shoved them into the bag.

"And his asthma medicine," Lillie said. She'd crossed to the top of the steps, scooped up the backpack, and was looking through the clothes stuffed in.

"I don't really need the medicine anymore."

"You wanna go?" Lillie asked her son pointedly. Then to Rayne she added: "I know you think I fuss too much. But this is the time of year he gets it. Weather changes, and boom."

"No, you're right. We don't want 'im fallin out down there. It's the country, Little Man. Your medicine might not have been invented down there yet." He spoke to Khalil, but motioned his chin in the direction of the boy's room, where Lillie was opening and slamming drawers.

Khalil made a face meant to show how ridiculous that sounded, but he also appeared just a tiny bit nonplussed.

"No socks, Khalil," Lillie shouted so that he could hear her. "No underwear."

Rayne raised his eyebrows. Khalil made an embarrassed face and batted Rayne's big hand between his smaller ones, hitting it back and forth to contain his excitement.

———

"I'ma go pack up the truck," Rayne called to Lillie.

"Oh, geez, I gotta put in more food." She came from the room with the backpack and an ancient half-sized duffel bag with Oscar the Grouch on one side. "Here."

Khalil groaned. He'd tried to avoid that bag.

"Nah, baby, we got food for the century. 'Sides, he only half eats anyway."

"You gotta make 'im eat."

"Not a problem, baby. Boy, Nana Selma will make 'im eat."

As if on cue, Rayne's cell phone rang. Nana Selma shouted into the phone from South Carolina: "Hey! You comin or what?"

Rayne grinned into the phone. "You cookin?"

"Your Chinee girl with all that crazy nappy hair, whatsername: I called the house earlier; she say you at the job. So I wanna know how you at the job and coming to South Carolina by supper?"

"Lillie. Her name's Lillie. I may not make it by suppertime," he said, using the old country meal designation.

"You certainly will *not* make it by suppertime. I be lucky you get here by bedtime."

"I had to check my locks, Nana. My foreman moved down South, and the other guys just don't pay attention."

"You sound like your great-grandfather. All right, Big Man, you handle your business. I'ma see can I put some clean sheets for you. You gonna be sleepin in your old room in the house or you wanna bunk in the trailer here with me?"

"How cold is it?"

"It's cold enough. But JJ fixed that little whatchacallit, stove; he fixed it and he said he lef' some firewood behin' the house. I ain't been out to see."

"The stove? What was wrong with the stove? Those things are cast iron. JJ doesn't know about those old stoves." She did not quite sound herself. Rayne wondered whether she was slurring her words.

"Box stove. That's it. No, he just cleared out the flue after some critter got in and made a nest. It was a mess. So where you want?"

"I'll stay in the house. But don't make up the bed. I'll do that when I come." He decided not to tell her that Khalil was coming, so she wouldn't begin to fuss about that, too.

"You come before sundown, I'm warning you, all you gonna see is weeds—they done took me over. First shoots of green: nothing but weeds. You just have to find me in the underbrush somewhere, peepin out, like that little old ant in the funnies. 'Member him?"

It was a joke that she still liked, a pantomime that she'd do in person sometimes: the tiny, antennaed black insect who popped up in the corner of old animated shorts, bug-eyed and with big white grinning lips, a wise guy inserted to give the smart-aleck, darky-style last word.

Who dat?

Who day say who dat?

Who dat say who dat when I say who dat?

Selma seemed even more amused when Rayne became old enough to take offense. This time on the phone, however, he laughed right along with her, glad to hear her tease after what seemed like slightly halting words: herself, but older.

"All right, all right, Nana. You still ain't told me whether you were cooking."

"I have told you before: I don't hardly cook no more for myself. Look, I don't know. Big as you is, it's hard to keep enough in the house."

"Grits, barbecue, sweet potatoes, greens: Nana, you know the drill."

"You better bring *me* sompin."

"Macaroni and cheese, rice and gravy. Anything. Nana, you're killin me."

She laughed easily. He could hear her tip her head back from the phone. "Honey, your Nana is just plain *old*. You don't seem to realize. Come on down. See how I feel today. You gonna be so late, maybe I'll just start getting things ready for tomorrow. I'll have a bite of sompin here tonight. Just get on the road!"

CHAPTER 3

Jewell tried to recall the pattern of one-way streets, but a tiny park and then a new-looking inner-city shopping mall had been built where she thought she should go. By the time she returned to where she figured her son's block should be, she'd driven instead to Market Street under the elevated train and into a construction zone.

The El roared. Jewell felt as if the roadbed underneath her were shaking. On either side of her were stacks of big-construction material: steel beams, concrete pillars on their sides, wide wooden planks. Dirt hills rose up under the elevated train tracks. Puddles gave a false surface to potholes. Beams, sewer pipes six feet across, and reclaimed timber blocked her way, forcing her to drive in a sloppy zigzag. After several blocks she noticed that not one other car was moving on Market Street. Somehow, she'd gone very wrong. Now and then a person walked across the street, looking everywhere so as not to step in mud or uneven concrete and asphalt surfaces. But each tiny street leading to and from Market was blocked. How had she gotten so lost in the city she thought she knew? This was a black alternate universe: and now a universe under construction.

She put the car into reverse to turn around. Red-brown construction clay was piled up behind her like an impromptu Indian burial mound. Next to it were a few municipal trucks and an earthmover. She had never liked backing up in this car, whose trunk was less easy to estimate than her old hatchback. She did not want to hit the dusty municipal vehicles parked haphazardly around the mound, so she swung her gaze from one side of the car to the other to avoid them.

Clearly she'd driven from *some* street into this muddy no-outlet mess, she was thinking, and there must be at least one street, if only that one, that could lead out. She was deciding to go the wrong way on that street if necessary, just to get out of there, when, at once, she saw a man who'd materialized between her car and the mound, and felt and heard him banging on her trunk and shouting at her to stop backing up. Jewell jammed her brakes so hard that she felt the ABS system buck over the slippery mud. But she managed not to hit him, a small, earth-colored gnome wearing a gray raincoat. She knew when he rounded the back corner of her car, bawling the whole way, that she had just missed hitting him, and that she easily could have done so had he not punched the car.

"Jesus!" he called out in a scratchy tenor voice that grated. "Jesus!" he cried again, now that she saw him. "What're you doin? Where you going? Ain't even no cars driving. How'd you get in here, lady? Jesus have mercy."

She expected him to move from behind the car, but he didn't. Looked as if he couldn't. The El roared over, rattling them both. He was yelling again, but she couldn't hear him, and the entire place, though deserted, seemed so busy and noisy, filled with so much grime and dirt, she almost couldn't stand it. As soon as the El passed, she felt, they'd be able to break out of their poses. She could get out of the car, he'd step out, and they'd both see that he was all right and that she was very, very sorry. She began to breathe.

Then, out of nowhere, at least half a dozen people emerged. *From where?* she wondered. As the El rumbled away, she could hear them clucking and grumbling, *chuff chuff chuff,* righteous group indignation. An officious man about her age, with large, suspicious eyes, caught her gaze, making sure to purse his lips pointedly and stare her down to show her his disapproval before he walked behind the car with exaggerated care. He was taking in her creamy car and creamy skin. Men had desired her since she was twelve and hated her for it. She could feel it.

He shouted: "Is that thing in neutral? Is it in park? Can you put on the emergency brake?" He escorted the still paralyzed older man to the side of the car. Jewell had lowered the front window, intending to ask the man's forgiveness. Now, with the little group of people turning into a tiny ad hoc crowd, she stepped out into the cold damp. The air tasted like suspended particles of dust. A few people popped out of a storefront and picked their way across Market Street with quick-moving excitement. At least two were drunk, with one woman calling out from across the street that she'd seen it all, that the crazy white woman in the Lexus was dangerous, that the man had been knocked over, that Jewell had been driving like a maniac, a bat outta hell, on the damn sidewalk and everything.

Jewell looked at the little brown-and-gray man, now held under the arm by his officious advocate. She wished that she were alone with the man so that she could apologize and ask him how he was without a hostile chorus. She wanted to tell him that she was sorry to have scared him, that she hoped she hadn't hurt him, that there was no way she could have seen him, with the mound, as big as a trailer, really, hiding him completely.

She imagined herself saying that she'd made some great connec-
tions *by accident,* including her husband. The little man looked
like the type who would laugh with her, friendly-like, once he'd
gotten over his fear.

Instead, the small crowd ringed the front of her car and stood
between them. The loud, drunk woman escalated her alarm.
"That crazy white bitch is comin out the car. Watch 'er hands.
What she grab her purse for?"

"She's scared when she get out the car somebody gonna
take it."

"Maybe she's tryin to pay 'im off."

"He could sue anyway."

"Pay *me* off: hey, for a thousand dollars, I ain't seen *nothin!*"

"Could be a gun."

"Tha's more likely."

"Crazy white bitches carry them cute little guns. Little
motherfuckin pearl-handle guns."

Jewell was shocked at the sudden vitriol—and something
familiar.

She did indeed come from a family of gun-toters, and she
felt it now, their presence, or at least their influence. She'd been
afraid as they'd started toward her. Now the woman's talk enraged her.

"What if I do?"

"White bitch *crazy.*"

"Whatever I got is legal for me to carry." Jewell found herself holding the clutch purse, which she'd grabbed out of habit,
above her head and shouting: "You back up. You back up and
let me talk to the man. And *I am not . . . white.* Stop saying that."

"Oh, oh, well, she crazy and the bitch almost kilt the man,
but she ain't white," the woman began to yell. "So now we safe."

"I feel safer already," said one man, beginning to snort.

In her head, Jewell could hear her lawyer husband, Jack, cautioning her to say nothing that people could use against her later. He would say that she'd already said too much.

The little gnome, who Jewell saw was holding a zip-covered Bible, let out a high-pitched rolling peal of laughter. The openness of the laugh communicated a mischievous goodwill that suddenly reminded her of video she'd seen of Desmond Tutu. Over the objections of his self-appointed bodyguard, the man reached out cold, gnarled hands and held her gloved fingers tightly. He looked up at her with his round face smiling.

"But, sir," Jewell said, "I am very, very sorry."

He reached up to kiss her. She bent down toward him. His face and nose were cold on her cheek. She breathed in his strong Bay Rum aftershave, a smell she remembered from her own father.

"Well," he said in a Caribbean lilt, "I am not dead, as we see, so all's well that ends well." Then he laughed again at his own wit.

Jewell thought of a way to get out of this situation. "If you're going to church," she said as the next El approached, "I can drive you there."

"What?"

People shouted the offer to him and to one another over the noise. The discarded bodyguard was shaking his head no, and making a lowing sound to signify that they were wrong to let this thing pass. "I wouldn't, sir. If I were you, I wouldn't. You haven't seen any documentation, any paperwork. You should probably get some information . . ." He reached into his breast pocket, feeling for a pen that Jewell suspected he knew damn well was not there.

The little crowd divided:

"She may not be white, but half-black don't mean she can drive."

"She ain't half, maybe a quarter."

"You can't tell."

"I can. My granmuvver were whiter than her with blue eyes."

"Black and blue, maybe!"

"I swear he should not get into that car with that bitch and the gun."

"What she gonna do? Shoot 'im now that we all seen 'er?"

"Oh, come on, the man grown."

"He better hold tight to that Bible."

"See, that's what you don't know: a prayin man don't have to fear."

"Not like niggers who get up on Sunday and have a drink!"

As they talked, the man thanked his advocate, shook hands with him, and allowed him to walk him, held by the elbow, to the passenger side of the car. Once inside, the man said, smiling, both at Jewell and at his audience through the windshield, "All right. Let's get out of here while we can. Turn around like you were doing and you have to go about five blocks to get out. I know where."

He told her to call him Jubilee. Together, with his strong aftershave circulating through the heating system and filling the car, the two navigated their way out of the construction area and back onto the streets. Once Jewell was headed toward his church, Jubilee sat back to enjoy the car's many features.

"Hey, what an automobile. I'm like the ambassador or the movie lady with Morgan Freeman."

"Driving Mr. Jubilee."

"Hah! Then tell me, what's this? Oh, it moves the seat up and down. Is this real wood paneling that I'm rubbing and getting fingerprints on? Very smooth."

"Help yourself, Mr. Jubilee."

"Much better than Morgan Freeman . . . Look, take a right here, go half a block to that little corner, see? And we'll go through the alley to Fifty-sixth Street, and then up to Fifty-second, and I'll take you through the park."

He opened the glove compartment, scanned the manual, and asked her to turn on his seat warmer. In about a minute, he lay back, closed his eyes, and chuckled his satisfaction.

They arrived at his church, an astonishing French Gothic cathedral in the middle of a tough neighborhood. Forcefully, he invited Jewell in, certain, he said, that God had brought them together for the purpose. Just as certainly, Jewell refused. She told him that she'd promised her husband, who was very ill, that she'd be home in time to make him a lunch. The old man ventured as how maybe that was what was on her mind under the El.

"Actually," she said, suddenly confessional, "I was thinking of my son."

"Oh, my dear. He is not well?"

"No, Mr. Jubilee. He is just fine, although it is no thanks to me."

"Oh, I see." He poked out his bottom lip and nodded thoughtfully. "Does he live over this way? Near where we met?"

"I believe so, yes."

"Oh, and you were looking for him, but bumped into me—almost bumped into me—instead."

Jewell pressed her lips together.

"Here." He handed her his Bible.

"Oh, no," she said quickly. "I couldn't take it. And I have a Bible."

"You can take it. You must. It will make me happy and make up for your frightening me to death. Besides, everyone has a Bible, but no one reads it. Put it in the bathroom. Then you'll read it."

She could not help smiling at him.

"On the sill. Leave it there. You'll open it out of curiosity. I have a thousand notes, and maybe one will catch your eye."

"And how is it good for you that I take your study Bible?"

"It will make me read through fresh, without my eye resting on the same passages I've underlined for years. This will be very good for me."

He made her stay while he went in and grabbed her a program, so she'd have the church's name and address. He brought it to her, encouraging her to put it on her night table and read it through; it would help her sleep. He asked Jack's name and said that he would pray for them both. And for her son.

"I've got children, and this is how I pray: Help me to be the father they need today, not before, not the last time I failed 'em, but *right now*.

"You haven't prayed like that, have you? See," he said, letting rip another run of laughter, "that didn't hurt, did it? Just ask. Just say: 'What shall I do?' Or remember this moment. That's a prayer!"

Then he asked whether she'd like him to put anything into the collection plate on her behalf, since she couldn't come in. Jewell handed him a twenty-dollar bill and called him a hustler for the Lord.

He hurled his pealing laughter out into the cold mist again and repeated her joke to himself as he left her: "You know who we are?" he shouted by way of greeting another worshipper, an old lady no taller than he, who was struggling up the stairs. "We are 'hustlers for Jesus!'"

The two laughed, and he gave her his arm to help her mount the last step.

Jewell watched them disappear. The front of the program quoted Paul's letter to the Romans: "So, then, you are no longer a slave, but rather a son; and if you are a son, you are also an heir by God's act of adoption."

The minister's name was the Reverend Ivy Needham Ivans; they shared Jewell's maiden name, Needham. It had to be, she told herself, a coincidence.

Jewell turned off what she would think of from now on as Jubilee's seat warmer. The scent of bay rum hung on the upholstery.

———

"Call 'im," Jack said after she'd told him the saga. "Call 'im today before you lose heart." Jack lay on his chaise longue by the fire, seven more chemotherapy sessions away from the hope of remission. He'd napped while she went son-fishing, as he called it, in West Philly. "What do I know? I'm an old white guy with no kids, but I think you should finish the job, Jewelly."

He lay back with his eyes closed, and she thought he'd dozed off again until he said: "If your father called here today and said: 'I was a heel, but I couldn't do any better. I love you. Let me try to make it up,' what would you say?"

"Until this morning I would have hung up on him."

"And then what if he called back?"

"He wouldn't. Not him."

Jack said nothing.

"But I could. Is that what you're saying?"

"Well, if you wanted to. You can do whatever you want to." He pointed to the dog-eared Bible. "What're you going to do with that?"

"Oh, I forgot. I promised I'd put it in my bathroom."

The scent of bay rum rubbed off onto her hands. Having reached out tentatively to her son, she'd drawn back the scent of her father. And now that scent was connected to the image that would play in her mind for as long as she had one: her son's rolling walk from the little row house stoop to the truck, and then the moment of impact when his body accepted the boy who vaulted onto his back. She'd jumped like that onto her father's back once, before he beat her and she hated him; before she'd left South Carolina to escape the swirling storm of his rage, and then sent her son back into it.

That big, happy young man in the truck: What could he possibly need from her now?

She heard Jubilee's voice in her mind: "Just ask." Now, *that's* a prayer.

CHAPTER 4

A t first, Khalil sat in the truck's backseat. It was hard and shallow, but Lillie had insisted. Rayne tried to reassure her, first that the truck had airbags, and second that they would not decapitate her son. When Khalil protested that he couldn't see anything, she brought up the old booster seat from the basement. It smelled of mildew, but when Rayne slammed it down, Khalil sat on it, because Rayne said that they had to get going, period. By the time they drove through Delaware, Khalil had eaten three bites of a sandwich, played with his handheld video game, drunk a bottle of water, and burned his mouth taking a sip of Rayne's coffee from the ribbed steel thermos. Soon, he had to go to the bathroom.

When they came out of the rest area, Khalil hopped into the front seat and watched pointedly for Rayne's response. Rayne reached behind them for the booster seat, motioned for Khalil to stand, and then slid the thing under the boy and motioned for him to sit. Khalil made a face at the smell.

"You wanna see out, don't you? No point sitting up here and looking at the dashboard. 'Sides, I need you up where the air bags can do some good. If you're too low down, they just knock you out . . ." Then he handed the iPhone to Khalil and showed him how to plug it into the truck's radio through a wire in the glove box.

"You got gloves in there?"

"Nope. My grandfather said that his father used to keep gloves in his—and a gun."

"A gun?"

"Yeah."

"They carried guns way back then?"

"Yeah. In the country."

"They were, like, gangster. They carry guns now?" He was feeling through the wires, half expecting a pistol to materialize in a corner crevice.

"Naw. Stop with the guns. Now, if you can figure out how to get the music on, then DJ for us. If you can't, though, we'll put on the radio, because I can't stop and look while I'm driving, and I can't stand no whole lot of questions that you can figure out yourself."

Khalil nodded his head seriously. They both knew that the last warning had been unnecessary. Although Khalil could chatter and play, given an adult piece of equipment or paperwork, such as Rayne's construction documents, and a stated mission, Khalil could also puzzle silently by himself for three-quarters of an hour or more. As he played with the dial and buttons, Khalil fingered the latch on the glove box, which he now called the gun box, and doled out other questions, slowly, one every few miles, and with as much nonchalance as he could affect. "So, Dad, you drove down here before? Did you used to, like, live down there, in the country?"

"Yeah."

"When you was my age?"

"Yeah."

"And then you left and came to Philly?"

"I went back and forth for a while."

"How come?"

Rayne didn't answer at first. He adjusted his back with a tilt to his shoulders and a customary impatience, releasing a series of pops that relaxed and comforted him. Then he sighed heavily. Lillie was protective of Khalil—"I haven't had any man since his father," she'd told him early on, "because I don't want him to be confused."

Had Rayne "confused" him, in their private times, here in the truck, alone, or crouching together under the overhang in the backyard, where they raked through architectural details of once-proud buildings, feeling a primitive enjoyment of the stored wealth in the plaster moldings, cast-iron ornaments, steel cable, and stone carvings? Should he have stopped him from calling him Dad in the first instance?

And since Rayne was not his father, what did Khalil need to know about Rayne's inner life, his family, or his past? Did he need to know about men going to prison and mothers leaving? Did he need to know how much Rayne did *not* know, and how it ached? Maybe Khalil didn't need to know any of it. Or maybe he asked because he already knew. That was the most likely. This fatherless child had felt the traces of Rayne's own abandonment; he'd sensed the loneliness that murmured beneath Rayne's life like an underground stream, threatening to erode every good thing he managed to build over it. Surely Khalil had whiffed it, like mildew coming off the booster seat. And surely he needed to know, if not now, then soon, that men, even young men, had to fortify themselves internally, to stretch supports from where they stood to whatever wall would hold.

———

If Rayne were Khalil's biological father, he'd say: this is the family curse, this clinging and abandonment—cutting off each other like soldiers in the Civil War lopped off diseased hands, only to feel each throbbing digit for the rest of their lives. These are the strengths: an appetite for work, the blessed ability, deserved or not, to sleep through the night, intuition, when we have the sense to trust it. These things you must guard against: stubbornness, alcohol, ear infections, athlete's foot.

In fact, Rayne didn't know Khalil's inheritance, only his young and certain ability to choose. And now that the boy had chosen him, Rayne felt himself responding, not with a warm, soft-edged love, but with a protective fierceness that stunned him.

He felt it at the school closing exercises, when the teacher forgot to call Khalil's name for honor roll. *What the fuck?* Rayne felt himself starting to rise up out of his seat, a six-foot-four-inch, thick-necked bulky black man who had barely perched himself on the folding chairs in the 1970s-era cafeteria-turned-auditorium. When the teacher saw him, she quickly righted herself. ("And last, but certainly not least, our own Khalil Nixon . . .") That evening, going home in the truck, Lillie and Khalil had laughed about Rayne's momentary lapse until tears slid sideways from their matching pairs of almond eyes.

He'd just felt it on this drive, standing in the Maryland House restroom, where a man's eyes lingered too long on Khalil's thin brown form standing next to him at the urinal. *You lost somethin'?*

He had begun to understand what he used to think was Lillie's overprotection of the boy. She protected Khalil from Rayne. She protected him from the sexual heat that had brought them together. Back in his downtown apartment, he used to bend Lillie over the kitchen counter on a summer night and spread both their arms out wide on the cool black stone counter, and they two would groan and buck and shout with abandon. Lillie's lanky, athletic body somehow complemented his big, bulky frame. She'd matched him in energy and need. Then, after the first year, desire bloomed into a fullness neither had ever known or hoped to sustain. But then he moved in, and she cooled.

He knew that the kitchen was out, but hadn't expected that she'd shush him in bed, reminding him that Khalil, in his room, on the other side of the bathroom, might not be asleep. He hadn't known that she would try to circumscribe, rather than welcome, his constant improvements in the house, as if to keep him from imprinting on the place. And he'd been hurt by her vigilant watch over his interactions with Khalil. He'd think to himself that Lillie went way beyond what was necessary. Then himself would think back: *How would you know?*

The boy began to imitate Rayne's turns of phrases, his hand movements, and even his big, rolling walk. Rayne felt both flattered and trapped—by mother *and* son.

But now that Rayne, too, had the boy's face and hands, his likes and needs, in his mind, he could begin to understand and forgive Lillie. At demolition jobs, Rayne reminded his men to harvest wooden balustrades and wrought-iron handles that the boy would enjoy. He knew his food preferences. Khalil loved old-time watermelons with black seeds, cheese tortellini from the Italian market; the flat section, rather than the drumette, of chicken wings baked in soy sauce and orange juice.

"I never had a father," he said, not answering Khalil's question about why Rayne had traveled back and forth between Philadelphia and South Carolina. "So I don't always know how to do this."

"Do what?"

"Answer your questions."

Khalil had found out how to search music on Rayne's iPhone according to listing by artist, song, and album. Now, as

Rayne tried to call up a set of criteria to determine how to answer a seemingly simple question, Khalil looked to see what he recognized. His mother liked Tracy Chapman, so he played one of her songs, and then made a face.

"Nah, don't change it," Rayne said. "That's almost country. And when I first used to drive down here, that's all you could get on the radio. That and Christian stations."

"This a long drive."

"Yeah, it is."

"Who drove you, your grandfather?"

"The first time, I think. Could've been more than that once; I can't remember. Prolly was." He made a memory, but the image that came back was the standard one that blotted out the others: his trying to pee into a jar in the car without spilling, so that they did not have to stop and risk his grandfather's running into any highway patrols or official people at rest stations. "But then after that, I drove myself. And I listened to a *lot* of country music!"

Khalil slumped in his seat.

"Look for Ray Charles. I'ma show you country music you'll like. Seriously. Fire it up."

———

Rayne's body was already remembering the feel of pounding down I-95 at sixteen years old, driving alone, scared, scared, scared, in Bobo's 1996 Ford Ranger pickup short-bed, in July, with no air-conditioning. At night, in his sleep, he could feel the road vibrating into his body.

Bobo bought Fords because King had bought Fords. This one had been new then, compact, so that they could park it in the city, "rough little cuss," Bobo liked to say, dependable, although dicey in the snow with its two-wheel drive. Rayne's current Toyota—not the big Ford he took on the road—was the contemporary equivalent, even smaller, able to park anywhere, and although built on a truck chassis, easy enough to steer so that Lillie could take it, without too much complaint, to Fresh Grocer.

In his mind's eye, Rayne checked the glove compartment, where they used to leave the keys back before crack moved south to make small-time rural thieves as crazy as urban ones. Bobo also kept the manual there, pristine in its plastic, and his many maps, the very ones Rayne had used to navigate, outlined in yellow from the AAA headquarters in Philadelphia.

Bobo had told him to use the cashbox under the bed and to stop *only* at national chain motels, and only if he had to. Though big, Rayne had a young face, so people wondered aloud where he was going alone, and why. He told them that he was being sent to his great-grandmother's farm in South Carolina to help her take down her old hog houses, and clerks and gas attendants and onlookers would laugh and joke about the smell.

"Boy, you got a job ahead o' you!"

"How many hog houses she got? You don't know? You gonna know soon."

Rayne didn't know how he'd come upon the hog house story, except that Selma had still kept a couple of hogs when he went down to live with her at age seven. It was years later that Rayne realized how well his dead great-grandfather must have built the several houses that stood strong despite years of moisture and muck. Even after Selma stopped raising hogs, the pens and the houses stood intact, giving off their complex stink. It was a shame, Selma said, because it meant you couldn't hardly use the wood for anything else. You couldn't take them down and build them into a shed or shore up a loose floorboard from underneath. So they stayed there.

Joking about the hog houses distracted people from paying too much attention to Rayne's big young black male self, or wondering why he was driving that self alone, or why he tilted with impatience as they asked him one question after another, or why he spoke, as people said in the South, as if he thought he was white. He'd tell them, if they asked, that he'd grown up with Selma in Sou' Ca'lina, which was true, but had moved to Philadelphia, where they all talked like this, which was also true, and that now he spent summers goin down to give her a hand, which he'd do this year, at least.

People observed his size and strength and his studied control and said that his great-grandmother, she must love to see him come and hate to see him go, that is if he put in a day's work like it looked like he ought to be able to. He'd smile a half smile and allow as his Nana Selma could work a guy pretty hard. Then he'd take his sandwiches back to the car with a couple of bottles of Coke, and make the next leg of his illegal drive across state lines, still scared and alone, with the Pennsylvania learner's permit that stated explicitly that the learner was permitted to drive only with an adult licensee in the car.

When he'd told the story of his drive to Lillie, he added, as an afterthought, that Bobo had called him from jail and told him to get the truck out of the city immediately.

She'd listened carefully and nodded. "So, at the time, did you realize that the truck probably wasn't paid for?"

They were lying together in bed. Rayne rubbed his hand back and forth over the smooth curve of her belly. "I don't know. I don't think so. But I felt so scared of being caught . . ."

"So, I guess so. You were, like, always trying to be the parent, weren't you?"

He'd shrugged, but in fact felt an unfamiliar recognition. *Who knew?* Selma used to complain that Bobo had never grown up, and warned Rayne not to follow suit. Lying in bed next to Lillie, telling her the crazy story of driving the Ford Ranger to Selma's, he felt something akin to relief.

Rayne decided that Khalil did not need to know any more about the circumstances of the drive. He didn't tell him about throwing the gun from the glove box into a ditch outside of Fredericksburg, Virginia, or the fear that made him want to relieve himself there, too, except that he was determined to be a man, and disciplined.

Rayne was determined to be a man for this boy, now, too, and he sensed that this entire situation was still fraught for him. It was hard to tell it nice and easy, or answer the likely follow-ups: Your grandfather went to prison? What for? For how long? Did he do it? Did he do what they said?

Ray Charles had finished and a Richard Pryor cut began to play. "Hey, Little Man," Rayne said. "Find some other music. Something with a beat."

"Like what?"

"I don't know."

Reggaeton came on and Rayne debated whether or not to make a big deal of turning it off, too, since neither of them spoke Spanish. While the music played, he remembered telling Lillie:

But what the hell else could I do? I was a kid. Somebody tells you to drive the truck to South Carolina, you drive the truck to South Carolina. That's not being a parent. That's taking orders.

Being a parent means taking care of things. You only had a learner's permit, but you drove the truck. You were down there in South Carolina, but you managed to get family members to clean his apartment, divvy up his stuff, and rent the place out.

If he hadn't been in jail, he would have taken care of his stuff himself. He was in jail.

He was in jail because he shot up his TV.

No, not because he shot up his TV, because the cops came, and he fought 'em at the door.

Same diff.

It's not; he's a black man in America.

He knew he was black when he picked up the gun and opened the door.

Let's not keep having this conversation.

But you still had to be the parent.

Yeah, well, I never thought of it like that.

Lillie had suggested that maybe it was easier for Bobo to blame himself than to take in the loss of King, the man the whole family spoke of as a legend, and, so far as Rayne could tell, the only man who had ever truly loved him. Bobo's personal Bible text, given to him during the Second World War by Selma's favorite old preacher, applied: "If the householder had known at what hour the thief was coming, he would have kept watch." No matter the explanations, however, or Bobo's culpability, eventually everything *was* taken from him.

Everything except that 1996 Ford Ranger pickup short-bed that Rayne drove to Selma's. In the Graterford prison AA group, and under the sway of an old lifer-turned-Muslim, Bobo likened himself to a woman who had been raped. That's what he said to Rayne on visits. "That's why people use that word: they get *fucked.* All this time, that's what it was to me. No matter what I did, I got fucked. My mother lef' me with Selma, then my daughter lef' me with you. Then the prison terms—for nothing. I have done things that I deserve being punished for. Make no fuckin mistake. But that's not why they got me in. They got me in on bullshit."

Then he asked: "But what was she wearing?"

"Who?"

"When a woman gets raped, you gotta ask, what was she wearing?"

"No, Pops, I don't think that's legal to ask."

"I'm talking about real people with common sense. What do *they* ask? You say: She got raped. They say: What was she wearin? The old-timer told me to *use* that common sense: look, if I got screwed, what did I do to invite it? I ain't say 'deserve' it; I say 'invite' it."

Dumb little shit. That's what you get. Rayne knew that this was not a new idea from some old-timer. This was how Bobo had always thought. It never occurred to him that Rayne could have been arrested twice over.

———

"Dad?" Khalil's touching his arm made Rayne suspect that he'd probably already called him once over the music, although tentatively. "Can I crawl into the backseat and go to sleep for a while?"

"Sure, son. Wait, lemme pull over," he said as Khalil threw himself, chuckling, over the seat back.

"Pull over? Dad, *c'mon!*"

CHAPTER 5

nto Virginia, once they left behind the Washington, D.C., corridor, I-95 started to feel more like going home. And with Khalil sleeping, Rayne's mind roamed from pounding the highway this time to the many times he'd pounded it before. For years now, Rayne would come down at Easter. In fact, he came the week before to do the chores she'd saved up for him, which he always protested were two-week work orders for three men. Then he'd take her to Holy Week services. If it was warm enough, they'd go fishing at least once, and eat the catch all week until the Easter ham. They'd walk the land, with her telling him his great-grandfather's maxims, so that by the end of the week, as Rayne told Lillie, he was so close to the man he'd never met that he almost expected him to walk in the door, or felt him to be waiting in the smokehouse, where Rayne had sometimes heard a sigh or a door closing, and where Bobo swore it was colder than other outbuildings.

It was.

Even Jones said so. He'd said it one Christmas after Rayne had finished Cheyney State. Jones told Rayne to come out and collect wood with him, and instead, took him to the smokehouse.

"You think this place is haunted? Well, it is. It's colder than shit in here, because King's still here, waitin for I don't know what, but I'm letting him know that I'm givin you this."

"Come on, Uncle Jones, man. Nana Selma already keeps everybody spooked."

"Stop talkin. Listen, I'ma give you a hundred dollars for Christmas just for yourself."

"Whoa. Jones!"

"Stop talkin, I tell you. Now, I'm only givin it to you to keep you from spending this other hundred-dollar bill I'm about to hand to you, but this here is not to spend. It's to keep. That's what I call the last gift I ever received from your great-granddaddy King. I'm just as superstitious as my sister deep down. You could say that, but listen up: you keep it, and it will bring other money to you."

Rayne had folded it into the copy of the business plans he wrote, rewrote, and revised each year as he went from demolition to demo and rough contracting to full-service construction. He'd clip it to the back of each budget that he made, line by line, before putting in a bid. Usually it stayed in an inner fold of his wallet. He never really forgot that it was there.

Rayne did not tell Bobo about the bill, because Bobo and Jones had never gotten along, and it would have pained Bobo to hear how close his grandson had gotten to the older man since Bobo's imprisonment. Still, it was Jones who'd taken care of the old truck's loan note, so that the police would not come and repossess it in South Carolina and jail Rayne for theft. Jones had sent money to Rayne in college, and he helped Selma with the taxes every now and then. He called and badgered her to tell him how things stood rather than suffer in silence.

Jones's work life, so far as Rayne knew, involved raising and breeding horses with a rich white man somewhere in upstate New York, and traveling with them when they were being raced or sold. That's why he could stay with Selma at Christmas, but seldom in spring.

Jones had told Rayne that he and Selma were orphaned children of King's sharecroppers, and that their parents and siblings, along with King's first wife and a third of the county, had died in an influenza epidemic. King earned their loyalty when he buried their family, and gave them the option of staying on, even though they were too young to command their own house and vittles. Jones worked with the animals ("the original horse whisperer," Selma called him). King sent Selma, who had expected to be put out into the field, to grade school.

"It's hard to imagine what it meant to be a black orphan in the Depression and to have a little shack to live in. Don't look like nothing, do it?" Jones once asked him as they stood looking at the stark two-bedroom wood structure, their first home on the farm.

No, Rayne had thought, it looked like a hog house, only bigger; it looked like the worst photos he'd seen in *National Geographic*.

"You gotta remember, we had no skills. I was sixteen and Selma was nine. Our relatives had already told us they couldn't feed not nary 'nother mouth. It was like slavery sort of, because where would you go, but live somewhere and do anything they said just for a roof over your head and a bushel of cornmeal? We was glad for it; glad for the meal, glad it don't have no mold, glad for no bugs."

Jones's murmuring baritone had a slow, low-country intonation, despite the years he'd traveled the world with his horses and their owner, Jared, a man Selma referred to simply as "White Folks." But Rayne never underestimated the sophistication of his analysis. "They said the difference between the Depression and slavery was that in the Depression if they killed a nigger, they hadn't lost an investment. It was a dangerous time."

"Is that why you left?"

"Sort of," he said, measuring his words carefully. "Mostly I left because, after King died, I couldn't stay still. I couldn't put in the crop and take it out year after year. I couldn't stand it anymore. My sister promised him that if anything happened she would keep his family's land. I loved your great-grandfather. I probably loved him more'n I loved my own kin. But I didn't promise I'd stay, she did, and, besides," he said, his baritone edged in a rare bitterness, "I knew who I was back then. How could I have lived *here*?"

————

Once Rayne finished the 395 loop around Richmond, I-95 stretched out ahead of him through North Carolina and South. He thought of stopping at a rest area, but decided instead to drive as long as he could while Khalil slept.

It felt like he'd been driving in a truck forever.

He took gulps of the coffee and ate two sandwiches, which Lillie had made with precise attention to his taste. She'd baked a turkey breast the night before, then sliced it very thin onto some small French rolls he loved, which she bought from a bakery downtown. She'd added different vegetable matter on each. He couldn't identify all the elements, but each sandwich had a distinct favorite flavoring: one with cream cheese and cranberry sauce she made fresh, the other with some sort of olive-y paste that oozed over the sides and dripped onto the big red-and-white napkin she'd packed for him to lay on his lap.

"The stuff you like is messy, baby." She always said the same thing when she showed him the bulge of napkins she rolled and wedged into the front seat next to him. Then, referring to their joke about his eating and driving, she'd say, "If you use this, then you won't have to jump around in the seat and curse when a piece of avocado slips out and stains your you-know-what."

Rayne ate and drove for as long as his bladder and the shuffle play lasted. Al Green's "Let's Stay Together" came swinging out with its romantic horns, big and round, seductive and earnest, after the driving intelligence of Nas, and the cool certainty of Miles. Rayne's memories fogged up from the landscape. The defrost system sucked them in to collect on the dashboard of his mind, as if he needed to drive the same territory again and again in order to discover how to escape from it.

———

It was the first lynching story Rayne remembered hearing. And it was the first, in fact the only, fight he remembered between Jones and Selma—over whether to tell it to him. It was the year he drove down Bobo's Ford, and Jones figured that since he'd been living with Bobo and boxing in Philadelphia, smelling himself, as they said, he needed to know how things had been. Selma came in to protest.

"Why the boy need to hear that old poison?" Selma asked. "How's that gonna help 'im?"

"He needs to know what he's up against."

"He know what he's up against. Isn't his grandfather in prison? Didn't his mother send 'im away like a sack o' mail? What else you want to lay on his shoulders?"

"He got good strong shoulders, like King. How he gonna get anywhere, he don't know where he come from?"

"He come from us," Selma shouted, her voice as low and harsh for a woman as her brother's was for a man. "He come from us, and he come from here. He come from King Needham, the only black man I ever met who said: Don't cripple children. Don't weigh 'em *down*."

"And all that means I can't tell 'im how it was that they lynched that boy? Come on, sis, they did it, and he needs to know that that's where it was—right out there where the golf course is now, runnin next to your east borderline, where whats-hisname got that dev'lish patch of hybrid corn.

"The boy got computers up in Philadelphia, Selma. He can find all this out if he's of a mind. You can't hide nothing! Ain't no secret."

Selma had withdrawn to her bedroom, and Jones, muted, went at the story he had begun to tell, but differently.

Rayne saw it for the first time. For years, he'd been caught in the memory of their fight, and then, in the terrible truth of the story itself. But something about being in the truck with the boy who had adopted him as Dad, and censoring his own story of Bobo's imprisonment, made him see that Jones had jogged onto a path that branched off from where he had started, although Rayne could not remember where that had been.

———

It had happened, Jones said, just around the time King married Selma, who by then was a lithe young woman, seventeen or eighteen, who worshipped the older man who'd saved her and her brother. As Jones told it, the lynching happened the night before they were to be married, which made King decide not to take his new bride away for a honeymoon trip, but rather to stay on the farm and watch his land and stock and outbuildings. Once the bloodletting started, it could sometimes make people crazy.

Jones said that he didn't tell Rayne this story to cripple him, but only to let him know not to believe how things look on the surface; people lie. The crickets and bullfrogs and cicadas make a racket all night, and folks never know what they're talking about. Likewise, the land tells its own stories. Bobo let it make him bitter. Jones suspected, he said, that Rayne's character didn't tend that way. But even if it did, secretly, then seeing Bobo's suffering should show him where bitterness leads.

———————

This happened. It was during the Depression, and who the hell knew why, but they lynched a boy the old-fashioned way. He was about fifteen and close to feebleminded. They said he killed a little white girl. Likely a lie, but everybody agreed that the girl was indeed dead. She was dead, and somebody killed her, and just because we didn't want it to be a colored kid doesn't mean it might not have been. That's how people talked about it to keep from going crazy.

In this case, the white men dragged the boy from his house. He lived down by the swampiest bottomland there was. If his folks had had two nickels to rub together, it would've been their first dime.

They took him to a field with a tree. They got up a crowd. Seemed like every so often they needed a lynching party. Jones said that he had told this to Jared once, who thought about it for a while and came back with the theory that Christians had an appetite for human sacrifice to cleanse themselves. Jones said that after a while, that made sense to him. It helped him keep from hating, which was as bad as going crazy.

But the people Jones grew up with, they told the story along fault lines of the teller's character, class, or experience. Compassion for the dead child or not. Possibility of boy's guilt, or the irrelevance of it. The logic of revenge or of repair. Jones told the story, and he tried to capture the collective sense of this tragedy, but it was hard to do so. The people said so many things:

—*And no matter what they do the poor child is still dead, the little girl.*

—*Fuck 'em.*

—*Don't say that. Dear Jesus.*

—*The boy's dead, too, ain't he? Fuck 'em.*

—*I don't think it was the child.*

—*Had nothing to do with the girl. They wouldn't get offa the land. The brother come from Arkansas told 'em they didn't have to. Said the AAA would protect 'em.*

—*Any fool knows better than that.*

—*Well, the boy they killed always had been feebleminded.*

—*I believe that's why they couldn't move.*

—*They gone now, ain't they?*

—*Jesus.*

—*Jesus.*

This may not be why those particular men did the thing they did, or why those people came out to the field like it was a damn barbecue, and brought their kids, or why they got a photographer right out there on the field to take pictures of the crime and then to sell 'em right there, but Jones wanted Rayne to know that behind all of this was the land. Same as the land his great-grandfather owned that probably some white men thought he shouldn't. The land was the hard, eternal truth underneath every law and every lie.

Jones remembered that not too long before this, the Agricultural Adjustment Administration in Washington had passed a law that prohibited landowners from turning sharecroppers off fallow land. The idea was that when farmers took crops out of circulation, the poor people would not be turned out to starve. In Arkansas, where sharecroppers were turned out by the thousands, they organized. The Southern Tenant Farmers' Union swept through the county, calling meetings. They distributed leaflets that people who could read were supposed to read to the others, quoting poems written by Negroes, but so beautiful you never could tell in a thousand years. In Harlem, Claude McKay tried to stuff the spirit of the times into sonnets: "If we must die, let it not be like hogs / Hunted and penned in an inglorious spot . . ." People printed these things, and so, eventually, poor people like Jones got hold of 'em. King helped him read them at first, then Jones would memorize them:

> If we must die, O let us nobly die,
> So that our precious blood may not be shed
> In vain; then even the monsters we defy
> Shall be constrained to honor us though dead!

The man from the Southern Tenant Farmers' Union insisted that thousands of black and white tenant farmers were banding together, taking to the highways, squatting there. Mrs. Roosevelt took up their cause, and word spread among them that the president would not let them die out in the sun like turtles on their backs. They wouldn't chop the cotton, period, they said. Weeds choked it; the rest went to seed.

Sharecroppers all the way in Mississippi heard about it: that at the meetings, when they said these things, slumbering men and women awakened to rebellion. And Mississippi talked to Georgia and Georgia talked to South Carolina. The hell with 'em! A family can only starve once.

But after the Agricultural Adjustment Administration man left, the black people talked sense back into themselves. Hey. Arkansas was *not* Mississippi.

But who went out and read this crazy, shining manifesto to the family of the lynched boy? Couldn't have been anything else emboldened them to turn up in the spring like lilies after the man told 'em to go? There they were, the father sick unto death, as they said, with TB, a grandmother crippled, one son run off, mother plowing like a mule to put in a crop of sweet corn and greens and potatoes, they say: something to eat, at least, since the land wasn't going to be used.

—*Wasn't going to be used? Was she crazy?*

—*Boy was just feebleminded; mother was insane.*

—*Well, what the hell she gonna do?*

—*I told you: you can only starve once.*

—*Maybe they figured something would turn up.*

However people could, they took it in. But they *did* take it in; you had to; everybody did. That's what the adults used to say when Jones was a boy, before the flu took his daddy, lying in his own sweat, eyes wide open to the flies. The children listened, afraid, Jones said.

"Mostly we were always afraid. That's why King was like nothing we'd ever seen. A big, giant colored man who did not seem to be afraid."

———

Selma's point was that she did not want the lynching from another era to insinuate its way into Rayne's mind and fill him with its terror. And Jones figured it was probably King who told her: if anything happens, do not tell the kids. King tried to stay buried in hope that his heirs would not have to mortgage their lives to the past.

Jones felt regret when Rayne told him that he could see it in his mind, almost, and that it made him want to blow up the golf course, whose green stretched out with innocent-seeming luxury over the crime scene.

It was true, in fact, that the lynched body, a lonely corpse in the wind, kept turning burning turning in Rayne's mind.

Sometimes for no reason he could figure, he saw it. Sometimes the smell of old joists in a metal trash can outside a demo job would light the fire in his mind, and he'd see it all over again, or close the door of his mind even as he knew that behind it, the body still burned. Lynching demands moving pictures—so we can be afraid forever.

See? See it? You can see it in your head, can't you?
See it? I can't hardly stop it. That's the thing; how you stop it?

———

When Rayne told Lillie, she did not think of the body, but the mob. Acting on the impulse of one ancient brain, they commenced the thing out in the open. As if that boy were theirs to do with as they pleased. As if God had given them dominion over this dull-eyed creature whose lips never closed, but hung akimbo like he'd forgotten what he wanted to say. That's how Lillie saw it; they acted like gods who'd been given the power to drive out demons, and he was the swine.

———

It was a picnic without grace. Every devilment you could do to a man's body, Jones hinted, they did to his.

———

Women brought food, and children watched. That's what Lillie couldn't understand. Children watched, and they had to remember. Even those who forgot, they remembered, too. On Sundays, they had to murmur, with his image turning burning turning in their minds, murmur together, shhhh, softly, whisper it together: *Grant us therefore, gracious Lord, so to eat the flesh of thy dear son Jesus*

Christ and to drink his blood, that we may evermore dwell in him and he in us.

Like Jared said: People need a sacrifice.

And those who missed the picnic itself could see it later. The photographer used a lightweight camera on a tripod: fast new shutter and clip-on flash. He pulled black drapes around him to makeshift a darkroom and developed photos right in the field. Men who got just five dollars a head from the hog-reduction program paid fifty cents for a print still wet.

The body smoked.

After they were outlawed as postcards, the photos traveled the world in envelopes and pockets, passed from hand to hand, lay in side drawers under baptismal records and bowie knives. They were inherited with possessions made affordable by black labor until, finally, "Four or five generations later," Jones begins . . .

"All of us know the outlines by heart," Rayne finishes. He has in mind the picture of a black man, neck to one side, hanged. An American icon. Now one could see it in museums and coffee-table books. Collectors collected the photos.

Dirty pictures. Who can touch?

———

Wash your hands.

———

Later, they shear off slices of the body. The pieces turn/turn/turn to dust in the men's wallets. Like that crazy hundred-dollar bill Jones gave him.

'Cause once you've sliced off a man's ear, Rayne thinks, what else can you do but keep it close? It's a relic. Touches your fingers every time you go for your money. Loose flakes rub off when you pick up your children. Shake hands with business colleagues to show your goodwill. Open hand, unarmed.

Charmed, I'm sure.

Over the years, the story had cooked inside Rayne's head, helped by the comments of the few people he'd ever told. You didn't bring it out too often.

But, wait. Here come the miracle. My Lord!

Jones holds in his voice the exact hopeful reverence of the sharecroppers who'd shared the news with him. They'd get to this part in the story and shake their heads—and this is what I want you to know, too, Jones says, referring to Selma's silence, because if Rayne didn't know the first part, then he couldn't know the miracle: that when the mob had done as much as you can do to a human being and him still be alive, a man pushed his way through the crowd, crazy as they were by now, crazy-mad with liquor and the terrible intoxication of blood— a *colored man* elbowed his way to the front and begged for the boy's life.

That was the part everyone repeated: *And then, do Jesus,* a black man *come up in front of them.*

And it didn't matter whether the listeners had heard the story before. They told it again, just as Jones told Rayne, and Rayne told his construction partner and later Lillie, because it remained a mystery. And because everyone wanted to know this and to learn, as Jones learned, what was possible.

Jones's words, present tense, because heroism exists outside of time: "He stands beside the boy's body, tied by now so that it won't fall flat. This black man says—listen what he say standing in front of all these crazy, drunk-up white people—he says: 'For God's sake, please, don't finish this. Whatever you meant to teach him this boy has surely learnt. And he'll never be good for nothin now anyway. Please, for pity's sake, just lemme take 'im down. Lemme take 'im home to his mother.'"

———

Where had he come from, this man who appeared like the black face of God speaking mercy?

———

The outrageousness of it would not be suppressed. It leached from between the rocks, seeped into the streams, soaked into the swamps. Finally, it ran in the papers, so they couldn't say it didn't happen. Jones was sure that Rayne could find it in the records, and one day, sure enough, he looked it up on the Internet.

———

Yes, they did hang the poor boy, anyway, just hanged him, what was left of him, and roasted him like a hog. They burned him like paper and breathed in the smoke. Particles of him went into their bodies and into the water. That's what Rayne thinks about sometimes when he starts getting south enough. Like the fish in the Pacific who turn up with plastic granules in their flesh, how many of the residents had drunk water in which was dissolved the ashes from this boy's body? And others'?

King dammed up the water running from that field. A wash field, they called it. Was it only because the lower ground was too soggy, or did he intend to erect a barrier? To keep his new raised tobacco beds free of the taint?

———

But because it ran in the papers, see, they couldn't say it didn't happen.

And people did learn from it. Black people learned that the terror was still abroad in the land, but they could choose to fly in its face. You only die once.

————

Rayne's business cell rang, and instead of Lillie's voice or one of the guys', his mother's purred into his ear like an announcer from a television commercial for something expensive. He listened for a moment. She repeated her name, and called him Lonnie, the slow, elegant voice coming through the phone and up out from his own psychic basement, which until now had been sealed. Where had he misplaced such a voice all these years? There was no other such voice in all the world. Mommy. His face felt hot. He'd thought when he wrote the letter that he'd be fine if and when the call ever came. But now he was not fine. He was in the corner of the truck, watching himself drive, telling himself, by remote control, to hang up the phone. Just hang up. The idiot in the driver's seat couldn't get words up out of his throat. Just hang the fuck up. "It's me," said the man in the driver's seat, the man who'd not been called Lonnie since his mother had left him on the train in Trenton, New Jersey, a city he'd always hated for that reason, "but I can't talk. Talk later. I'm driving." Then he clicked off.

CHAPTER 6

That's what you get.

That's what Jewell heard when her son hung up the phone, after his deep voice, sharp-edged, cool, and dismissive, told her that he was driving. He had a productive life in progress, and she'd interrupted. Like her father, Bobo, would have said, *That's what you get.*

Well, what else had she expected after more than twenty years?

"He hung up?" Jack asked. Jewell's husband was so thin now that the two of them lay together like spoons on the chaise longue by the fire, which she'd built directly upon coming home.

"Said he was driving." She shrugged into her husband's bony chest, where the lung cancer had been, and where he now had one lung, maybe growing cancer of its own, maybe not. He'd wanted to go to Mexico again this year for Easter, but their doctor had warned them off. This week, he'd felt stronger, and they'd been thinking of going anyway.

Jack rubbed his wife's shoulder-length brown hair. At forty-seven, she was still a striking woman, tall, slow-speaking, and elegant, with an olive complexion and deep-set, dark eyes. She'd taken up running in the last ten years, which seemed to have made her quiet moments more still, like a cold-water lake. People who didn't know her thought her aloof. Once, she'd admitted to him how guilty she felt to be getting stronger . . .

"While I get weaker," he'd supplied. "Let's just say it."

Theirs had been a romantic, impulsive, and long-lasting marriage. He'd been an inveterate liar—he liked to say "an invertebrate liar"—in his youth, as Jewell knew, and figured there was only a short time to redeem himself. Honesty mattered a great deal to both of them now.

"Call the other number," Jack said. "You can leave a message for when he gets back."

"What can I say?"

"I don't know . . . Say: 'This is your mother. You okay?'"

She laughed in her throat.

You okay? You okay? It was one of his recurring jokes from what he called Cancer World. *You okay?* Mostly now, he asked: "Do you want the long answer or the short answer?" People sorted themselves out with surprising honesty, the few people whom they were really close to.

"What are you afraid of? Right now?" That was a quote from Jack's favorite visiting nurse, Barbara. *Right now,* she'd always say, and without making him admit to it, she'd let him see how many were the fears that throbbed through him, like pain, and how fast-moving.

"My old family," Jewell answered him after a delay so long he'd almost forgotten the question.

"But you're only talking to the son."

"He brings 'em with 'im." She hadn't thought of that until she saw him.

"Maybe it's time," Jack said, but his wife wasn't listening.

Instead her mind watched as her younger self boarded the train in New York and then combed the cars to find the perfect Negro schoolteacher to exploit, a plump fifty-year-old spinster wearing a white cardigan sweater over her shoulders, and headed home to Beaufort County, South Carolina, for the summer. Jewell had explained, with easy-to-conjure tears threatening behind her eyes, that she had only enough money for two fares, that she wanted the boy to get out of the city for the summer— it was unhealthy in the city, but she had work here. If he stayed, he'd get into trouble; the other boys ran wild; she needed him to know his people back home. If Jewell continued all the way there, then, to return, she would have to borrow. Or she'd hitch- hike, because they barely had enough to go around, and now another mouth to feed.

With that the schoolteacher had insisted Jewell get off the train in Trenton, go back to New York, and cash in her ticket. She commandeered the goodwill of the black conductor, a ge- nial round-faced man, also in his fifties, and together they fussed over Lonnie until all three agreed that he could be and *would be* a big boy for sure. If he was very good, the conductor said, he would take him to visit the driver of the train, and Lonnie could sit up on the rail by the window and watch the train plunge into tunnels, shoot out into the open, and climb over the high bridge with a drop of a hundred feet. Big boys could do that, not babies.

"Oh, boy, oh, boy."

Jewell convinced herself that, beginning with this train, her son would be riding into a new, wholesome boyhood. "He's bet- ter off," she told herself through the years. And, well, obviously, he had been.

Of course, it was Jewell who'd ended up better off. She and Jack didn't really need the dog, friends joked, because they were each other's pet. And until these last few months' descent again into Cancer World, it had never occurred to her that they had no help, no heirs, no sons or daughters to pop in on Thursday evenings like her friend Eva's grown daughter, who came to help with Eva's mother.

That first time in Mexico, when she and Jack had climbed the hill, she'd felt a warm redemption that pulled out of her a promise to live better. She'd stopped smoking and convinced Jack to join her, which the doctors said had probably earned him his last few cancer-free years. All well and good, but now, trapped by the moist, low-ceilinged sky, Jewell found herself remembering the rest of it, for which there was no pardon. She heard herself moan. She was crying. Jack held her as close as he could.

———

They lived in New York, where she had come after a night when Bobo had beaten her. Her baby was two, and New York seemed exactly the right place to take him to find the unexpected life-changing opportunity that a young woman, stunningly beautiful and headstrong, fully expected to discover. Instead, New York offered her the chance to clean office buldings at night. She left her son with the big woman next door who had her own babies and loved having another one each year.

Jewell started smoking when Lonnie turned five, and by the time he was six, he would go into her purse and find the matches. She told herself that he was not a firebug, just curious. It was a fluke, a onetime, then an occasional, thing. Four times in all. Small, aborted fires, except the one.

But at odd moments through the day, his dissatisfied little face told her how desperately he wanted her to be different, and better. When she came home late at night, she'd stop to collect him from next door and carry him to his own bed. He'd have been awake, and she knew it, but he would keep his eyes stubbornly closed in order not to acknowledge her. She saw his eyelids flutter, and she played along, too tired to engage. Then he would watch her when she wasn't looking. He became a suspicious child, at once sulky and vigilant.

She tried authority: "Lonnie Freeman Rayne, you touch these matches one more time, and I'll smash your fingers." She had, indeed, made him hold out his hands for her to hit with the wooden spoon, and at other times, she had lost all control, beating him with anything she could find, sometimes not even recognizing how enraged she was until she was spent. He'd be crying, screaming, or finally just blubber-babbling things at her that she never would have dared say to an adult: that she was mean, that she couldn't make 'im stop, that she could hit 'im, but she couldn't make 'im do anything; that he would do it, whatever it was, again. She slapped his face to shut up the snotty torrent.

She'd become her father.

The summer he was six she'd returned to South Carolina for a month. Lonnie had set fire to hay in the smokehouse. In the chaos that followed, she'd beaten him something awful. Nana Selma pulled him away. Later she tried to talk to Jewell: "I'm afraid that I'll always have that picture in my head, girl, of you holdin that boy up by his arm and beating on him like you fight a grown-up."

"Well, I can't help what's in your head. All I can do is try to keep him from burning up everything we own," Jewell had said, although she owned nothing except some share of the land that Selma promised would one day come to them, when she went "from work to refreshment," or, she said, when she swam back to Africa.

Jewell returned to New York, with no money and no job, and a boy even more sullen than before. He'd loved the farm and the chickens. He loved the truck. And he loved Selma, who took time with him and who, he informed his babysitter, "didn't hit." For a while it was the question he asked everyone he met, child or adult: "Do you hit?"

Their last argument, when he was seven, had been a fight practically of equals, him screaming hatred and need, Jewell shouting back again and again, "So you want somebody to take care of you like a goddamned baby?"

"You *don't* take care of me," he'd said.

———

Jewell wiped her nose on Jack's sleeve and snorted and coughed, but each thought took her back. She got up to throw a few more logs onto the fire, hoping to pull herself out of the sucking memory that was taking her down.

During that last fight, she'd moved to grab Lonnie and he'd thrown up his hands, mimicking the boys next door, like a little boxer. Jewell remembered that exact moment of insanity. She'd been drinking. She wanted to grab something and beat him until the pain in his own perfect, demanding little body made him understand what he should expect from life.

Nothing. Nothing. Not a goddamned thing. *That's what you get.*

That's when it came to her: send him away. She'd been threatening it—*I'll send you away.*

No, you won't.

Oh, yes, I will.

I'll come back.

You think you could find your way?

I could.

This time she'd do it differently. She slipped out of herself and watched the scene from the corner of the shabby room. She could see the room now: its dirty woodwork and three pieces of used furniture. She could smell it: like grease and old food, like cigarette smoke and a thousand thousand roach droppings. She saw herself back up from Lonnie and sit in her accustomed trough on the couch. She saw herself call him, coax him to her, and put her arms around him. If the argument had been between equals, so, too, was the making up. She was about to lie to him, as she would with a negotiator who held cards of his own. Mommy was not being a good mommy, she said, and she knew it, and she was sorry. Now she would be a good mommy: she would find a way to make enough money so that they could have a nice house and he could have a daddy.

He was curled up tight, wanting her caress, she could tell, and not wanting to show it; wanting to believe her, and not quite able to do so. She cradled as much of his big, seven-year-old body as she could hold on her lap and let it seep in that she was acknowledging the legitimacy of his grudges. She reminded him that Nana Selma had land as far as you could see, and chickens, and Granddaddy Bobo was down there with the truck that he could ride in again. She'd send him there for the summer, she said, then see how well he liked it when it came time to go back to school. "How 'bout that?"

"When?"

"When?" She had no idea how to answer him. There was food money in the jar, but nothing more. "Tomorrow." The word popped out of her mouth and gained instant, impulsive authority. "Tomorrow morning." She'd smiled on him like sunshine. He loved her to smile. He'd clown and roll on the floor to amuse her. *(Laugh, Mommy, laugh!)* "I'll wire them now. We'll go together."

"Are you comin?"

"To South Carolina? No, baby, I gotta stay here and find work. But if you're good, Granddaddy'll let you feed the hogs."

"I don't like the hogs."

"They'll have piglets, maybe, from this spring."

"I don't like piglets."

"Okay."

"You say he still got the truck?"

"Yeah, he's got a nice pickup truck to haul things from town."

"The red truck?"

"Yup."

"I wanna drive the truck."

"You ask him."

———

When the train was about to leave the Trenton station, Lonnie buried his face in her belly. The schoolteacher next to them sucked her teeth. On her son's behalf, Jewell already hated all the people who would tell him to be a good boy, a big boy, and who would begin to heap shame on him, but nothing like her shame. Her father had predicted this when she got pregnant, when she'd followed Lonnie's father to Charleston and then come back. Bobo was clever about finding other people's short-comings: ungenerous, for sure, but usually correct. He found satisfaction in sensing the undertow of disturbing truths that other people overlooked. He'd said that a cat would be a better mother than Jewell, and that she would end up sending the boy to be raised by Selma, just like his wife, her own no-good mother, had done to Jewell. Yup, he said to himself, he sure knew how to pick 'em.

And so it was. Jewell squeezed down on the shame to try to contain it, but it had dribbled out, warm, and run down her legs.

———

Jewell stood, making sure not to lean on Jack as she did.

"You gonna call the home number?" he asked. "Maybe you should do it now before you lose heart."

"Not while I'm still sniveling," she said. "I'll run the dog, and then I'll do it when I come back. Promise."

"Want me to do it? Hi, I'm Jack Thompson, your mother's white husband. I'm just calling to ask you to be nice to her."

Jewell laughed. "Oh, God. That'll fix it."

"Or, hi, I'm your mother's husband. What's my angle? Well, I've got lung cancer, and even if I beat it for now, well, I just figure it'll be good for her to have some more family. Even if it's complicated."

Jewell knelt down next to the chaise and kissed Jack. His breath had almost lost the sickly medicinal taste. "I'll do it when I get back. I will, really."

————

In the cold air, toxic memories rose to her skin as sweat. She'd move the blood faster. She opened the parka and trotted up the gravelly path. Jack used to ask her what she was trying to outrun, and she hadn't had the decency to tell him, this man who'd loved her all these years, until the letter had arrived last month.

————

Right in her belly was where Lonnie had buried his face when the conductor had appeared. They held up the train for a minute or two while he reminded Lonnie how fast the train would go, and how he'd soon see it all from the engineer's seat up front. Lonnie's arms eased. Jewell bent down and rested her hands on his shoulders. She looked up at his battered luggage, and the conductor followed her gaze and nodded—*Yup, he'd see to it.*

She was sweating into the white piqué blouse and gray suit that her neighbor had let her only borrow, even though, after five children, she'd never fit into it again. With their faces close together, she kissed the boy's cheek and gave him the only thing she had—a smile. Just for him to keep. It was smallish, fresh, a touch sad.

"Good-bye, sweetie," she said.

"September, right?"

"Lonnie rhymes with Mommy!"

"Almost."

She held her secret smile. The muscles around her eyes strained to keep it in place for him when she looked back before she stepped off the car, and then as the train pulled away from the platform.

Good-bye, sweetie, she mouthed, smiling and waving up to the open doorway where Lonnie stood, his wild, uncut hair in bold, shaggy relief against the conductor's starched white shirt. She wanted that last moment to trump the others stored in his memory. That one, at least, would square with what she knew Selma would tell him years hence, because she heard her say it about her own mother: *It's the best she could do for you, honey. She knew you'd be better off.* Better off. Selma would say it so as not to hurt him. She'd give him plenty of work and a safe, regular childhood. Jewell was pretty sure that Selma would be able to resist trying to make Lonnie hate her. Bobo, she knew, would not.

CHAPTER 7

&

When Rayne's construction cell phone rang, Lillie almost didn't answer it. She was studying for her nursing midterms. The most important, in her mind, was Senior Integration, a title that no one but the black nursing students thought sounded funny; it referred to students' integrating classroom learning about drugs and disease with their clinical learning about direct patient care. The faculty also threw in an intensive review for the dreaded NCLEX licensing exam. Why they chose Easter week, Lillie could not figure. Public schools were on vacation, and nursing students with children scrambled for child care. Otherwise, she might have made more of an objection to Khalil's going with Rayne without her.

Instead she decided to stop fussing and be grateful. Except that, really, she hadn't stopped fussing: right as they left she'd insisted on their taking the old booster seat, and Rayne had put down his construction cell phone in the vestibule to take it from her.

She knew he worried about the new job. He had left a message with his foreman about the locks, and left the keys, labeled, with Lillie. For that reason, she'd clipped his cell next to hers on her waistband. When it rang and vibrated in a loud buzz, she startled and answered abruptly: "RayneDance Construction."

A woman's slow, liquid voice asked: "Hello? Hello?"

Lillie repeated more slowly, "RayneDance Construction Company. May I help you?"

Speaking in a low voice, and minding her words, the woman answered, "Yes, please. My name is Jewell Thompson. I'm calling in response to a letter from Alonzo Rayne. Do I have the right number?"

"Yes, you do. Oh, my goodness," Lillie answered. "You certainly do."

————

Jewell perched on a settee next to Jack's chaise. He was inspecting her lemon wafers, which she'd begun to make for him when the chemo made him nauseous. The wafers seemed to stay down. Besides, he said, even if he couldn't eat them, it was worth it in amusement value to watch Jewell take them out of the oven: cursing the papery wisps as they cooled and began first to scrunch and frill, then to tear, then to stick fast to the cookie sheet like so many bits of dripped plaster.

Jewell patted his arm to let him know that this was the correct number. He opened his eyes in acknowledgment.

"Oh, so he's not there?" Jewell said. "I got the other number, and he said he was driving. I was hoping that maybe he'd arrived wherever he was headed."

"No, he's not. He just left this morning to go out of town. Oh, you know where he is—I was about to do a whole explanation, but you know: he's going to his Nana Selma's for Holy Week."

Jewell thought: *All those years, while we did Mexico, he went to Selma's.* It was an eerie feeling, connecting the two. Of course, he was going to Selma's. Selma had raised him. Jewell tripped her teeth: "Oh, Selma's."

"I'll give you his cell. He should be there in, maybe, like, around six more hours or so. And after that, you can call Nana Selma's landline. The reception, when he's down there, out in the country, can be kinda iffy."

"Thank you, my dear. I know the number, unless something forced Selma to change it since Truman."

"Excuse me?"

"Nothing, dear."

They exchanged numbers. Jewell was eager to end the conversation: "Evenings are usually good, you can tell him. Thanks so much. Good-bye."

"Was it a she?" Jack asked.

"Yes." Jewell sat up straight on the settee.

"His wife?"

"Something makes me think maybe not."

"Everything okay?"

"Yeah. He and the boy I saw have gone down to Selma's for Holy Week. The young woman suggested that I call him there, but I think I'll wait. Talking to him is one thing. Selma is another story."

Jack patted her hand and smiled crookedly. "The whole family: you said it."

Then, because he'd slept badly the night before, and could finally relax, Jack dozed. And Jewell, although she meant to get up and plant tomato and pepper seeds indoors, lay down next to him as if there were nothing else in the world to do. *I've exhausted us both,* she thought as she, too, fell asleep.

When she awoke, Jack was watching her. Jewell thought he looked more rested—less sick, actually, than he had in weeks. "Did you dream?" she asked.

"It was one of those funny dreams. I think it's the drugs. I was back in the hotel, remember, when we decided to get married . . ."

"*We* decided?"

"Whatever it was. I was back in the room, thinking to myself: *If she says yes, we're gonna be all right. This is gonna be a blast.*

"How did I know that?"

"Is that really what you were thinking?"

"I was also thinking—although this wasn't in the dream—that this was going to be the best sex of my entire life."

"And was it?"

"Yeah," he said earnestly. "It was." He realized that he'd been out of the cancer bunker and time traveling. It hadn't been simply a dream. He'd been back there, and, at her simplest suggestion, he was in bed with her again, this time in Barcelona, with her lips and tongue tasting of anisette. Why that moment, he wondered, after the train ride where they'd teased each other in the bathroom with little signs telling them not to drink the water in the sinks?

"Remember Barcelona?"

"Oh, my God, yes, I remember Barcelona." Jewell stood, stretched, and began to tidy their area, as if she could not sit still with the memory. "I remember the last night when we drank that licorice liquor and got so drunk that we didn't put in my diaphragm, and I was scared to death for a month."

"I'd forgotten," he said, although now he thought maybe that was why his mind had indeed picked that moment.

Jewell bent over Jack's face to kiss him. His eyes were closed. Tears had formed in the corners.

Barcelona was their celebratory trip, the one they took after his first cancer episode went into remission. "You didn't want me to be pregnant, did you?" The thought had never occurred to Jewell before this moment. She tried to recall whether he had said anything or indicated anything that she should have noticed.

"No," he whispered, too tired to voice the words. "But right about now, a son might be nice, so I'm glad you have yours back . . . At this point, the mind goes where it wants. I'm sorry."

———

Khalil, who seemed to be sleeping on the back bench seat, threw himself forward to grab Rayne's cell phone when it let out Lillie's ringtone.

"I thought you was 'sleep," Rayne said with only half-hearted pique.

Khalil giggled into the phone as he answered, his hearty, throaty laugh: "Hi, Mom. We're in Virginia, and while I was 'sleep, Rayne ate up all the food.

"*Sike!* But he did eat the oranges . . . I know I don't eat oranges. But maybe I might like to try some."

"Tell your mom they were good."

"You hear that, Mom? He said they were good. The oranges." Then to Rayne, he said: "Mom says it's impor'ant. Can you talk? Or you want to call 'er back?"

"Tell 'er there's a rest area in fifteen miles. Can it wait, like, fifteen minutes?"

Khalil was holding the phone up in the air. Then he put it to his ear. "You hear that?

"Okay, she says, don't forget. Mom, you know *I* won't for-get." He turned the phone off and sat stiffly with it in his hand.

"You gonna come up front again?"

"You wanna know the truth?"

"Sure."

"I gotta go to the bathroom pretty bad."

"What? And you're afraid to jump over the seat?" Rayne looked at Khalil in the rearview mirror to see how much tension his face revealed. "Can you make it another ten or twelve minutes?"

Khalil shook his head no. Rayne drove on, looking for a stretch of road with a good shoulder and some bushes. He told Khalil the criteria, too, hoping that watching the side of the highway would occupy his mind. As soon as he'd finished explaining what makes a suitable pull-off, Khalil shouted, "Dad, look, right here, right here."

Rayne steered the Ford to the side of the road, as close to the grass as possible. Weather threatened. A gray sky and damp air made them pull on their coats as they crossed the weedy strip to the bushes, Khalil trotting to keep up with Rayne's wide strides. They found a spot, used it, and walked and ran back to the truck. Khalil allowed as how he was ready for a sandwich.

"Where'd your mother put the hand sanitizer? Hey-hey, *do not* touch that food without wiping your hands." He shouted it at Khalil's back, because the boy was sprinting to the car.

Not sure whether Khalil had heard him, Rayne jogged to catch up.

"Here." Khalil sat sideways in the front seat, facing out the open door. He held out a small tube of antibacterial lotion in one hand and a bottle of similar stuff in the other.

"What's the difference?"

Khalil shrugged. Rayne wiped his hands and gave back the bottle. A truck's wake rocked the Ford. Rayne swiveled Khalil's body forward by the knees and closed the door. He was chilled by the time he walked around the front of the truck, so he turned on the engine, blasted the heat, which was still warm, and took the cell phone that Khalil handed him.

"Hey, babe," he said, waving at Khalil simply to hand him any sandwich rather than point to each one. "What's up?"

"Your mother called."

"Good. That's real good. She called me here, and I couldn't talk. I'll wait to call back," Rayne said evenly into the phone.

"How can you stand it, not calling back? Don't you want to hear her voice? She's got a great voice. It's like honey."

He heard Khalil opening the door, looked over to shake his head to say *no*, and saw the boy slip down off the seat, pantomime peeing again, and turn away. Then Rayne snapped his fingers loudly to get the boy's attention. He did not want to shout at him and have Lillie go ape because her son was out on the highway alone. "I heard her voice. Look, baby, me and Khalil are sitting on the side of the road, the trucks are rockin us every time they pass, and I've got another seven hours to drive. Lemme just drive it in peace without, like, drama."

"Yeah, I hear the traffic. You got the windows open?"

"Unh-huh." In fact, Rayne was watching Khalil slip down from the passenger side and motioning for him to leave the door open, so that he could watch him go back to the bushes to pee again. Every few steps Khalil would turn around. Rayne made big dips with his head to nod okay.

"Isn't it still cold there?" Lillie continued, nervous. "It's just, like, awful here. I'm about to call the number for those body bag Snuggie things. Hot pink. You come home, I'ma look like a big ole fuzzy tongue sittin on the couch reading about electrolytes."

Rayne laughed. "Don't sound like you."

"Dear *Lord*," she asked, "is that all highway noise? Sounds like a racetrack."

"Yeah, it's loud, all right."

"Still, you could close the window and call 'er real quick. She's easy to talk to. At least on the surface, I mean."

"Yo, baby, all I wanna do is one thing at a time, okay? She and I been waiting twenty-something years. We can wait a few more hours." Rayne was watching Khalil, thinking that the boy had not gone back to the exact spot the two of them had used the first time. It irritated him.

"Okay, okay. I thought you'd be excited. I was excited."

"Yep. I know. I thought I would be, too."

"Everything okay?"

"Yeah. Khalil's got to pee again. Lemme go."

Lillie laughed. "That's just a George-of-the-Jungle pee, 'cause you probably let 'im go in the bushes, and I make 'im go in the ladies' room with me."

"No doubt. I'll call you when we get there."

Before Rayne hung up, Khalil scrambled back into the truck and slammed the door.

"What was that?" Lillie asked.

Rayne frowned at Khalil, who was rubbing hand sanitizer with ostentatious care into his palms and over the backs of his hands up to his wrists before taking off his coat. "That's your son playing games. I gotta go."

"Want me to talk to him? No, I know, I know. Okay. Drive safe. It's been a hard week."

CHAPTER 8

R ayne spoke sharply to Khalil about leaving the truck while he was on the phone. He poured a cup of coffee from the thermos into the convenience-store travel mug Lillie had packed, and the two rode away in silence. When they passed the rest area full of cars, Rayne drove by, glad that he did not have to stop, and realized that he hadn't thanked Lillie for the food. Khalil sat quietly, chastened only a little, playing his handheld video game.

Rayne put in an old homemade CD of heavy reggae hip-hop and dance hall music. It *had* been a hard week, especially for Lillie. He and Lillie had sent a card and a check to the lady up the street who watched Khalil. Ten years earlier she'd awakened to find her husband dead in the bed beside her; last week, after her daughter had failed to respond to calls, Mrs. Towers had gone to her apartment and found the forty-two-year-old dead, where she'd collapsed, the medical examiner said, the day before.

Mrs. Towers kept saying that she'd just saved up enough money for her husband's gravestone. Her daughter had helped.

Then, Lillie's best friend Temika's two-year-old was diagnosed with a rare form of cancer—detected after Lillie told her that the child seemed to tire too easily and might have an infection. Lillie filled a basket with violets for healing, because she said she didn't know what else to do.

And Beanie, the young boy, just twenty-two, who'd been working with Rayne since he started his business, had died on Sunday night after riding with a cousin whose license was suspended. Rather than pull over when cops flashed their lights, the cousin tried to outrun them, crashing and killing Beanie and another passenger. They'd had a funeral in a driving rain in North Philadelphia, where the grief and the storm drains backed up into the streets and spilled over onto the sidewalks, sloppy pools that splashed everyone nearby.

That was why there'd been the haphazard handling of the padlock at the job: with one foreman having moved to Atlanta and Beanie dead, his two most conscientious men were not on point to run quality control.

———

Rayne turned up the music and searched through different songs for the grittiest he could find, the harshest voices and heaviest bass lines. Too much. This morning, after they had made love, and knowing that Rayne would be leaving, Lillie and Rayne's fears returned: that two people without happy nuclear families might just be kidding themselves that they could succeed in creating their own; that this island of calm and pleasure might not be real, or else that it couldn't last; that they would ruin it out of ignorance; or that it would be taken from them. They felt it most when they were about to separate or when trouble struck near them, which it did so often that it became regular, like girls having babies. It was more regular in their lives to hear of deep stresses and tragedy than not. So they were always afraid.

Lillie said the way trauma packed itself into their community this last week reminded her of how she'd been taught to pack gauze into a wound. That's why so many people couldn't feel much of anything, but only watch one another as if on a video. This week Lillie called, delivered food and cards, and said the words; and when they did feel it, she asked him, how would they know? Rayne answered simply that he'd shouted at a bike messenger who had come too close, but that so far, neither of them had shot up their TV. They laughed sadly.

Rayne could feel the sex, that he could feel. He could feel the music, but only if it was natty dread and loud. He could feel how the surprising flushes of irritation threatened to derail him: right now, it was with his mother for calling at a bad time; and with Khalil for cavorting on the side of the highway while he was on the phone. The irritation was out of proportion to the offenses; he knew it, and yet, hey, there it was, threatening. Like Lillie, he had thought he'd be happy to hear from his mother. He'd assumed he'd be relieved, satisfied. Instead, he was dragging up the week's tragedies, as if to confirm what he already knew: that she'd gone somewhere a long damn time ago and had nothing to do with his present life; the time Lillie shaved off her heavy black hair for kids with cancer; the restaurant job when he cut through ten pitas at once with a cleaver and took off the tip of his finger; the first time he plowed Selma's corn and soybean fields by himself; the time when Magic let him go three rounds with the giant Panamanian who everyone said would kill him—and Rayne won.

Why would his mother up in cushy Bucks County, or wherever she was, call on a weekday afternoon as if he were sitting by the phone, unless she knew nothing about anything in his life? "Voice like honey" was the last thing he wanted to hear.

He dragged every grievance, every sadness, out of the drawer, spread them out, and examined them for an hour until Khalil pulled him out of his head.

"Dad?"

"What is it?"

"Look."

"I'm driving."

"Just for a minute, look."

Rayne's countenance was more severe than he meant it to be when he turned. The boy flinched slightly. Without words, obviously scared, he held up hands to his face. Light traces of red were forming. His eyes were swollen. Rayne swiveled his eyes back and forth between the boy's reddened, puffy face and the highway.

"When you walked into the bushes, did anything hit your face?"

Khalil nodded. Tears had collected in the corner of his eyes.

"Does it itch?"

He nodded again.

"Fuck." Rayne knew that they were just five or ten miles past the last rest stop, but maybe twenty or thirty miles from the next. He maneuvered the truck into the left lane, hoping against hope, and made a U-turn in the next opening in the median. No state trooper. He aimed the truck in the other direction, waited for an opening, then jammed the pedal to get them up off the grass and into the left lane.

"Don't touch your face, hear me?" he kept saying. "I know it's hard, but do not touch your face."

When they drove into the rest area parking lot, Rayne grabbed Khalil's duffel bag, shouted to him again not to touch anything, and walked him into the men's room. There he stripped Khalil's clothes down to his underwear, wrapped them inside out in his coat, and threw them away. Khalil was too afraid to say anything. Rayne leaned him over the sink, first washing his hands and arms with what seemed like a hundred squirts of pink bathroom soap, then his forehead, cheeks, and chin, each area separately, with soap. He tipped Khalil's head different ways to keep the soapy water, carrying the poison ivy oil, from running into his eyes. Khalil tried not to cry, because Rayne told him that the tears could conduct the oil back into his eyes. He shivered, because without his clothes he was cold, and tried as hard as he could to follow Rayne's directions.

Rayne left him in the handicapped stall to dress while he went out to try to buy calamine lotion. The cashier flirted with him, bending low to give him an eyeful of tattooed cleavage as she reached beneath the counter. She had a little boy, too, she said. He had been a beautiful baby. "I make pretty babies," she added, giving him this as a special assurance with his change.

"Yeah, I bet you do."

Then Rayne went back for Khalil, draped his big coat over him, and bought five giant cups of boiling water at coffee/tea prices at the Roy Rogers, one cup of ice for Khalil's face, and a twenty-five-cent courtesy cup, which he instructed Khalil to fill with pink liquid soap. They walked to the car, and Rayne told the boy he was to stand with him, watch, help, and touch nothing. Still damp, Khalil began to shiver.

It went on for half an hour, what felt to Rayne like a ridiculous cleanup, with big-gulp containers as buckets and paper towels as rags. Finally, so that he could really scrub down into the plastic upholstery, Rayne sacrificed a T-shirt from his own bag. He recalled bitterly the exact location of his buckets and Pine-Sol at the shop and, in fact, all his supplies: rags, scrub brushes, even Lava soap for the boy. Khalil helped as best he could, mutely, guiltily, truly chastened.

"Put the ice on your face," Rayne said, and Khalil obliged, though the weather was cold and he was still shivering.

Rayne bagged up the T-shirt, cups, and paper towels to throw them away, draped his extra hoodie on the seat, and went back inside to wash his hands and arms again. Khalil started to climb into the truck, but Rayne wanted to keep him where he could see him. "Come in with me," he said.

When they came out of the men's room the last time, the flirtatious clerk was standing there. She said: "My little boy did the same thing last summer. You from around here?"

Rayne started to step. "No, baby, I'm on my way to South Carolina."

"Well, here," she said, holding out two individual packs of Benadryl. She looked over her shoulder. "Take 'em."

"I don't need to do that," he said, reaching into his pocket to pay.

She made a pushing motion with one hand. "Just give 'im some. It'll keep down the swelling."

"Thanks a lot. I wouldn't have thought of that."

"I know." She flashed him a dimpled grin and turned away with a bounce.

Khalil was happy to take the pills, submit to the calamine lotion, and lie quietly, no video game, faceup, on the backseat. Rayne adjusted the heat, so that the cab felt warm and intimate. After a little while Khalil was hungry again. They drove together and ate, under the influence of the music. Then, pronouncing it a "really long ride," Khalil slept soundly.

Yellow jessamine and forsythia began to appear here and there along the roadsides, and sprayed yellow in luxurious profusion in the last light of sunshine that began to slant through the atmosphere. Solid cloud cover in the north now opened up to big white cumulus clouds with dusky rose bellies rubbing the stubbly tree line.

Once over the South Carolina line, Rayne regained his equanimity. He bought four bags of spiced pecans from a stand outside a rest stop, dropped one in Khalil's duffel bag, and ate two as he drove. He swigged the last swallows of lukewarm coffee and hoped that Selma had cooked for them.

———

Once upon a time a boy just like you was sent to find something for the family to eat in the place where the woods met the water. He was getting big, and it was time that he learned how men take care of their families. Because, as his mother said, That's the way of the world.

He laid a trap and caught a rabbit, but the rabbit said to him: "If you let me go, I'll show you where a big old crocodile is stuck in the swamp nearby. He'll be a much bigger, and, might I add, a much tastier, meal than I."

The boy said to him: "I will not go back to my village empty-handed. If you are lying to me, and there is no crocodile, I will catch you again and kill you."

With such rough bargaining, they struck a deal.

"That's not how Grandma Bett would say it," says King, "but go on. Bett said whoever tells it tells it."

"I like it this way, too," Selma says. "Kinda fancy. Go on."

The rabbit was indeed as good as his word. He led the boy to a place in the swamp where a jagged tree stump, felled by lightning, had created a natural trap. The big crocodile had waddled into it and was jammed fast, so that he could not pull through or back out.

That's the way of the world.

"Too bad for you, Mr. Crocodile," said the boy, and before anyone could say another word, that fast boy took off running to get the men of his village to help him kill the great beast and carry him home.

They could not believe it, but they followed the boy to humor him, and when they saw the huge animal, they killed him and, using heavy rope, strung the croc on two poles stretched across four men's shoulders to spread the weight. They would eat his meat and tan his leather.

"That's the way of the world." The family says it with Rayne-bo. He stops, smiles, and looks from one face to another.

"Go on," Selma says. "Keep reading. We know the story, too, you know."

The men sang as they walked with the beast swinging. They sang an old song and put in new words: about the clever boy, and how he'd been sent for a rabbit to feed his family and returned with a crocodile to feed the village. Oh, he was part of their history now.

The vain little rabbit, hearing their song, came out from the bush to remind the boy that it was he, Rabbit, who'd shown the crocodile's position. Rabbit wanted the boy to tell the men so that they'd sing about Rabbit and immortalize Rabbit in their history of great feats in the village hunting life. One of the younger men who was not carrying the crocodile was watching the edge of the bush intently, as he always did, for movement of prey. When Rabbit stood on his hind legs, the hunter raised his bow and arrow and—zzzzzing-pfft!—shot him dead. Then he picked up the rabbit and gave it to the boy to take home to his mother.

Because (and here the family joins in) *that's the way of the world.*

CHAPTER 9

◦◦

"We *home!*"

Rayne yelled out the traditional Needham family hallo as he stepped out of the truck and into the mild South Carolina spring night. A discreet moon shone just enough light to reveal the weedy gravel and a whole front yard overgrown.

Selma could see them from the old house, where she'd gone in the late afternoon to make the bed and try to freshen the place a little. The girl she paid to help her had promised to come, but hadn't shown up. So Selma had tried to clean and cook, but it had been too much for her. It was ten o'clock, and she could barely stand. And now she saw that he'd brought the boy, too. She wondered if she had another set of sheets. People had been going into the house for months since she'd gotten ill last year. Every time she looked for something, she discovered something else lost.

Oh, well, she thought. Nothing she could do about it now.

She could just try to enjoy him while she had him. Was a time when she would have run around fussing about the sheets. She reached into the cupboard for a second glass. Like everything else in the place, it no doubt needed washing. So she filled a little bowl with hot, soapy water, and plunged in a juice glass for the boy. It was hard to see into the dark, but she could tell Rayne's jacketless outline in the moonlight: the familiar big, thick body rocking with remarkable lightness on the balls of his feet, Jesus, *so* like his great-grandfather King. For a moment she felt disoriented, as if weather had settled on the estuary and she were fogged in, alone.

Rayne was showing the boy the trailer that Jones had purchased with 50 percent down, and Selma had insisted on finishing paying for. He didn't stay in the trailer after he moved in with the man named Jared who had been his boss with the horses, but whom he now called his partner. Selma had never met Jared, and she doubted she would. In any event, she didn't ask. She couldn't see over to the trailer, but she waved two or three times anyway, thinking maybe Rayne would look her way.

He called again, "Aw, c'mon, Nana Selma. You gonna make me come find you? Where you at?"

She felt giddy. It might as well have been his great-grandfather's teasing, serrated voice that snagged her memory.

————

You don't know how beautiful you are, do you?

No. What she knew was that she was black and skinny.

C'mon, Smoky, lemme show you.

————

Others had said it was weird, how her eyes, the color of brown beer bottles, matched her skin, like a snake or a witch. King called them smoky eyes, and she loved him for it. *Well, Smoke, look like we the only ones to raise this little fella.*

He'd said it about Bobo, but she'd thought it to herself two short generations later when Bobo's daughter sent Rayne to her. And now she'd done it, she thought to herself; she'd won out over Rayne's feckless mother and grandfather and made him into the man he was born to be.

She remembered how she'd sat him down on the porch when he was a boy, and told him that one day he'd be a big man, and nobody could take anything away from him, and that, out of the kindness of his heart, he'd come over on Sunday afternoons and take her for a drive in the country. One day, when she died, the land would be his.

And here he was.

She knew, now that he was back, that she should have told him about her fall. It had seemed right just to keep going and not worry him when he was on the phone, twelve hours' drive away, but now she knew he'd be hurt to know she'd kept it from him. This trip, they'd have to have a sit-down, she told herself. Talk business. The place was coming apart around her ears. Most times she made sure not to notice, but at bottom, now that he was here, she knew how it would look through his sharp eyes.

Just one more thing. That's how to stay ahead.

Okay, she said to herself, just set the table for another place, so you can feed the boy, too. One thing at a time.

But she was so tired, she could hardly even face going across the room to fetch another plate. And she'd been too proud to ask the girl to bring over the little wheelchair she mostly lived in over in the trailer. Then she corrected herself: the trifling, lazy-behind girl hadn't come; that's why she was so tired.

So, a little more work.

More work, never less, had been King's answer to what he joked was the "ongoing inconvenience" of being black. As a seventeen-year-old sharecropper's daughter, Selma might not have understood the words and phrases he used, but she did know how to work right along with him: two-man days, he called them, hard, long days that few people could sustain. She kept up with him through heat and cold and rain, focused like prayer on doing his will. And then she kept up with him at night, too, happily, in an outsize desire unlike anything she'd ever known before or since. She did everything with him. She could still hear his contented breathing as he slipped into sleep, when she could admire and adore the mountain of him lying next to her, and stay awake to absorb the last warm embers of pleasure. Which may have been why God took him away.

———

Selma tried to watch where Rayne was going. It was dark, but she thought she saw them aim east, toward the raised beds where she'd taught him to tend tobacco as a boy.

And hadn't he fought her all the way? Starting with suckering the plants. In the first few weeks, she'd take him out to work with her. She showed him how to reach down at the bottom and snap off the suckers. The plant oozed sticky tar, so he had to work carefully. But fresh from New York, and never having done a lick of labor, he made sloppy grabs at the bottom leaves and ripped them off. After an hour, he had himself covered in tar. He sulked, stopping finally to try to pull the goo off his eyebrows.

Selma slowed down to coax him to move on to the next plant. The hired men passed them. Their children stayed in a pack with the new boy, encouraging for a while, until their fathers barked at them to move on. Selma remembered wondering why King's nieces and nephews could not be counted on to help raise the boy in Philadelphia, where most of them lived, but the fact was that they didn't. They had stopped coming down, stopped sending their children for the summer to learn the land, stopped sending money to help with taxes. Bobo helped when he was home, but he was heavy-handed and bitter, and drove trucks across the country most of the time anyway. Like it or not, it was her job to bring the boy along.

C'mon, baby, we ain't milking the plant; we gotta sucker it.

Rayne wiped his hand and wasted more time observing the jagged edge where the suckers had been and trying, it seemed, to decide whether any others were the right size to be torn off.

Selma hissed with frustration. *I tol' you like this. Just snap it and move.*

He reached out a limp hand.

Snap and move. Snap, doggone it. Like this! The others turned the row and were gone. It was as if Selma were alone with the lazy boy on a jetty of won't-do. She had told herself that he had never been taught to work, and that God only knew how his mother had failed him. Selma wanted very much to beat him, but she had vowed to King that she would not beat his children. This boy, the spit and image of her husband born years after his death, and with no idea how to live up to his legacy, was indeed still one of his children.

"Pig won't jump the stile, and I'll never get home tonight," she said. It gave her a minute to collect herself, and stop her palms from itching to smack him.

"Ooh, tell me the story. *Please.*"

"Well, when we gonna work? We sit out here telling stories, we can't bring in a crop. Don't make a crop, we don't eat."

"Like the story. *Please.* I'll work if you tell me."

"I got news for you, Lazyboy: you gonna work either way."

Selma secretly suspected that the children in this family would have done better with a few more whippings, but King's word ruled. Black people had been whipped enough without doing it to their own, he said. *Why do you think we stand for it, Smoky? Why? Because our parents teach us firs' thing: Bam! And then we say to 'em: See there? That's whatchoo get.* When Selma had argued that the children were arrogant, he snorted. White people were arrogant, he said, *but we don't begrudge them their children's freedom, just our own.*

Still. Junior went off to war and died. Charlotte had run away; Bobo went to jail; Jewell just went bad was all Selma could figure, spoiling her boy rotten and then throwing him away, and it looked like little Rayne was close to ruined.

"All right, then," she said, looking at him hard.

"I can see through your eyes."

"One story fast, and then we work. Or else."

"Or else!"

"Now. Th' old woman finds a coin and buys a little piggy, but the pig won't jump the stile and she thinks she will not get back home before dark." Raynie was afraid of the dark, Selma knew; she could see that he understood the old woman's fear of being out on the road alone in it.

"What she do?"

Selma answered the boy with as much excitement as she could muster, even though her mind was clicking off the wasted time.

"Well, she finds a dog to bite the pig," Selma answered, fixing him with another hard look.

"What?"

"You wouldn't want me to fin' a dog to bite you if you didn't work, would you?"

Rayne shook his head slowly. "But he didn't bite 'im."

"Nope, dog wouldn't bite pig, so the old woman go find a stick. Say: Stick, stick, beat dog. Dog won't bite pig, pig won't jump the stile, and I'll never get home tonight."

And on it went. She found a fire to burn the stick, water to quench the fire, and an ox to drink the water.

"Then what?"

Selma tells him what he knows: "She went out and found a butcher-man."

And then, finally, the bloodthirsty magic that Rayne had been waiting for commences.

So, the butcher begin to kill the ox;

ox begin to drink water;

water begin to quench fire;

fire begin to burn stick;

stick begin to beat dog;

dog begin to bite pig,

and then, finally, oh my goodness, the pig jump over the stile—and the old woman finally gets back to her home that night.

Selma sighed, and sat silent for a moment, letting the story end before she drew the natural parallel. "Okay, boy . . ." She was ready to go on, joking, cheered herself now that the old woman was home, no longer stuck by a recalcitrant animal, dependent as she, and rural women everywhere, were on the creatures in their care. She'd queued up her nicknames all in a row, ready to list them, laughing: "Okay, Newboy, Littleboy, Lazybonesboy, Bigboy, Bigolebutterboy, Sillycityboy, Nana's Boy, Nana's Best Boy, okay. Let's move 'em out, and show me that you can be a Goodboy, be a Farmboy . . ."

Selma stood. The boy did not rise with her. "Suckerboy," he mumbled. "I wanna go home."

"This the home you got now, boy. You home now." Selma mustered her last shred of patience. *Up, uppy!* she thought.

He started to shake his head no. She reached over his shoulder and snapped a sucker. With her tar-sticky hand, she grabbed his collar to stand him up and move him along to the next plant, wanting to get some momentum going before he could slow

their process yet again. He needed to get some geography between him and the starting point, or else he'd never know the
simple satisfaction of the job well done. Or even poorly done,
but done. "C'mon, boy."

Rayne reared up at being touched, lost his balance, and
pitched forward. His elbows splayed out and his face plowed
into the ground.

"Oh, Jesus. C'mon, child, get up."

Mouth full of dirt, Rayne jumped up and flailed his body
around, spitting out the soil as best he could and cursing: "Shit,
shit! I wanna go home! I wanna go home. I want my mommy. I
hate this damn old farm! Damn stupid dirt. Piece o' shit farm. I
hate it! I hate you!"

The children came running back to witness the tantrum. *Oh,
my gosh, looka him. He spoiled.* They'd never seen or even dreamt
of such a naked display of temper to an adult. *Spoiled.*

By the time the hired men appeared, Rayne was lying on the
ground, screaming and crying, face full of snot and tar, unable
to catch his breath to cry more than "I want . . . I want . . . I
want . . ." on each jagged inhalation.

JJ picked the boy up by his shirt and carried him to where
the others could not hear them. They saw that he held the boy
up to his face level, shook him hard once or twice, then dropped
him to the ground. He turned and strode back to the others.

"Let's go." Selma fell back in behind him, and the others
fanned out according to their usual places, their children gos-
siping behind.

"Whatcha tell 'im, bro?" one of the others asked.

"Same thing King always said," JJ answered solemnly. "Hope
Selma agree."

"What's that?"

"'S what he doesn't know yet . . ."

Selma finished the sentence so that all of them could hear

her say it and know that she'd enforce it: "'Gotta work to eat.' In't that right, JJ?"

"Yep."

The children chattered among themselves and sneaked looks at the spoiled child paying them no mind, not working and certainly not contrite about not working. JJ threatened to beat any of his children who slowed down to talk to the outcast, and one of the others lectured them about working harder. But they could not help but look over at the boy now and then, sitting on the ground in the thin shade, methodically pulling tar from his eyebrows. He had done the unthinkable, and he seemed to have gotten away with it.

At dinner, after they had all scrubbed with Lava soap and scrubbed him, too, Selma sat him under a turkey oak twenty yards off from their outside table and gave him a mason jar of fresh water. From there, Rayne watched them eat boiled pork backbone stew, field beans and rice, corn bread, and cucumbers. King would not have let him eat *or* move. Selma let him walk back and forth under his tree, but he could not go farther, and, of course, he could eat no supper at all. His was a big boy for his age, always hungry.

"Gotta work to eat," the grown-ups repeated, as if to keep Selma's resolve.

————

That night Selma did take the boy a bowl of bread and milk, which he drank down too fast and vomited up. To put him to sleep she told another story:

Once upon a time a boy just like you was sent to the place where the woods met the water to find something for the family to eat. He was getting big, and it was time that he learned how men take care of their families. Because, like his mother said, That's the way of the world.

"That's not how you told me before," Rayne protested.

"This the old version, like Grandma Bett told it. 'Cept I'm tired of talkback, so that's it. Tell it to yourself."

"I'm sorry. I'll be quiet," Rayne said, humbled after the day's events.

"Too late, Cityboy. Nana's had all the talkback I'ma take. That's the way of this world. You gotta start takin it in."

Selma remembered years later lying in bed and talking to King as if he were alive, asking him to help her raise the teenager who had learned to work, but not yet to love. Rayne would get up at dawn before school to do his chores; he no longer whined, and did not need to be awakened or reminded. But he was cool, closed in on himself; he was correct, but unyielding. King's answer came to her in a dream. Selma knew it was King talking to her because it was his exact brand of wisdom, and something that she'd never have thought of herself: she had to picture whom he might become—and then she had to trust him to grow into himself.

Her brother, Jones, said something similar years later: you can't raise a boy to be afraid of what he'll become.

The implication for her was not just to love the boy dutifully, but to delight in him *as if* he were that glorious young man to be.

She tried. Now and then it came naturally, when she'd catch him out of the corner of her eye across the field. Then she saw King in him, and admired the kernel of the man she sensed he could be. Later, although she always said it would kill her, Selma gave him back to his family in Philadelphia for college, and she prayed God that the hoity-toity Negroes wouldn't ruin him. Now here he was, just as she had imagined him.

It seemed to hit her all at once, as she waited for the night to yield him up. Nothing solid existed anywhere; everything melted into everything else, and she with it. The back door banged open, and his big, heavy boots stomped, and his voice filled the air, and the child next to him jumped up and down.

The fifty-year-old juice glass in her hand, the one she'd gotten out for Khalil's table setting, dropped and shattered just as she reached for it.

CHAPTER 10

Selma was thinner even than Rayne remembered. In less than a year her braided hair had gone from salt-and-pepper to gray-white. Looking older and stunned, she stood at her kitchen sink, hands hanging loose at her sides, one dripping soapy water, one blood, onto the floor. Her smile drooped a little on one side.

"Why you standing there lookin simple at me, you big ole Rayne Man?" she asked in greeting. "Come on and gimme a hug."

"Nana, look at your hands." Rayne caught her wrists as she lifted her arms toward him. He turned her palms upward. "What happened? I'm out there callin, and you're in here cutting yourself like a teenager in a documentary."

Selma didn't know what he meant, but the energy and humor in his voice made her happy. "What're you talkin 'bout? Hey, baby; is this our new young man in the family?" She grinned even as she took in the fact of her bleeding hand. She had to think about the cut to feel it. Now that he mentioned it, it stung. "Oh, Lord, I done cut myself and wasted the glass. That was your great-grandfather's wedding present from his first marriage, too." She looked over her shoulder at the glass in the sink, then down at the hand, at the bloody semicircle around her thumb that dripped both ways, toward the fingers and wrist. Once she studied it, the sting deepened into a slicing pain.

Together Rayne and Selma held her hand under cold running water. Khalil stood on her right side. Selma turned to him and said: "You must've had a long, long ride today. And what's that on your face?"

"Poison ivy, I think," Rayne said.

"Yeah, I see you still got a little calamine on. Come on, need to put on some more. Do I got any in there? Probably all dried up. Look and see. And if it's dried up, drip in some water and let it sit and shake it up. Warm water. What you should have is some jewelweed, 'cept it's too early. Jewelweed be better."

"We got some fresh calamine in the truck." Rayne wanted to take Selma to the hospital. "This looks deep."

Selma shook her head: "You just the nurse o' everybody today, ain't you?"

"My mom's gonna be a *real* nurse."

"I heard that. When she graduate?"

"This summer."

"Then she can stop doing those tattoos?"

"Mommy says she might still do both, because some of the Eagles players came to her first, and now some others come and ask for her, special. They like going to a nurse, 'cause she won't give 'em diseases and stuff."

"I think we need to get stitches at the hospital," Rayne said.

Selma made a dismissive snort. "Shoot. I ain't thinkin about no hospital. You just walk in the door, and we goin to drive another hour and sit up in that meat market with all the crazy Negroes been shootin each other? How's that feel? And I got a plate full of food for you sittin on the pilot? Boy," she said to Khalil, "you wanna drive another hour?"

Rayne shook his head at Khalil to stop him from answering. "All I'm saying is that it looks deep."

"And I'm sayin that this boy gotta eat. I bet you been eating junk all day."

"Nope," Khalil said before Rayne could catch his eyes. "My mom packed us lunch and snacks and dinner. We had sandwiches and oranges and Pirate's Booty."

"Pirate's Booty?"

"It's good. She sent chocolate milk for me, too. He had coffee. And water."

"He give the whole inventory," Selma said, laughing. "Better not do nothin you don't want reported. This one'll tell."

"Okay, no hospital tonight," Rayne said. "But if it's not mending tomorrow, we're going first thing. Even if they do suspect me of elder abuse."

"Oh-ho! Come down and they put you in jail. Just like your grandfather."

Rayne did not answer. Instead he read and answered the text that came in from Lillie, checking on them. He typed: *Just arrived & nana cut finger. Getting bandages now.*

Lillie asked a few questions, and then told him to ice the hand and make her hold it up. He smiled to himself as he picked the sharp shards out of the drain and dropped them into a paper shopping bag from under the sink. Next to that bag he saw the one-gallon mayonnaise tub in which for years Selma had stuffed plastic produce bags. He grabbed two, lined one with the other, and filled them with ice.

"Your supper's right there, Khalil. Your mama call you Lil? Lil Boy? You too big for that. Lil Man, maybe. I go for that. I made plenty, so there'll be enough for two," she said, waving the hand. "You don't eat like Big Man, here, do you?"

"No, ma'am," Khalil answered. "Nobody does. My mom says."

"Oh, some people do, I guarantee you that. And a couple of 'em lived right in this house."

Lillie texted back: *Calld ur mother?*

"Here, Nana," Rayne said to Selma as he read the text. "Sit down and hold this ice on."

"Yes, *sir.*"

"Go on, go on," Rayne bossed her gently. He fastened the bundle with rubber bands from the back doorknob and placed it into the trash. No jewelweed, he thought. Then he texted back: *No time to self. Tomorrow.*

Selma sat heavily onto the kitchen chair and pressed paper towels into the wound. "Will you get me the bandage stuff?"

Rayne ducked into the bathroom for adhesive strips, and went to the second shelf in the medicine cabinet that he now recognized as an old silver cutlery box that King must have installed sideways onto the wall and then inset with an oval mirror. The floor was a crazy quilt of off-white tile shards with the occasional black or red and a rough, uneven circle of red pieces in the center. Rayne remembered the feeling of the floor on his bare feet, how he marveled at the many sharp edges, all submerged in grout so that none snagged his skin. The floor was cool in the summer. Rayne wondered where King had salvaged the tile, and a shudder of recognition went through him. "Say, Nana Selma, where'd Great-Granddaddy get the tiles?" he yelled.

"Same place he got the rest of it: anywhere where they was tearing down. He'd take the mules and load up the cart. Naturally, when we got the Ford, he'd take that and fetch stuff with it. Stored it in the shed where you used to go play and get into trouble. Whenever I need a part for something, I still go in there and look.

" 'Course JJ's not creative like King Needham were. Or like you. Very few people are."

———

They bandaged the cut after two more trips to the bathroom and one to her old bedroom to find witch hazel, ointment, gauze. Selma fussed that skinny old ladies could only have but so much in them to bleed out, and Khalil followed behind Rayne with the cell phone ready, if only they'd give him the go-ahead, to call his mother for nursing consult.

"He still remember where everything is," Selma said half to herself and half to Khalil. "Well, I guess he would remember the Band-Aids, seein's how he went through 'em like Grant through Richmond."

"Did he fall a lot?"

"Fall? Child, he fell, he knocked, he scraped, he ran over things, he dropped offa the roof. He got wedged underneath that old yoke-plow, tryin to see could he lif' it. Everything you can imagine."

Then, loudly, to Rayne, her eyes wide with righteous indignation: "Oh, listen, you know they tryin to pass a new ordinance," she called. "Lemme tell you what they tryin'a do. They wanna make it illegal to have a bathroom off the kitchen!"

"Yeah, lotta places say that," he said.

"Do they call it unsanitary, like we all dirty?"

Khalil read a text from his mother. "Lillie says to hold your hand up higher than your heart."

"She is so right. How'd I forget?" Selma raised her hand over her head.

"Thank you very much," she said, chin pointed in the direction of the phone. "Can she hear me?"

Khalil shook his head, frowning.

"Stop staring, Khalil, and text your mother thanks from Nana Selma."

"Why do you do that?" Khalil asked when he looked up. He appeared far more comfortable with Selma than Rayne had ever seen him be with a strange new adult.

As if in answer and to amuse him, she tilted her head toward the ground and fixed her face in a far-off look. Rayne laughed. It was a family joke, an imitation of an Indian holy man in one of the many *National Geographic* photos that King had cut out and tacked to the wall. "Go into Rayne's old room, right there, across the parlor, and bring me back the picture that look like this. Take a butter knife."

Khalil frowned. "What for?"

Selma would not dignify the question with an answer, but swiveled her eyes instead toward Rayne, who picked up a worn stainless steel knife from the table and handed it to Khalil. "You'll see."

"Why children think we don't know what we're talkin about?"

Rayne nodded at Selma, and then smiled when he heard Khalil in the bedroom exclaim at the sight of all the photos.

"I found it!" As he worked the staple out of the wood, the house was quiet except for the child's groans of exertion and the sounds of the knife edge scraping the old staple.

"Want help?"

"I got it." Khalil came running back into the room, studying the picture. He bumped into the table. "Sorry."

"Can you read the caption?"

The caption said that the holy men kept their arms raised above their heads for years, until the arms shriveled—Selma anticipated his trouble and said the word as he got to it—from lack of circulation. The nails on the raised hand sometimes grew so long that they pierced the monk's fists. In a family marked by King's insistent discipline, the swami had become an iconic jest, but only half joking, about determination. When more hard work was needed, or when someone knew that he or she was failing in fortitude, they raised their arms and turned their eyes heavenward as a reminder of the outer limits of human will: ridiculous as the shrunken-armed swami, but possible! It was the sign for buck up, do better, get strong—*"Keep working. Hah!"* as Selma wrote in the one or two cards she sent each year.

Rayne barked out a laugh, even as he noticed how very thin her small arms had become. The two of them sat laughing in the kitchen, enjoying Khalil's first discovery of the persistent swami, and also remembering, and reassuring each other of who they were together, which was different, even in this most tiny and atrophied of families, from who they were apart.

"It's cold in here," Khalil said.

"Yeah, it was fine while I was cookin," Selma said. "But now, you right. It is cold. Bet you didn't think South Carolina got cold. And when I was your age, half us didn't have shoes."

Khalil opened his mouth and eyes wide.

"Ray, you think you feel like firing up the stove?"

"Sure. C'mon, Khalil."

At the back door they grabbed empty milk crates that served as kindling baskets and went outside and across the old kitchen garden to the mound of sticks from cleanouts of the underbrush and teardowns of old outbuildings.

Khalil pointed to it as they approached: "If that's an old Indian burial mound, we can't disturb it."

"Nah, man, if anybody's buried there, they're not Indians."

In the moonlight, Rayne could see one very large branch. He snapped off a twig. It made a dry crack.

"That's how it should sound. If your twig's not dry like that, it won't burn."

Khalil hung back.

"Come on, Lil Man, what?"

Khalil eyed the pile.

"Lil, listen. This is a bunch of wood, and Nana's in there cold. See, this is why they used to send city kids to the country," Rayne said.

"So they'd be haunted?"

"That, too. Here." Rayne put Khalil's hand onto the log as if to connect him to the mound and break the spell. "We'll work on this one. I'll give you a twig and break it up this long. You lay it up against that cinder block, and then snap it with your foot, like this."

"Whoa, ninja!"

"Yeah, ninja. But before you do that, gather up like an armful of little twigs about the thickness of your finger. That'll get us started."

They worked together in the moonlight, with Khalil cracking the branches until they were too thick for him. Then Rayne took over.

———

Now what? popped into Rayne's mind.

Never before had he worried about Selma's ability to take care of herself and the farm. *You leavin me?* she'd say every August when he got onto the bus that said NEW YORK on the front but that would drop him off—that's how Selma always thought of it—in Philadelphia for college. *You leavin me?* And he'd walk away smiling at her pitiful little voice, knowing that she was as strong and as capable as anyone half her age and twice her size.

This time he'd just arrived, and already he was afraid to leave her alone. The land was too much, too heavy for her to keep pulling from its productive past to some future where she imagined it would once again support their extended family, with Rayne, like King, at the center.

As if to answer his question about her capacity, however, by the time they returned, Khalil carrying the kindling and Rayne the small logs, Selma had somehow already rolled the newspapers in the bottom of King's old stove with one hand and adjusted the damper. A box of wooden matches lay on the ledge.

"This gonna feel so good," Selma said, mostly to Khalil.

"I'm not even cold anymore," he said.

Rayne laid his careful latticework of twigs, and then medium branches. "I didn't get anything too big," he said.

Selma finished his thought. "Because it's too dark. And I had 'im put away the little hatchet I used to keep in the basket so somebody wouldn't steal it. Crack came in, and, honey, they steal everything. They liable to grab the hatchet and chop me up just to get the ring offa my finger."

Khalil glanced the question over to Rayne.

Rayne shook his head no, but felt his gut contract.

The fire flared, and the old stove's cold metal pinged as it warmed. They watched until the twigs had burned down and the two small starter logs had caught before putting in a larger log and two jagged triangles of half-rotten pine board.

Then Rayne closed the stove door. He got up and walked back to the bathroom to put away the antibacterial cream.

" 'Course," Selma continued, as if they'd never left the subject of bathrooms, "that's where us all got our bathrooms, 'cause that's where the pipes is. I mean, what they think people gonna do? Carry the pipes over t'other side the house? Who got that kinda money?"

"Don't they give out waivers for old construction?" Rayne asked. King had built the one-story, hip-roofed house in the 1920s onto the old shack his father had dragged to this spot forty years earlier on a wagon flatbed. Plumbing came later.

"Waivers?" Selma said derisively. "What's a waiver? These people down here don't know nothin about no waiver. You may have waivers on your construction jobs in the city, but down here, all they know is taxes. That's why I had that job taking care of Pettiford on the weekends, 'cause of the taxes. 'Cause if I miss—if I miss one deadline—they'd be more'n willing to take the whole thing away, *all* your grandfather's land. They be *happy* to take it away."

Khalil asked whether they could please eat.

"Aw, man. Yes! I can't believe it's eleven o'clock at night."

"Oh, Jesus, eat," Selma said. "You know me: a boy should eat."

CHAPTER 11

K halil ate every neck bone. Selma encouraged him to pick them up with his fingers. He sucked them noisily until they were clean. His mother, he said, didn't serve meat; he'd have to tell her about neck bones.

"You do that," Selma said mischievously.

He ate every grain of rice. He ate down to the last fingerful of corn bread and then mopped the essence.

Selma grinned happily. She was comforted by their appetites, and by Rayne's simple and sure answers to her questions about his business. *His own business.* He told her that he'd be working on the newly designed memorial at the house where George Washington and John Adams lived before the capital was moved to D.C. It was going to be a unique National Park Service building, for once commemorating the enslaved Africans, not their rich and powerful masters.

"Oh, really?" Selma did not appear as impressed as Rayne had expected.

"People protested outside the place; they'd go there and pour libations and shout, and there was a group of white historians who were working over the Park Service meanwhile. It's a big deal, Nana, to talk about the slaves and not just the founders. And it is a *very* big deal that I got a piece of the contract. Not the whole contract, but still, a piece of it."

"Jones carried me up to Mount Vernon once," she said. "And the black lady—she was in costume, pretending to be one of the slaves—she acted like, I don't know, like she was just so proud to be one of the general's people. That's what she kept sayin: 'We was the most trusted of his servants.' Make me sick. It's not gonna be like that, is it?"

"I don't think so," he said. "But really, I'm just working on the basic stuff: floors, curbs, the low walls around the borders. They've got a special company who're designing a system to put video and sound outside in the open. I want to learn that: sound design."

"Like Times Square in New York, where the ball drops?"

"Yeah, sort of, on a smallish scale. If everybody can get along. There's a new fight, because the architects have moved some of the walls, like two feet one way or the other."

"Why they do that?"

"'Cause the street has been widened since 1790, for one thing."

"Well, are they gonna tell the people that ole Washington had his slaves' teeth extracted to make his dentures?"

"What?" Khalil choked on his spoonful of food, and Rayne pumped his back until a grain of rice flew from his nostril.

They laughed until they couldn't breathe, then they caught their breath and laughed some more.

"You didn't know that, did you?" Selma said after they'd collected themselves.

"No, Nana, I don't think there's documentation for that."

"They document anything they want, baby, when the lions tell history."

———

Selma's vision was fading, but she could see that Rayne's neck and jaw had thickened, and something in him felt more sure. He *felt* more like King. Selma supposed that now that he had his own business, Rayne was learning things that King had understood, especially about having to support a family and workers, and having to tend the physical and social networks that make up a going concern. Other people said they understood, King had told her, but, when the deal went down, most of them had not stood in a field of tobacco that had been flooded and counted out the loss in their heads, or worked all night to set smudge pots next to fruit trees facing a late frost. Most people got to blame others and curse the sky, he said. If he made an error, even if there had been no way to know better, his mistake could take down his family and everybody who worked for him.

Rayne had also inherited King's spirit of adoption with the boy here sucking neck bones. It's what King had done for her and Jones, and what she'd done in turn with King's children's children. Selma knew that Rayne had grown into his own because he'd inherited the spirit of adoption.

———

For his part, Rayne observed that Selma was much weaker than she'd been the year before. She tired more easily, leaned harder on the table to stand, wobbled a little when she walked. Carried not two plates but one at a time. The house, though she'd cleaned it, had dust in the corners. The top of the fridge, he could see, was black. And every so often she wiped away with her handkerchief, stuffed up her sleeve, a little drool that collected in the right corner of her mouth. He wondered whether she'd had a stroke, and he wondered whether she knew it and had kept it to herself, or didn't know, or whether the doctor had told her and she'd denied it. The last was very likely. Or maybe she was right that that's what younger people always thought: that old folks were having a stroke every time they caught a cold.

Selma's dinner was fine, but not spectacular. Rayne used a little more hot sauce than he usually did, but tried not to let her see.

"Good?" he asked Khalil.

Eyes and hands puffy from the poison ivy, Khalil nodded vigorously. "Don't put hot sauce on the rest of the meat, please," the boy pleaded.

"Why, you think you gonna want some more?" Rayne asked.

"Yeah!"

The homemade canned peaches, however, were perfect, just the right combination of peach flavor and sweetness and gentle, golden-red tang. Of all the food, they tasted precisely as they always had, back from when he was a little boy and he'd pick the peaches and help Selma spice them and set the bottles into their boiling bath. Selma would wipe sweat from Rayne's forehead and tell him that in winter, they'd remember the hot summer afternoons when they'd preserved peaches in these bottles.

"It'll be chilly and col', and we'll say: 'Could it *ever* have been that hot that the sweat run off us like rain?' Be so col' and gray we won't even b'lieve it."

And sure enough, when winter came, they'd recall that very moment. Then she'd repeat the recipe: "Peach, lemon, cinnamon, sugar," said like a song so he'd remember. And he had. A faraway sadness called, like the whispered roar of the waves as they traveled toward the ocean on a small boat on the estuary. One half peach was left in the jar.

"You want that last one?" he asked Khalil.

Khalil nodded enthusiastically, and Rayne scooped the shiny golden half onto his saucer. "Only if you stop scratching."

"I shoulda had some cream with that," Selma said. "If JJ had come by, I woulda asked 'im to run pick some up for me. Or some ice cream. But cream is better. I get so tired so fast. Like I can really only do three things a day, two, really. Sometimes one."

"That's all right, Nana Selma," Khalil said. "It'll be okay." He patted her hand, and then took the mason jar to his mouth and sipped the sweet syrup.

"He like a little ole man," Selma said. "Looka him, telling me everything be okay."

"Come on, Nana," Rayne said. "Let's walk you over to the trailer."

———

It was close to midnight by the time they started to make the hundred-yard walk to Selma's trailer. The moon had migrated to the top of the sky. A light breeze came toward them from the east, carrying the scent of fire. Running ahead, Khalil was the first to catch it.

"What's that smell?" he asked.

"Farm trash. Smells like somebody's burning it off."

A hint, at the start; it smelled to Rayne like quintessential country, preparing the land for planting. Then the wind picked up, and the smoke came at them so heavily it burned their eyes.

Selma was holding on to Rayne's arm hard with her one good hand and the bandaged hand aloft. She could not see her feet. She thought to say to him that the county had outlawed that kind of burning, and that the farmers knew damn good and well that they were not supposed to burn off the fields, which is why they did it in the middle of the night. But then she felt that telltale slip, as if her leg were going out in front of her of its own volition, and her arms did not respond to the certain knowledge that she had to grab on to something. And the smoke caught in her throat, in her eyes and nose, just as it did before. *Don't breathe it in.* She was shouting from inside, but they couldn't hear her. *For God's sake don't breathe it in.*

Selma's panic rolled up into them both, as if whatever they were breathing would shred them slowly from the inside. Khalil turned, coughing, and shouted: "She's falling."

Rayne grabbed her up. *Shhhh, shhhh.* He held her tight and close against his chest—*Come on, no; come on*—and after a few minutes the quivering, gulping, choking subsided. She quieted. He strode to the trailer.

Once inside the tidy beige interior, they smelled the strong scent of smoke that clung to their clothing and hair. Rayne did not know what to do with Selma, until with her trailing hand she indicated the thin wheelchair she'd left on purpose by the door. It was a child's chair that JJ had found at a yard sale. Anything else would have been too wide for the trailer. The last time Rayne had visited, she'd had it folded in the corner. He hadn't noticed.

Khalil started to wheeze. And he was touching the red welts on his face and arms. Rayne felt in the breast pocket of his parka for the Ziploc bag of inhalers that Lillie had insisted he bring. Khalil made a face. Rayne knew that he hated the medicine: he said that it made his heart pound.

Selma, meanwhile, needed to go to the bathroom.

"I can do 'em myself," Khalil said, reaching for the inhalers and the long spacer chamber, a plastic tube through which to breathe in the more powerful steroid medicine.

Rayne hesitated.

"I could do it right. You don't have to watch me."

Rayne handed him the bag. Then he pushed Selma's wheelchair a few yards into her tiny bedroom, and aimed the chair toward the open bathroom door.

"I'm all right now," Selma said, obviously not all right. "Go on outta here, unless you wanna look."

Rayne returned to the tiny parlor, and observed Khalil finish his protocol of inhaling, waiting, and inhaling again, twice for each inhaler. He wanted to bundle the boy and the old lady into bed immediately, simultaneously.

"Hey, Lil Man," Rayne asked, "listen, you think you can go across the yard and across the driveway by yourself and put some ice into a bag for your face?"

Khalil shrugged hesitantly. He did not want to disappoint. Neither did he want to walk out alone into malignant smoke that could slip among the long black shadows of the moon and clamp down the tiny airways in his chest.

"How bad is the wheezing?"

"Not too bad. I can feel the medicine. I feel dizzy, though."

Rayne hoped he was not being self-serving when he remembered and then reminded Khalil that Lillie often preferred him to sit up for half an hour or so after taking the meds. "Okay. Sit over there, and close your eyes. The air in here is clean, okay?"

Khalil did as he was told, even though the air in the trailer did not seem especially clean to him. In fact, from the bedroom doorway came the faint odor of urine. But Khalil would never say so, because Nana Selma was old, and that would be rude.

Although the tidy trailer did not cure Khalil, it had an immediate effect on Selma, who was breathing nearly naturally within five minutes of returning, in her wheelchair, to her little parlor. The shuddering that so frightened Rayne had lasted no more than a minute or two.

They sat for a moment until Selma gathered the strength and the determination to say: "Now, this is business. Listen, this farm is on two separate pieces of land. One part your great-grandfather bought from Old Broadnax the drunk, and they tried to steal back from him, but we kep' it. That part is over by the golf course, and I lease it to Pettiford, the greedy grandson, and now he wants to buy it."

As far as Selma was concerned, she said, and the phrase stuck in Rayne's mind: "As far as I'm concerned . . . ," which meant that maybe her ideas did not square with others' or law or custom, but as far as Selma was concerned, she held the land in trust for Rayne. What she needed him to do now, she said, was to figure out how to get clear title on the heir property so that they could transfer ownership, properly, in writing, while she was alive to tell any judge, if it came to that, that King bought out Brother Amos's share, and that Brother Richard had forfeited his by leasing it out in some kind of long-term deal with Pettiford that they'd kept secret between them.

Selma talked fast, her low voice even lower. Rayne wanted her to stop talking, and he shook his head gently as if to ward off more information.

Selma continued trying to explain: "Okay, so that's the Broadnax field. Now, the other part is the heir property. That's from way, way back. Used to be shared across the three brothers, and the people at the county claim that everybody owns it now: all the heirs, every single soul descended from them three. How's that gonna be? Everybody gone, everybody paid off a hundred years ago, and now I gotta go ask Mother-May-I to pass it on?

"You know they don't tell that mess to nobody but black people. They say everybody owns it, and then force a sale for a price that can't nobody but a big developer can pay. That's why ain't hardly none of us got any land lef'."

"Nana," Rayne said, pleading, "I'm here all week, and we can talk."

"I'm finished. That's it. I ain't tryin to overload you. But just so you know: anybody wanna come down here and live, you know it's always been open to 'em. And I hope you'll honor that, 'cause it's only right. Economy like it is, hey, worse come to worse, they can always come on down, fix up a little piece of shack, get a trailer used or something, okay. But *some one body* has got to own it is what I'm saying, or else they can always take it."

"Okay, Nana, but what are you trying to get me to do?"

"So what we gotta do is go through the papers we can find, and prove that King owned this land, and that he meant for it to go to his issue. The county and the state—it's none of their business."

"So, Nana, wait a minute, you're telling me that if we wanted to sell the land, we couldn't. It cannot be sold by you or by us or Granddaddy Bobo or my mother or any of us?"

"Your mother?" Selma made a snort. "Well, do Jesus, where'd that come from?

"To answer your question, no. That's what I been tellin you. 'Cause the county keep saying we don't have no clear title. The county say that Amos and Richard and all their children, and all of King's issue, right down to you, they all own the same itty-bitty shares. For fifty years, where have they been? And before that?"

"Nana, you don't own the land?"

"Me? No, baby, *me* ownin the land was never the issue. I been *holdin* it, is all, but I'm the second wife with no children. I am not an heir. Not noways an heir."

"So, they say everyone owns it?"

"They are a forfeit, baby. Listen, man and woman live together for fifty, a hundred years, when he dies, the state say: she's his wife. All those years count the same as a license. Same with land. Everybody knows that. Possession is nine-tenths of the law. Your great-grandfather farmed, and sent Amos a share until finally Amos wrote 'im said: take my share. 'At's a quitclaim, same as.

"And Richard leased his part to Pettiford, for fifty years—and it's over. Lease is up. It's a forfeit, I tell you. You hear me?"

No, Rayne did not hear her anymore. All he'd heard was that she did not own the land. And if she didn't own it, then she couldn't—and he couldn't—sell it, and his loosely formed idea of using the proceeds to set her up in a long-term-care facility wouldn't work. And, he could see, she had no Plan B. In fact, her Plan A required him to set aside his life and attend to this land.

Now Rayne spoke firmly. "I gotta get Lil Man to bed." He indicated the boy with a nod and stood.

"I know they talk about me like a dog up there," Selma continued, "'cause I ain't Needham blood, but best proof, I'm here, ain't I? I'm here payin the taxes and they up there eatin Twinkies.

"But it's gonna be yours. I was gonna talk to you tomorrow, but might jus' as well start it now. Case I'm not here in the morning."

"Oh, Nana."

"Might as well say it. Okay, and here's the thing. They keep talking 'bout you need a will. I gotta have *his* will in order to prove I own the land to will it to you. Now, here's the thing: I could have swore your great-grandfather wrote his will and put it in our strongbox under the stove in the kitchen. Under the floor there under the stove, so no one could get to it by accident. Please look and find it while you're here. Lookit: then we can go to a lawyer while you're here and get started."

Rayne transferred his weight from one foot to the other. He was too big for the trailer. And he was sorry to know that Nana Selma, who above anyone else in the family had always looked out for the children, could not stop herself from talking even when Khalil needed to go to bed. He'd wanted Khalil to feel the delicious gift of Selma's total, delighted, fixed attention. But she could not collect herself to give it to this new adopted boy.

Then it occurred to him that Khalil didn't need Nana's care

as he had or as his grandfather Bobo had. Khalil's own mother paid him that attention, and so could Rayne.

"I've gotta get the boy back to the house," he said firmly.

"Okay, I'll shut up."

Now what? was being answered on Selma's terms. He'd been thinking about her care; she'd been thinking about the land. A will in a box under the floorboards? Heir property? Golf course lease? Rayne had private contracts, a municipal contract, a girl-friend, Khalil. This was the day he'd dreaded, when Beaufort County came to call.

As if reading his thoughts, Selma said: "JJ and his son are pretty good with most of what you need. The place can still support a couple crops a few years till you get yourself together, decide what you wanna do. Funny," she said, shaking her head, "those little nana goats are good business again. I used to have goats and they laughed at me. We got a young white couple make goat's milk cheese and sell it to restaurants for something like twelve dollars a pound, *wholesale.*"

Khalil's wheezing had slowed, but not stopped. He looked up at Rayne, beseechingly.

"Okay. Night-night."

"Unh-huh," she said. "Just sleep on all this. I been meaning to talk to you for so long. And out there, seem like something said: 'What are you waitin for?'"

"Okay," Rayne said to Selma. He propped Khalil up on his feet. "Okay, Lil Man," he said to Khalil. Then to Selma again: "We here the whole week. We can talk some more."

"Will you look for the strongbox for me?"

"I guess. Sure." He and Khalil shuffled around the wheel-chair, which sat between them and the door. Selma caught Khalil's hand.

Then, even as Rayne opened the door, Selma talked to his back: "Or, since you're a builder, maybe you could use this property and develop it. Whatshisname, Pettiford's grandson, he made a go with the new golf course. So, if you don't wanna keep farming, you could develop the land. Every time you see development, it's *them* makin money. *You* could build a resort same as they can."

"Whoa, Nana, I have *got* to get this boy to bed. Look, I think the medicine helped his asthma, but it got his face itching again."

"Did you drip some water in that calamine bottle?"

"I told you I got a fresh bottle in the truck."

"You told me that?"

"Yeah. Come on, let's all go to bed." He crossed to her in a long stride, squatted down, and looked her in the face. She had never been a big hugger and kisser, but she appreciated ceremony, and they did a traditional hug to signal good night. Rayne enveloped her and the wheelchair in his long arm. "Good night, Nana," he said quietly, into her ear.

"I'm sorry, baby. It's too much. It's just that I can't never talk to you so far away, and then I call on the cell phone and you always on the job." Then, as she put her face into his collarbone, she whispered: "Listen, Ray, you think you can move my bathroom?" Before he could answer she said, "But, nah, don't bother, 'cause then what I'm gonna do in the middle of the night? I mean if you move the bathroom?"

"Well, here, we'll mark off where the old bathroom was and then we'll have to lay out a big old litter box for you."

"Hah!" She laughed and then patted his chest. "Been a long time, Rayne, since you come see me and make your old nana laugh," she whispered. "I don't know what happened to me out there. I just couldn't breathe." She breathed deeply again and looked at Khalil, who stood with his hand on the slightly open door. Smoke seeped in.

"Has that happened before?" Rayne asked about her collapse. Later, he would tell Lillie as much as he could glean.

"Yeah. Took me down out back of the old house. Last year. Fell right over. I woulda fallen out tonight if you hadn'ta caught me. I think I can pull a full day's work, and then I get winded. Plus they not supposed to burn all that damn farm trash. 'S why they do it at night. Good wind come up, they burn up they own barns."

Khalil pulled at Rayne's hand.

"I feel your heartbeat," Selma said.

"That's the good news."

"I always said you should be a comedian."

CHAPTER 12

Khalil sat in the hard little wooden chair that King had made for Bobo while Rayne took the sheets off his old bed and, at Lillie's request, slipped the thirty-year-old mattress into the plastic cover she'd packed. Puffs of dust wafted into his face as he worked.

"How the hell did she have time to pack this thing?" Rayne said with wonder and irritation as he got onto his knees to close the stretched zipper.

Khalil answered him: "Mommy keeps it in the closet in case Melvin comes over."

"That the boy who wets the bed?"

"Not anymore," Khalil said, defending his friend.

"I used to wet the bed," Rayne said.

"Did you?"

"Yep." Rayne made himself remember how to fold corners on Selma's thin flat sheets. The bottom one had a seam down the middle where she'd repaired it once already. "I used to think that was why my mother sent me to live down here."

"Why did she?"

Rayne indicated the calamine lotion they'd grabbed on the way in. He sat on the side of the newly made bed. It made noisy plastic swishing against his weight.

Khalil came to stand where Rayne could reach his face and hands with lotion. "Why did she?" he repeated.

Rayne could not think of an answer that he wanted to stand by. "I don't know, Lil Man."

"You gonna call and ask her?"

"Maybe. But you know whose mother does have to be called."

Rayne had rubbed onto Khalil's hands and face enough calamine lotion to make him feel as if he were wearing a mask. "Mine."

"And I've got to explain how you got asthma and poison ivy all in one day. We haven't even been away from her for twenty-four hours. Shit."

"You cursed a lot today. How come? Are you mad at me?"

Rayne laid a threadbare towel over the pillowcase. "I will be if you don't stop talkin. Jeez. What they do, put talky pills in the water down here? Here, lie down. Least I can tell her that you are 'resting comfortably.'"

———

Lillie's phone was off, which made Rayne think that she might be in a late study session at the hospital, where they regularly turned off their phones, or that she'd picked up a tattoo job, thinking to grab some extra "pin money," as she called it, while she had no one to look after. He sent her a text saying that he'd be awake to talk for the next hour if she wanted. He hoped she wouldn't call, and that when they talked in the morning, Khalil would be well enough so that this evening could be just a day-one blip.

But first, he had to fall asleep. And with his heart beating fast from the inhalant, his skin itching, and his mind full of the day's adventures, Khalil was having a hard time. He came into the kitchen, where Rayne was sitting at the table checking e-mails on his phone.

"This the longest I been away from my mother."

"Man, stop it. You spend the weekend at Melvin's and that other boy's house—what's the little blond boy's name been playing with you since T-ball, him and his sister?"

"Zachary Smith."

"You stay with Zach and Sam all weekend and don't wanna come home. This hasn't even been twenty-four hours."

Khalil edged his eyebrows up and down as if to massage the skin on his forehead under the calamine lotion.

Rayne looked down at the floor so as not to laugh. "But this *is* probably the *farthest* you've been from her."

"Yeah. *Really* far. This really *is* the farthest."

"Feel like it, too, don't it?"

Khalil's eyes threatened to tear as he said: "And I forgot to bring books. I'on't even have one of my favorite books to read to go to sleep."

"Maybe there's one at the bottom of the bag."

"No, 'cause we rushed my mom. Otherwise, she always remembers." His breathing got more jagged as he got closer to tears. "And the pictures on that wall are weird. It's weird in there. And I just met Nana Selma and all, and then she fell out and look like she'd gonna die . . .

"Plus the mattress smell bad, all the way through the plastic. It smells funny. I can't sleep here!"

Rayne started to laugh.

"It's not funny." Khalil perched on the edge of tears. "You're making fun of me."

"No, I'm not, Lil Man. Look, Nana Selma's okay. True enough, the mattress is mildewed. So's the pillow; I'll bet that's the real problem. The damn pillow."

"Damn blanket, too."

Rayne laughed harder. "It's a rough end to a rough day. But come on, I got something for you. Get my coat."

"No, I don't wanna go outside anymore. It's scary."

"Get the coat, Lil Man. I'll give you a piggyback ride."

When Rayne squatted to offer his broad back, Khalil brushed aside the heavy dreadlocks and reluctantly climbed on. Each step Rayne took vibrated Khalil's own jangling body from underneath. Khalil laid his masked face at the base of Rayne's neck, and then he closed his eyes. The warmth from Rayne's body seeped into him. They walked to the truck. Rayne opened the cab and reached for the pillow and fleece blanket that he kept in the backseat.

"Here," he said, "this'll keep your face off that stanky old mattress. Then tomorrow, if it's not raining, we'll take the slipcover off and put the whole thing out in the sun, okay?"

Khalil nodded into the nape of his neck.

"Okay, so now we're going in. You know the drill: butcher begins to kill the ox; ox begins to drink water; water begins to quench fire . . ."

". . . Fire starts to burn the stick; stick starts to beat the dog; dog starts to bite the pig, pig jumps over the stile—"

"And the old woman gets back to her home that night with a new pillow and blanket and a face full of calamine lotion and goes to sleep. Like you gonna do."

"I miss Mommy."

"Yeah. Me, too."

"Can we call 'er?"

"Her phone's off. She probably in the library, okay? Lie down, be quiet."

Rayne walked around the trailer on the way back. Within five minutes he could feel Khalil's head bob and his arms relax. He took him to the house, laid him on the bed, and put the truck pillow under his head. He folded the fleece blanket into a pillow for himself, and lay down with the dust and mildew in his nose anyway.

Selma had talked for so many years about "passing the land" to him that he'd assumed she owned it, and that it would pay for her retirement. Now that he knew she did not own it, he had to find out who did. Really. Not just in Selma's willful mind. Although, Rayne knew, as Selma had always told him, if she hadn't been willful from the start, she'd never have had the nerve to imagine herself with King; she'd never have raised his children and grands—and great-grands. She'd never have been able to hold on to it.

Rayne fell asleep and dreamed about large dogs that tore at the bottom of a raggedy wooden door. It was a vaguely familiar dream, except that this time Khalil was with him, sleeping on the top of a bunk bed. Somewhere in the room, Selma was sleeping, bundled in blankets. Rayne kept watch. He could see the dogs; snarling teeth under the door. They were huge dogs. He was wearing a sweater that Selma had knitted. He didn't know how long the door would hold.

———

In the morning, Rayne lay in the old bed that had been Bobo's, then Jewell's, then his, and determined to accomplish two tasks he did not want to do: call his mother and go to the town hall to begin to investigate the legal standing of the Needham land. So, he told himself, do them today, and get them over with. Later in the week, he'd take Khalil and Selma fishing, which promised to be a funny dockside pairing. He lay in bed for a long time, unwilling to begin. He imagined himself calling his mother's number and just opening up gonzo-style, like: "Yo, this Lonnie. You know who the fuck I am. And you know why I'm callin . . ."

Khalil was breathing easily now, face muscles relaxed. Seven years old was when they put children out in the field. Quarter-hands, they used to call them. But no one sent them out alone.

"Yo, Jewell, you lef' me on a train by myself. Like, what the fuck was you thinking?"

———

Across the field, in her trailer, Selma went into and out of consciousness. She'd felt this before. She'd told Rayne about the fall, but not the other spells, because there was no way to explain how the feeling came from inside, as if she were an old motor, and one of her distributor caps had come off and she simply lost power. Then, something inside would right itself again, although there would be that interval, and she might fall or fall asleep or slump in her chair. Over time, she had to create exercises for herself to get her strength back. She sat in the chair and moved her right arm up and down, holding a can of beans. She smiled into the mirror, first one side, then the other, forcing herself to move the right cheek up high to bring it in line with the left.

Then, because she found herself craving fish after these spells, she had the girl buy her cans of sardines and mackerel to keep on hand. She thought they helped her heal better than other foods. On her toast, she spread the cream cheese with salmon. She made the girl buy her tubs of those, too, three or four at a time, because the supermarket didn't always carry it.

This morning, lying in bed at dawn, she felt like death warmed over. She didn't usually let the word *death* into her consciousness, but it was sitting there now, at the foot of her beige-and-brown bed that matched the trailer. Last night's spell had taken everything out of her, and all the cooking for three days to make one simple meal, and staying up late, even though she had napped in the afternoon, and being in the old house in the cold and damp before Rayne lit the stove. Too, too much for the old woman she was. Too much for the woman who wished every day that she'd never carried to her husband the poison gossip that Old Broadnax wanted to sell his farm so badly that he said at the general store, for everyone to hear, that he'd even sell to a nigger if his money was ready.

Selma turned to sit on the side of the bed, stood, wound her nightgown in front of her, and stuffed it into its own neckline to free her to pee into her bucket. She wiped with a tissue from her night table, and then scrubbed her hands with one of the baby wipes, which she hung on the side of the dispenser to use a second time.

Then she made her way into the kitchen for a snack, because she could tell that the Old Broadnax field would not leave her head. She got out her crackers and salmon cream cheese and poured herself a small glass of orange juice, all clumsily, with the bandaged hand. Boy, that was silly, too. Then she wheeled herself up to the little table and plucked from the center of the table the napkin she'd saved from the snack that had served as her evening meal. She spread a Ritz cracker and took a bite. It took awhile for the taste to register. Jesus, everything was going. But finally, it came to her: the creamy cheese, the briny tang of the salmon, the familiar buttery crunch of the cracker. Here she was, despite the dark that wanted to pull her into it. Still alive. Despite the Old Broadnax field, and losing King and losing babies, and runaway children, and Bobo in prison, and Needhams who left old black Selma stuck as the caretaker. Her brother, Jones, was the only soul in the world who remembered. Every now and then they spoke about it long distance, him on his fancy cell phone, and reminded each other that they two were neither crazy nor alone.

Selma spread another cracker and closed her eyes as she ate it. But the Old Broadnax field was waiting for her behind her eyelids, as if everything that happened were always happening, in an excruciating present, eight-tenths of a mile south, as if, with enough faith, she might could open her mouth and swallow back every wrong word and snatch from her mind every thought that led to every wrong word, because each and every word had to have been utterly, horribly wrong, or else none of it would ever have happened.

————

Jones heard the dog before he could tell what was wrong. Everything was as he and King had left it halfway through clearing the Broadnax field. Stumps lay upturned throughout. Heaps of dirt marked the space between pockmarks in the ground. He couldn't see around them. But a dog whined insistently, frustrated, grieving. He followed the sound.

"Oh, my God." Jones whispered it as a prayer. "Oh, my God, don't let 'er be dead."

He knew it had to be the white girl who'd been coming to watch him work. He had not smiled at her—he was no fool—but he knew it.

What could he do? The stump was so big. And since she was under it, he could not get into the hole to find leverage.

"Oh, my God!" On his knees by the hole, Jones looked for a miracle. Her dog paced and cried for him to help. He saw the girl's eyes move. "You're alive!"

King was not around. He had gone to deliver his only son to the army. Jones felt panic crawl up from under his scrotum and into his gut. What should he do? What could he do? Try to free her, and then go for help? But he could just make it worse. Go for help first so that someone else could witness what had happened to her? Colored help? White help? He had no protocol to consult. Only a list of consequences. And no time. She was slight, pale, slim, very hurt. He ran across the field and up the hill to get Selma, who, being a woman, could touch the girl to help pull her out if he could hitch a mule and a pull hook.

———————

That's what he came in bawling to her. She was canning peaches; four bushels so far, a total of nearly eighty quart jars. By the time he got to the house, Jones was so out of breath and frantic that at first Selma could not understand him. A pile of peach skins lay on her left side, a fleshy huddle of baldhead fruit on the other. She worked fast in batches so that they would not turn brown. The sweet, peachy steam made her feel hungry and a little sick. Then, when she could understand him, she could not believe him. Jones told her his plan.

"Oh, Jesus." It was all she could say. How could such a thing have happened? Her stomach flopped in terror. She wanted to run. Steam from the water bath joined their sweat. They shone at each other, desperate, thin brown siblings with high cheekbones and almond eyes, wild with terror, looking around the kitchen for some scrap of hope that might be lying around, close to hand. "Who is she?"

"I'on't know!"

"We gotta go get somebody else. We can't do this thing alone. What if she dies?" she asked. "We can't carry a dead white girl into town."

They stood together in the main room of the house—the kitchen, dining room, gathering place—looking at the wide plank floor. Who was this who had brought her foolhardy self into what King called the U.S. of Needham?

"Jesus. Oh, Jesus. Is she unconscious?" It occurred to Selma to leave her to her own devices. Do what they would have done had Jones not heard the dog. There was no reason for her or Jones to have gone to that field. People had seen King and his son Junior leave with little Bobo; King had stopped in town to fill up his extra tank with gasoline. People had said good-bye to him. Somebody swung by and told Selma some old gossip, and said piously that she was praying for Junior's safety. Everything that day was wrong, however, and Junior never did come home. King was planning to return the morning after next. By that time, the girl could be dead, and someone else would have found her.

"What if we mess around going to find people, and she dies and we coulda done something?" Jones showed tears collecting underneath his eyes. He'd been thinking about himself and Selma and the Needhams. Now, being Jones, with his good heart, his mind went back to the girl's pained face, the brave movement of eyes below translucent lids, the barely rising torso. He felt her dog's hot-breathed panic as if it were his own. Selma rocked her head from side to side, looking past him through the open door, counting something.

The problem with leaving her, Selma thought, with brutal calculation, was that she might *not* die. And if the girl lived to remember that Jones had found her—and left her there—then everything was over for Jones.

Selma knew the girth of the stumps they'd been removing. The two of them could roll one all the way over her—if she could convince Jones to do it. But even then, if people didn't find the body for a couple days, God knows what that sight would do to people. You could say dead is dead, but how a body looked would work on people's minds. Besides, Jones would never do it.

"Selma!" She remembered Jones shouting at her.

"Who is she?"

"I tol' you. I'on't know!"

"You sure she was alive?"

"Yes!"

"From where she is, could somebody see the Schoolhouse Road?"

"I dunno."

"Put it like this: If I'm driving the School Road, would I be able to see *her*?"

"You could see the dog."

"Dog? Jesus. What dog?"

"Her dog was with her. That's how I heard, remember?"

"Right. Jesus. Jesus. Jesus . . . Okay. This what we gonna do. Listen, I'ma tell you. We gonna go into town like we need dry goods. Take the rubber-wheel buggy wagon and the mare mule. Then in town we gonna bus' a tire, y'hear? Then I'ma get somebody in town to bring me back. Try to get a white person to carry me back here, and we'll come, naturally, by the School Road. Maybe old Mr. Mortenson at the General Store; he don't be doing nothing."

She stopped for a moment to run through in her mind her choice of the potential driver. Mortenson was middling good-hearted in Selma's estimation, neither particularly friendly to coloreds nor hostile. Because King had done a good business with him for twenty-five years, he treated Selma with rather more than less respect, given the differences between them. He was chatty, so he'd tell everyone what he'd seen, and, more important, white folks would believe him. She hoped he'd be there. She did the calculation quickly: she went into town once a week. Since January that would mean nine months, and she could remember not seeing him only twice. Two out of thirty-six plus the three extras, one each in January, March, and July this year. She didn't like that it wasn't even. That should have been a sign right there.

"You'll stay in town with the buggy wagon and the mule. Then, I can look over the field and see what happened and make 'em stop, if the other person don't see 'er firs'."

Tears rolled down Jones's face. By then the girl could be dead, he said, and they'd be as good as killed her. Selma could see him thinking of her alone, with rain threatening and the crying dog.

"If we nail a big ole roofin nail into the rubber buggy tire, will it go down by time we get to town?"

Jones shrugged.

"Or will we just break down afore we get there?"

He shook his head and shrugged again.

Selma pursed her lips and looked at him.

"We can't kill 'er." He said it in the tiniest whisper, as if the wind would carry their sin through all eternity.

She whispered back in a hissing sound that she could see stung him. "Did we ast her t' come in and mess around with some stump twice her size? What would happen if some niggers was to mess around on some white gentleman's land? She did this to her own damn self, and don't put it on me!"

"It's her or us. Or King. You know that, don't you?"

No. Jones hadn't thought about King, he later told Selma, but of course, they'd hold him responsible. Still, Jones suspected that if the white girl died, the sound of that dog barking, the slow flutter of her translucent eyelids, would never leave him.

He went to the wagon barn, took out the rubber-wheel buggy, and hitched the relatively affable mule, who would never perform like their old gray-and-white mare with her sweet nature and wide shoulders. Of course King needed a big horse. Jones drove a nail into one wheel. He remembered learning from King how to shoe the mare's big hooves. When the air made its initial sigh, Jones jumped, as if blood would spurt from the puncture.

In town, Selma headed for the store and sent Jones to tell

King's brother Richard what was happening, but to tell him not to do anything. He was to pretend that everything was normal. Jones didn't want to go. You could never trust Richard. But somebody had to let him know, and Selma had to get Mortenson.

She told Prentice, the storeowner, that King had gone to take Junior to answer the draft. Yep, he already knew. And, of course, she knew he knew. Then she gabbled on. The horse breeder and trader in Cherokee Falls had asked for them to apprentice Jones to him, 'cause he was so good with horses. Chat, chat, chat. She said that King promised to come back in three days, and everyone knew how King was about making his time. She got nervous then, because usually she didn't talk so much, and Prentice, the storeowner, was looking at her funny. There were other people in the store. She couldn't decide whether that was good or bad.

She apologized, but said she didn't know what to do with King gone and Junior gone and the buggy wheel busted and she thought that maybe they'd help.

"Do you think maybe if I ask Mr. Mortenson real nice, he might ride me out to our place to get the replacement wheel? I shoulda had it. King tells me to always carry it underneath. I shoulda put it on."

"Where's your brother?"

"I already sent him to help my brother-in-law who's working Mr. Reid's field over west of town." She tripped her tongue. "If I'da seen the wheel . . ."

"Go ask Mortenson. Did you see 'im on the porch?" Prentice asked.

She nodded but couldn't move. Trembling. On the verge of tears.

"'S just a buggy wheel. Come on, you always been a sensible gal. He won't bite'cha. Here, I'll ask 'im for you. Say, Mort. You ain't doing nothing special right now, are you?"

———

Mortenson chided Selma for undoing the replacement wheel, which had to have been her, because King knew better. Plus, King had always been the most particular Negro you ever met, and so he told Selma, as if these were facts about her husband that she did not know. He'd seen King drive that rubber-wheel buggy, and Mortenson could swear that he'd seen the tire on the bottom there, right where it should be. Well, he figured, she'd have hell to pay when the big red Negro got home and found out his little black gal had been driving the buggy around carelessly. Because he was always *so* particular.

Replacement tires and farm management led Mortenson to why everybody wasn't cut out to own expensive things and why there was a reason some people were tenants; and he named people, first black, then white, who had owned farms and lost them, and others likely to lose them soon. Selma's heart banged. She counted her heartbeats, twice normal, and cut them into the rhythm of Mortenson's old horse's hoofbeats. The peach skins she'd eaten threatened to spill up from her stomach. She forced them down. Then she counted the peaches she was losing: three bushels peeled, sitting out in the heat; twelve more unpeeled, all on top of one another in the kitchen. She'd likely lose half the peeled, and maybe a tenth of the unpeeled. It distracted her for a few minutes.

As they approached the south field Selma realized with terror that Mortenson was talking too much to notice anything. Her heart flailed around; she gulped at the air so loudly that he asked what was wrong with her. As clearly as she could, she said: "Mr. Mortenson, what's that? Can you see what that is over there on Old Broadnax field?"

"Jus' a dog. 'S not your dog you making all that fuss about?"

"No, sir. That's the funny thing: I don't know that dog, but

I could hear it all the way over here. Look like sompin wrong. Sound like it's whining. Oh, God, Mr. Mortenson, I gotta bad feelin about that dog."

Finally, and with a sigh to show her his annoyance, Mortenson stopped the buggy. Together they noticed that where the dog was circling, a stump had toppled into its hole, the only one to have done so.

Selma got down. "Here, Mr. Mortenson. Shall I see to it? I know you think I'm a silly gal about this . . . I'll see to it, shall I?"

"Well, what's the point of me comin with you if we run into something and . . . ?" He struggled to get down fast enough so that he didn't have to tell her to wait. "Come and tie up this horse, Selma. Don't want three emergencies 'steada the two you already got goin. If this is one, that is," he said under his breath, "and not a silly gal cryin wolf."

She waited for him just inside the field. "Mind the blackberries, sir."

"I ain't so old I can't see a bramble bush."

And there she was. It was no playacting for Selma to shout when she looked on the smallish face, brushed with red dirt, eyes closed, dirty blonde bangs to one side. Everything was wrong. Everything wanted fixing. Selma stood, transfixed, unable to feel anything but her own fear, unable to do anything but contain it, control it, push it into a dry corner, shut the door, then pay attention to Mr. Mortenson, huffing and puffing, now next to her, the dog circling, excited, ready for a human solution.

Then, without warning, the eyes opened.

"Oh, Jesus!" Selma screamed, and Mortenson let out a startled grunt.

Selma's fear burst its chains like the dead on Judgment Day and flooded her body, circulating round and round so fast that she went dizzy. The eyes stared at her, through her, as if they knew that she'd contemplated leaving her to die.

"Thank God," Mortenson said.

"Thank God," Selma echoed, the voice belching from her as if she'd been kicked.

"You one of the Broadnax grandchildren, aren't you? You hear me?"

The eyes flickered. Tears began to run from the corners.

Selma counted seconds to stop herself from vomiting.

"We gotta get her outta there," Mortenson said.

"Can we lift that thing together?" Selma asked. "I get on that side, you get on this side, take hold of the roots?"

"And what happens if we drop it?"

"Mr. Mortenson, what'll we do?"

"How long you been there, chile?" he asked.

The girl did not answer. Her dog pawed at the hole again, splattering fresh dirt onto her face. The eyes closed.

"Stop that, Dog," Mortenson said. "Stop, you.

"Selma," Mortensen said seriously, "look, can you handle my buggy?"

"Aw, Jesus, Mr. Mortenson. I can drive anything." Selma heard her own words come out garbled. She hadn't realized that she was crying.

"Now, look, Selma. We both gotta keep our wits, girl. Come on, gal. You blubber, I can't think."

"I drive, Mr. Mortenson. I'll get the pull hook and rig." She took off running as she spoke.

Mortenson knelt carefully so as not to lose his balance and fall onto the girl. He stayed just like that, talking to the girl.

When Selma got back with the rig, it took everything he had to push himself up to a standing position and walk around again. Selma twitched with anxiety. She walked Mortenson's nag up and down, saying it was to pull the rig through, nice and easy, no back and forth. And then they did it, the old porch gossip and the skinny colored woman: they hitched Mortenson's horse to the rig bought for King's 1,200-pound mules. They sank the hook into rotten wood so close to the girl's young flesh that they shuddered. Mortenson shook as they lifted up on the pulley, to suspend the stump three inches off the ground, and off the girl's body, which they saw lay mostly in a depression underneath. Selma pulled the horse's bit just hard enough to keep the stump moving back away from the hole, over the prone body, and onto flat ground beside her.

The girl was scratched and red. The bruising would spread everywhere. She was shaking weakly. They covered her with the horse blanket. The dog sat next to her, panting and finally quiet. Stiff and afraid, Mortenson sat himself down again to one side of the hole and brushed the girl's bangs back every so often. He mumbled little phrases he said to his own children while Selma drove his team hard to fetch the white doctor and white men to help.

The white men came fast. They examined the scene and the stories that Mortenson told, and then that Selma told in answer to their questions. *This was life and death right here,* they told Mortenson. And *Well, I tell you what it was, it was nothing short of a miracle . . . Thank God they saw 'er . . . Don't know what she was doin there . . . Probably just wandered in to take a look.*

Mortenson puffed up. He reared back on his heels and rocked and shook his head as he told again how they would have driven right by had he not heard the poor dog whining and howling something awful . . .

It didn't bear thinking on, although, of course, they could think of nothing else.

Selma dared to hope that they had pulled it off.

———

Although the two crackers with salmon cream cheese had been so comforting, Selma lost her appetite for the third. She wrapped it in her napkin and placed it in the center of the table. The Old Broadnax field felt to Selma like the Bible's field of blood. That's why she'd borrowed against it. If mortgaging the one could help her keep the other, whose business was it? And if there was blood on the money, well, at least she hadn't spilled it.

CHAPTER 13

t took Rayne most of the early morning to figure out how King had put in his box stove originally and then how JJ had jerry-rigged its repair. For one thing, JJ had installed the male end of the stovepipe up, no doubt assembling the pipe to follow the smoke. But as it was, black creosote was oozing down into the stove. Eventually, it would gum up the opening. Rayne took newspaper from under the sink, laid it on the floor, and then took the stovepipe apart, hoping that he would not need another part when he reversed the relay. Then he cleaned the drippings and tried to see whether he thought it possible that a strongbox would be buried under the bricks that formed a rough foundation for the stove. He couldn't tell.

What he could see was that someone had taken up several of the planks around the stove, and then nailed them back. Whoever had taken them up had put the original nails back into the original holes. Only one or two nails showed hammer indentations. He'd probably used a blanket to keep from marring the old heart pine floor. But none of the nails had been sunk, as King had sunk them, it looked like to Rayne, with a spare nail of the same size. Well, Rayne thought to himself, it was as likely to have been Selma herself trying to get to the box as anyone.

Two layers of brick had been laid, one on top of the other, into a tight boxlike holder cut into the plank floor, which was itself raised up off the dirt by joists. Rayne had begun to pick out the bricks and mound them next to him on the floor when his phone vibrated in his pocket. Since it was early, he assumed it was Lillie. He put the phone to his head without checking the caller ID.

"Hey, babe," he said, happy for her company, "I missed you last night after the Energizer Bunny finally ran out of gas. I'm tryin to man up to the single-parent thing, but baby, you got me."

"Oh, Lonnie, I'm sorry. This is your mother, Jewell."

"Oh, whoa. Whoa. I thought you were my girlfriend." Two minutes before, he would not have been able to conjure the sound of her voice, but it was her, all right. One time he had heard a cello concerto on the Temple University station in his doctor's office, and the instrument had so reminded him of that voice that he had had to walk out. What the hell could he say? "Good morning."

Jewell felt as if she were barely inside her own skin. Learning that he and Lillie were not married gave her information to focus on. Was the boy his? she wondered. "I probably should have done something to warn you."

"Well, what else could you do? You talked to Lillie. She told me you called yesterday. And I do have a cell phone. I just didn't look at the number, because my hand was full anyway."

"What are you doing?"

He heard her voice—it curled around in his head and purred and nuzzled—as if they'd talked last week; it seemed that familiar. Her question, though simple, however, drove home to him their distance. *What was he doing?* How to answer? She knew the very stove, and had likely heard Selma brag about it: that King's Grandma Bett, and her second husband, Slim, had carried it from an auction of the contents of their former master's house on a borrowed cart. Rayne's mother probably knew that Bett had died here in this very room, napping next to her stove, bundled in her wedding quilt, on a Christmas evening, having eaten half her holiday dinner and asked to save the rest for her to eat the next day.

Rayne was pretty sure that she did not know about the strongbox or the will. But then she might.

"Sorry. It's none of my business," she said, when he hesitated. "Are you able to talk now, or is this a bad time?"

"I'm fine for the time being."

They did not say anything for long enough that she asked him: "You still there?"

"Yeah, I'm still here, not knowing what to say."

"Is there something you'd really like to say, like, I don't know . . . ?"

"Yeah," he said, "you do know. My girlfriend's son asked me last night why you gave me up. I told him that I used to think it was because I wet the bed."

"Oh, Lonnie."

"I did. And I was a bad kid. I know that now. When I see him, I know how bad I was."

"I didn't give you up because you were bad, Lonnie. I gave you up because *I was bad.*"

Again, they were silent. Rayne's elbows were on his knees and his head hung down between them as if he were trying to catch his breath. His hair slipped out from where he had tied it and hung around his face like a dark tent. The anger sent up soundings from somewhere very far below the surface of his current, everyday life. Very faint.

"I was a wreck, and it's taken me years to become, I don't

know, a full person, I guess. Except I wasn't a full person, because I didn't find you and tell you this. You had to come find me. You deserve great parents. But you got me. All I can tell you is the person you've found is better than the person who left."

"And I've got Selma. And Bobo."

"Of course. They raised you. Of course. I didn't mean to slight them . . . You're there now?"

"Right now? Right this very second, I'm here in the old house workin on the stove."

"Oh, don't tell me the old stove's still working."

"You know it is."

"Is Selma there? I hesitated to call, because I figured she didn't want to hear my name."

Rayne started to demur, but he knew his mother was right. Instead, he said simply: "Nana Selma's not here in the house. She's in the trailer."

"The trailer?"

"Oh, right. You haven't seen the trailer. Jones bought it a few years ago now, for when he came to visit. Mostly Selma stays there now. It's compact, air-conditioned, easy to heat, easy to clean."

"What about Jones? Oh, Jones, my God."

"Why are you crying?" Her crying affected him. She'd seemed cool until now, almost too perfect. And yet, had she simply cried about her own guilt, he would have wanted to smash the phone.

She sniffed and said in a higher range: "To hear you, to talk like this, like we're still a family."

"We are. We are. So, I'll tell you about Jones. He stayed for a while. We thought he would retire down here with her, but then he got a lead on a great job: the best job for him. It's like the gig you wish he'd had all his life."

"Horses?"

"Yep. There's a rich guy who raises and sells them to people all over the world. Jones breeds 'em, raises 'em, and goes with 'em when they're sold to help the new owners learn about 'em. He's like a different guy. Truth: I think they're a couple. That's the way it sounds. But, at any rate, he's happy."

"Hunh." Jewell's mouth was dry: something about Jones coming into himself at, what, eighty? She conjured his deep, sharp voice asking her how much money she needed to live up there in New York. His right hand, with its missing pointer finger, peeled off five twenty-dollar bills. *Listen, baby,* he'd said, *you act like you all alone in the world, but you got family. Don't forget that.* Then he laughed. *May not be the family you woulda chose, but we here. You got a home.*

"Jones deserves to be happy. My dad thought he was gay for years."

"Yeah. Well, you know him and Selma; they're, like, indestructible."

They laughed together, and it felt good, although Rayne had to go back and correct himself. "Except that Nana Selma's showing some wear and tear. A lot, really. I think it's hard for her keeping this place up. She is, uh, she's *not* happy."

"My dad always said that she hasn't been happy since King died."

"I think sometimes she and I were happy," Rayne told Jewell. "We had some good times. Maybe. I guess you'd have to ask her."

Every exchange chastened Jewell. Of course the two of them had been happy together. And of course, she couldn't ask Selma anything at all, so she'd continue to ask her son. "Selma used to have a man there who rented a place over on one corner and worked it. My dad said it was modern-day sharecropping."

"Mr. JJ. He's still here."

"Jesus."

Rayne laughed. Her voice and humor and memory were bringing him comfort. It soaked in like a slow rain. "I know. Mr.

JJ's like the oldest handyman in America. No, seriously, he's like a hundred and fifty years old."

Jewell made an alto yelp of delight. "Is he still as sloppy as he always was? He would fix things, and they'd do the job, but it wasn't pretty."

"Are you kidding? That's why I'm sitting here with the stove-pipe in pieces on the floor."

More laughter: his, hers. They egged each other on: JJ's fence posts at half-mast; JJ's doors that wouldn't close, or wouldn't open. The lock on the toolshed installed upside down. Then quiet, companionable, as if they were in the same room. Easy.

"I'm glad you called," he said.

"I'm very grateful you wrote. It was an act of enormous generosity."

"My girlfriend is the one who found you."

"Lillie?"

"Yeah, Lillie. You talked to her yesterday, right?"

"Yes, I did."

"She's the one did the research. I just sorta said: 'I wish I could tell my mother about this contract.' It really isn't easy to get a contract with the city, you know, and I was feeling . . .'"

"Proud?"

"That sounds sort of, um . . ."

"It sounds absolutely natural to me. And I am so proud of you, too. I am."

"Thank you." It was funny thinking back to the months before, when he began this search, with Lillie's help and encouragement. He did not know what else to say.

Jewell did: "Lillie sounds lovely."

"Yep. She is. And hardworking. Smart, too. She's almost finished nursing school."

"That's great. That's just great. This spring?"

"Yeah. Just a coupl'a months. Well, finished nursing school, but she wants to be a midwife, so there's still more. But she's, like, in the top ten of the class."

"Wow."

"Yeah, no joke."

"Wow," she repeated, slowly, contemplating. "And my father?"

"Granddaddy's in prison again."

"Did he hurt anybody?"

"No. Just himself." Rayne did not want to gossip about his grandfather to his mother, just as he no longer nodded in agreement when his grandfather complained about the daughter who left him with her child to raise. "Yeah. He's pretty much converted to Islam."

"Oh, Lord."

"No, I think it's a good thing for him." ("All-merciful," Bobo had once said to him. "*All*-merciful: If I could believe that, how would that feel?")

"Well, good." An embedded bitterness curled gracelessly at the edge of her own voice. She heard her son hear it. "I'm sorry."

"Bobo's had it rough."

"Please, tell me what happened."

"It's hard to say, exactly." He shot up his TV, and the cops came, and he jumped stink with a gun in his arm? The summary would sound like making fun of him.

"Yes, I'm sure. You don't have to bother. I just wondered . . ."

"You know that stand of scrub oaks—I'm not sure what they're called—by the road as you come up the drive?"

"The one between the heir property and the Old Broadnax fields?"

It took Rayne aback to hear his mother use Selma's exact language. He hadn't thought of them as the boundary, but, of course, they were. "Yeah. Well, when I drove up yesterday, the same thing happened to me that happened when I drove here in his truck when he went in the first time."

"How old were you?"

"Sixteen."

Bobo had spoken of it as a great forest, Rayne told his mother, where he had gotten lost once as a very little boy. Jewell made assenting noises to indicate that she had heard this story, too.

Bobo always called himself "a dumb little shit" for not obeying King and getting himself lost. Very lost. Even as a grown man sitting in Graterford prison, learning to pray to Allah, the all-merciful, Bobo suspected that had he gotten home sooner as a five-year-old, things would have turned out differently.

But it had to be a wrong memory, Rayne said to his mother. In part, he wanted to hear from her even a splinter of compassion for the grandfather who did his best by him, miserable though he often was. But he was also fishing for family facts, like an adoptee searches medical records.

"Here's what never made sense to me about that: like, sure, people then gave kids more responsibility, but the King they described was, like, he was like the only black man I ever heard about from back then who would not beat his children. I cannot believe he would have put a five-year-old out onto the road alone to find his way home. This is like a crazy bum rush, I know, but I've never been able to ask anybody, and since you mentioned him . . ."

"Yes, he has told that story all his life, and truth to tell, I always dismissed it, because I figured that my dad's story is that he's always the victim. Period. I've never thought about it this way before. You're way ahead of me in terms of generosity."

"But think how he talks about himself: dumb little shit. That's how he described himself."

"Yes. Did he call you that?"

"No," he said. That wasn't where he was going, and it wasn't until later that he realized that Bobo must have called Jewell something similar, or maybe worse.

"Here's another thing, since you've brought it up about him," Jewell said. "My father always paired that story with his own personal Bible text, the one that Selma's favorite old preacher gave him. Did he ever tell it to you?"

"I guess, probably . . ."

"'If the householder had known at what hour the thief was coming, he would have kept watch.'"

"Yeah, yeah, he did."

"I always figured he was showing me that it was not his fault that life had robbed him. The way he talked, it was like God Himself was the Great Thief." Jewell regretted saying it the minute it left her lips.

"Lillie says that maybe it was easier for Bobo to blame himself than to take in the loss of the man who loved him."

"I do realize," Jewell added quietly, "that no matter what his part in it was, eventually everything *was* taken from him."

"Everything except that Ford Ranger . . ."

"Even you," she continued, "and I imagine that having your company and your respect must have been very important to him." She knew at that moment something else she'd never thought about: how very hurt Bobo must have been by her scorn, even though he'd earned it.

———

Closing his eyes, Rayne saw himself again that night, around the corner from his grandfather's apartment at his friend Malcolm's, smoking a joint when the others rushed in.

Yo, man, the cops on your porch. Your grandfather come at 'em with a gun. C'mon!

He'd run, light-headed, stunned, and yet expectant, arriving home in time to push through the neighbors and see in the jaundiced yellow streetlight his grandfather being dragged off the porch, hog-tied, ridiculous: screaming that he'd rather be dead than go back to prison. His soft, naked belly scraped the sidewalk. He left an almost imperceptible smear of blood.

———

"I am so proud of you," Jewell said again.

"I may need to ask you some questions about the heir property," he said.

"Anytime. Feel free. I think the law says that everybody in the family owns it, whether they're there or not. I'm pretty sure that's what it says. But Selma doesn't agree. I don't know what you can do about that."

"Me neither."

"Well, call me again anyway. I'll try to be more help."

"This is help. Just this. Believe me."

"I do."

CHAPTER 14

◦

J ewell had gone to the park to make the call, and now that it was over, she and her dog began to trot slowly on the muddy paths. At least she had managed not to burden Rayne with any more of the story of her leaving him on the train—and especially not the tawdry, self-absorbed plan to kill herself after she had sent him south. Nor did she want to speak just yet of her undeserved rescue: how she wriggled out of the bed she'd made and into a false, velveteen life that eventually came true.

Falseness was what she remembered from that time that she usually chose to forget: the unbearable distance between whom she portrayed and the cringing girl inside. At the New York train station, after Jewell had abandoned her son, busy people hurried past her to their trains: men in suits, well-groomed wives who were free to screw them or not, as they pleased, at the end of a tarragon-and-butter roast-chicken evening, she imagined, with no consequence to next week's allowance. They turned discreetly to observe her, the tall, gray-suited beauty who stood apart, indifferent, wondering, no doubt, what was her story.

As she stood in Penn Station, still on the platform, everything, it seemed, began to pull away from her before she had a chance to do anything about it. Like a scab. She picked at it at first, and then she peeled off the colored-out-of-wedlock-mother mask and threw it onto the tracks. Another train would come soon to mash it against the rails.

Which is what she should have done with the rest of her had she not been, well, too afraid. She remembered being tired, as children whose mothers don't put them to bed are tired, so worn out that they sit in the middle of the floor and cry. Like her own son would do, because he stayed awake waiting for her.

Bad mommy.

"Ma'am, you sure you don't need he'p?"

"My goodness, I'm still standing here, aren't I?" She gave the old redcap a dollar for his trouble, went upstairs to the counter, waited in line with people who were in a rush, but she wasn't. She cashed in her ticket, which would cover the money she owed her roommate and the babysitter. And nothing else.

So when she left the great columns of Penn Station on 34th Street, she had to walk back to 125th Street in Harlem in the heels that were giving her blisters. It helped her bear it to know that when she got home, she'd leave the money with her neighbor, put her head into the oven, and be done with it. Just like that. Done.

———

The bars were open on Forty-second Street. Against the white heat, their dark doorways emitted an old, boozy, smoky smell, some vulgar cousin to the polished-wood scent of her hotel lounge.

Outside one bar a tall white man stood in a summer suit, right hand in his pocket, smoking. He was about thirty, fit, debonair. Jack Thompson looked as if he'd just stepped off a magazine cover. He watched her coming toward him and touched his two fingers to his forehead in a silent salute when she came to within three feet.

"I wish I could offer you something you might want right now." He said it quietly as she passed.

She slowed, feeling a tiny, hopeful thrill, the little match girl's first tiny flame, and he stepped across the sidewalk to meet her.

"Is there anything a stranger can offer a princess?" His was a smooth baritone radio-announcer voice.

"Nothing at all, thank you," she said. She perked up despite herself, despite suspecting a con job and worse to come, but it didn't matter now, because she was going home to the oven, so nothing mattered anymore. For a moment she was free, a feeling so delightful that she smiled quite spontaneously. Then, "You could offer me a cigarette," she said. "I'd like that."

He took out his pack, shook one out, lit it with a silver lighter, and handed it to her. From inside the bar Jewell heard a fight. She wondered that she hadn't noticed until now.

"Thanks," she said, turning her face away from his eyes toward the ruckus inside the bar.

Immediately, a white man with red hair exploded out the doorway; a second followed him. They wrestled, hit each other drunkenly, cursed. A third lumbered after them, a once-powerful man gone to fat, carrying a hammer.

"Botha you. I'ma clean house today. I'll fix botha you," he said.

She remembered thinking that the hammer was just a threat.

The first two rolled about on the sidewalk some more, now bent not only on hurting each other but on staying out of the way of the hammer as the big man approached.

Jack cupped Jewell's upper arm gently and guided her away from the melee and out of the crowd, most nearly drunk, who gathered around the fighters.

Suddenly, one of the two wrestlers on the ground broke away, ran down the street, and ducked into an alley. The redhead was left. He stood confused, cursing at the man with the hammer, who swung the tool at his face, catching the side of the redhead's jaw with the hammer's claw. The big man's follow-through carried him down to the ground, where he hit his head. The redhead, wobbly but still standing, felt the bottom of his jaw, which was bleeding.

"Omigod. Gotta get 'im to a hospital," someone yelled.

Others took up the cry. "Hospital. He needs a hospital."

"Needs a drink," he answered them. Pointing to the hammer man on his knees on the ground, he said triumphantly, "He needs a hospital." Then he kicked the man on the ground and wheeled back into the bar.

"What are you doing here?" Jewell asked Jack.

"What *am* I doing here?" He pivoted, whistled for a taxi, and then guided her into it. "I'll drop you off," he said, as if in answer. "Where are you going?"

"Nowhere," she said. "I'm going nowhere."

"That can't really be true." He scanned her hair and suit and shoes appreciatively.

She acknowledged his look. "You're right. I have to go to my friend's apartment and give her back these clothes." She told him the address, which he relayed to the driver.

"Then what will you wear?"

"Nothing. If you're not going anywhere, you don't need to wear anything, do you?"

"You could come with me."

She dismissed the suggestion with the tiniest bat of an eyelid. He lit two fresh cigarettes and handed her one. She lay back in the taxi and inhaled deeply, because it was such luxury to ride in a taxi and to smoke a fresh cigarette, to have it lit by a man with money in his pockets who didn't ask for anything in return.

She was told that her mother used to say something will turn up. For her, something always had.

Jack took a thin silver flask from his breast pocket and offered her a sip of whiskey. She liked the idea of having a drink before she did the deed.

"Thanks for the ride *and* the smoke *and* the drink," she said prettily when she got out.

He ran a quick eye over the place and registered no emotion. "Our little adventure." It was a dump, but so was the bar. "Look, won't you come with me?" he asked, as if it mattered to him. "I want to take your photograph. So I can see you whenever I want to."

"People have taken my photograph. No, thank you. You'll just have to remember me as I was."

He frowned. "What's that about?"

"Good-bye," she said as she swung her long legs, ankles together. Then she got out, and blew him a kiss.

———

Upstairs, she gave the neighbor her money. Jewell cut their conversation short. Inside her apartment, she took off the suit and hung it on the bedroom door. She put the rest of the money into the shoes and lined them up on the closet floor. She washed the blouse with dish detergent and hung it to dry on a hanger on the doorknob.

Then, very quickly, before she lost her nerve, she propped the coffee table at an angle to the oven, and blew out the pilot light. She felt a thin but thrilling satisfaction that she was actually going through with it. She looked into the oven to double-check the size. It was filthy with coated grease and blackened cooking drippings. Feeling a rising panic, Jewell ran into the bedroom, grabbed her pillow, and laid it on the rack. There was only one. She turned up the gas and lay down, resting her head on the pillow, hoping to God to be asleep, which is how she thought of it, before any roaches appeared.

She closed her eyes and breathed, waiting for stillness to descend again now that she had everything, everything, under control. The smell of gas and filth made her nauseous at first. She remembered Selma's scrubbing her oven with steel wool and lye soap. The thought of Selma made her face and bowels feel hot. She tried to keep herself from despair. She'd hidden it from herself. The gas jet made a hissing sound. Interesting.

She squeezed her eyes to keep them shut as tears ran toward her hairline. Behind her lids, she saw the picture of Lonnie in the little white christening suit her father sent, no doubt at Selma's urging. Jewell had the photo taken, but never accomplished the actual christening. She had not believed in heaven or hell until this moment.

Bad Mommy.

Night–night.

———

Then she heard that smooth voice at the edge of her conscious-ness, where shame and hilarity bled together. "Stay there. And keep the neighbors from gawking."

———

Jack stepped off the magazine cover to pull her from the oven, turn off the gas, wrap her in his jacket, and take her downstairs to the cab. They drove with windows open, and he spoke sharply to the driver. She heard him say that she'd had a little too much. She woke in a hotel, dizzy, sick to her stomach, looking up at a ceiling fan.

"Oh, God," she remembers saying. "Oh, shit." She knew that she would never have the courage to do it again, and that she would never stop crying. The grief felt endless, as if it had started before she was born and would continue beyond her, irreparable; she was its vessel. "I can't stand it."

He sat next to her for a long time while she cried. When it was dark, he ordered deli sandwiches and coffee and more cigarettes. Then he spoke.

"Look," he said, "I need a wife. It would do me a great good to return home to Boston with a wife."

"You have some lies goin?"

"Yes. I lie. I lie all the time, but that's the worst of it."

"You have money?"

The hotel had to cost plenty. She squinted to see whether he was lying about the money. He nodded to reassure her. "I do have money," he said, seeming to take no offense. "Some. Some money. My father's will leaves me a trust fund, but with two conditions: I must have a job and I have to get married. My mother's been indulgent, so I've studied and traveled.

"But if I don't marry by the end of this year, the money goes to a fund for the protection of wildlife. Not my wild life, obviously.

"So, I have secured a job with Philip Morris. I'm being transferred to Boston."

"I wish you hadn't taken me out."

"Can you forgive me?"

"That's so stupid."

"Why?"

"There's no such thing." It was too much for her to be bothered. It seemed like a nasty joke. "I could be black, you know. You don't know me at all. I could be a Negro."

"Better and better," he said. He lit a cigarette and handed it to her. "My father's father owned minstrel theaters. So, we're connected. It's poetic justice. I knew I had to go back for you." He grinned. "You are quite perfect."

"Blackface?" She couldn't quite take it in.

"Of course you are black or you wouldn't have said it. This is very funny. But you have it, a very rare quality. You know it, of course. It's star power. Will you marry me? And move to Boston with me and take college courses and give dinner parties? We'll know what kind of marriage it is, and therefore we'll just have fun instead of trying to fix each other. Let's." He reached toward the lamp in order to see better her beautiful face.

"No, please, don't turn on the light." The only thing she wanted was to sit and smoke quietly in a dark room. How else could she gain the courage to go to Boston to marry or pretend to marry, who knew, a tobacco executive whose inheritance came from coon shows. "My family used to raise tobacco," she said. "My great-grandmother told me how they stayed in the smoke barn flue-curing tobacco for three days, watching that the leaves didn't dry too fast or stay too moist. They had to turn bunches of leaves on the string and keep the fire just so."

He was watching her take it in. "I know," he said. "There are a lot of disincentives. But the whole deal is perfectly absurd. That's why it's perfect. I know it." He laughed to himself. Then he got serious.

"Look, I'm not a bad guy. Once, at boarding school, I pulled a kid out of the ice. No, really. Truth." He put his hand up in an Eagle Scout pledge. "I knew that the ice was bad where he was. I told him not to go there, and then when it started to crack, I'd gone the other way to the dock, and I knew the rope was there, and that if I tied it around myself, I could grab him and pull the two of us back.

"It's the only other good thing I ever did, and I was absolutely certain about it. I'm certain about this."

"Because you like to rescue people?"

"Maybe. Hadn't thought of it that way. It occurred to me today that—"

Jewell was listening now that he was speaking to her from behind his cool façade. She wanted some solution. The place where Lonnie buried his head against her still burned with shame.

"What?"

"Have you ever been honest with a man? I mean, my parents' marriage was really an exchange. They talked about love, but I never felt it between them. I've been behaving like a kid about this—you know they say, 'Eat your vegetables,' so you spit them out."

Jewell laughed grimly, but said nothing.

"What I objected to about marriage was the pretense, but maybe we could do less of that, and in a year, if we don't like it, we can split."

Jewell asked: "A real marriage? Legal?"

"No point otherwise. Besides, maybe I do like to rescue people." He ran his hand along her arm. "And I could look at you forever. Maybe we'll have a ball. The signs are auspicious."

He lit another cigarette for them to share and handed it to her, and began to rub her feet.

Jewell lay back on the bed, smoking, enjoying his hands. As far as Selma and Bobo would ever know, if they ever found out anything, she'd been carried out of the building and disappeared. It might as well be a suicide. She'd be gone, she thought, and whoever she became would be something else: a creation. She wondered whether this was a chance to make herself over and get it right. The man sitting opposite her remained as he appeared earlier, cool and magazine-handsome, matter-of-fact, amused by the day's work, but also suddenly almost credible. "Remember the redheaded man at the bar? Remember how he went back inside when everyone said he should go to the hospital after the guy bashed him with the hammer?"

"That's how you feel to be alive again? But, my dear, you were not going to the hospital. I thought about it, but you looked like you were coming to. That sounds as if I were gambling."

Redeem the time. Selma used to sing a hymn with that phrase. She'd sing it low and off-tune, with more lyrics Jewell could not recall, but that urged them to work harder. You could never work hard enough for Selma. How could this man be talking about getting a trust fund that he hadn't worked for? How could she simply step off one track with nothing and onto another with sandwiches and coffee and hotels, talking marriage to a white man who took taxis on a whim?

————

After her run, Jewell returned to her vestibule full of moist dog smell, and to the man who had started marriage as a lark, and then grown into it, as she had, with sincere gratitude for a chance to give and receive love.

But she could still see Jack as he'd been that night in the hotel, sleek and amused: he unbuttoned his shirt. "So, how long have you wanted to pass for white?"

She started to shake her head no.

"C'mon, now. Don't kid a kidder." He undid his belt and button and zipper and slipped off his pants.

She shrugged as he approached and laid a condom on the bedstand.

"Let's not do kids, shall we? You don't have any, of course?"

She shook her head. Now that he'd confessed to being a liar, she could lie without qualms. She was a cicada shell, stuck on the side of a tree, tiny bulging casings over the eyes, claw casings holding on. Whoever was inside had fled.

He stood her on her feet, and ran a hand lightly over her torso. "You can say no," he said. "But I thought that we'd just get married and pretend to be a perfect couple. Who knows? Maybe we can beat the odds and enjoy it. I can stop cutting off my own inheritance to spite my father. And meanwhile, we'll have lots of sex and chicken salad sandwiches. That's at least as good as your alternative."

She shrugged again, and he began to undress her, checking as he did for her assent, and admiring her flawless body. "If we get married," she asked, "can I go to college?"

"Sure. That's the idea. So, if you don't like me after a while, you can do as you please.

"I like this place," he said, referring to the hotel. "It's warm."

He rubbed her so lightly that it almost tickled. "Were you going to go through with it today?"

"Maybe."

"Why?"

"I wanted to disappear."

"No, you don't. You want everybody to look at you and feel just as I do right now."

He's never been black, she thought. What she said was: "Today's my birthday."

"Mine, too."

"That's a lie," she said.

He laughed, kissed her, and slipped in a finger in one deft, delighted movement.

That's when she decided to do it. She would lean her despair against his delight and rest in it.

———

Now, how can she tell her son, the thirty-year-old builder with his first city contract, a truth more stupid and pathetic than any lie she's ever told: that she decided to marry a white man she didn't know because, at that moment, she felt certain he wouldn't hit her.

CHAPTER 15

When Selma awoke, it was past 10:00 a.m., bright sun and mild. She'd dreamt of her married youth. Lying very still on her side, she prolonged the dream and held off the certain awakening into aloneness.

Check your damn fences.

Like a feudal lord, Needham is everywhere on his land at all times. He and the boys and Selma and then Bobo, together with brother Richard and his family, and Amos and Mary's children who come in the summer: they invest each acre with their presence—their plows, threshers, mills, hitches, wagons, and trucks; their homemade blacksmith operation; their mules and mare, the nanny goat and kids, the big brown-and-yellow milk cow the brothers share, the chickens that lay green-and-white pullet eggs; their voices sing in time to the implements and change with the rhythm of the season; the stench of their fertilizer and the whiff of brown creek water that collects behind their sticks-and-stone dam and runs through ditches across the new orchard; the hum of bees from the hive boxes they build at the edge of the south field. Whatever they can buy or claim stamps Needham into each tidy corner.

———

Then the present knocked on Selma's trailer door, and called her name. Selma's voice was croaky, and she knew that if she moved too fast, she'd have an accident. So she lay in bed, answering Rayne and Khalil, as if they could read her mind, to stop banging and come on in like they had some sense. Soon enough, they did.

"That's why I gave you the key," she said, as loudly as her morning voice would allow, "so you wouldn't have to stand out there bangin like a buncha crazy people."

"Yeah," Rayne answered, "I know." They shouted through the thin trailer door to her bedroom.

"But we're two guys," Khalil explained in his most reasonable singsong. "We can't just barge in on you."

"Well, now you see I keeps the bedroom door closed at night, so you can feel free. Help yourself to some toast and cream cheese. I got grits up in the cabinet if you not too lazy to make 'em, Ray. Take me a while to get dressed."

"Well, maybe I am lazy. Listen, Nana, just so you know, I put the mattress out in the sun. Nothing happened to it, it's just been in the house and needed to get some air."

"Yeah, 'cause you know I don't heat in there in the winter, and it probably got mildew. And you know I can't haul it out and beat it. Did you beat it?"

"Yep, plus Khalil's been beggin for McDonald's since we left."

"McDonald's no good for you," Selma said. "I say we go fishin and get some real good eatin."

Khalil raised his eyebrows inquiringly at Rayne, who opened

his arms, palms up, and shrugged. Then he asked: "You up to fishin?"

"Wouldn'ta said it otherwise," she said confidently. "Especially if I got somebody to take all my gear. I'm as bad as takin a baby. Got the wheelchair and the whatchacallit walker, and we got to take bottles of water for me so I don't pass out. It's terrible. I been waitin all year for this. Who else gonna put up with all that to take me fishin?"

Rayne walked three steps to Selma's bedroom door across the miniature living/dining area, cracked it open, and said quietly: "I found your strongbox."

"Oh, thank you, Jesus!" Selma came to the door in her bathrobe, leaning on her night table with one hand, and carrying a toothbrush in the other. "It was under?"

"Not under. Behind. He built it into the back of the chimney, where the decorative plate was."

"You look in? Is the will there?"

"Looks like it. And some other papers. A couple strange ones. Listen, I'ma leave them here with you to read carefully while I take Khalil for breakfast."

"Well, hang on. Can't he wait a minute while we go through the box together?"

"No, he can't. Maybe he could, but he shouldn't. We'll be back soon. Oh, and I'ma stop at the Goodwill and get him a coat, since we lost his on the way."

"Lost it? How the heck did y'all lose a coat? Can't he wear something over to the house? We got jackets there."

Khalil shook his head violently back and forth until it was wagging on his neck and his eyes spun back and forth. Rayne laughed and grabbed him to stop him before he got dizzy.

"Nana, I'll be back."

———

Rayne used the errand to stop in at the county courthouse, too. In the register-of-deeds office, he asked a young woman whether she could explain the current laws governing heir property. The deed he found in his great-grandmother's strong-box listed as owners ancestors whom he'd heard of, but who'd been dead many years. She said simply, "If you have a deed in the name of some ancestors who are deceased, and the deed has not been changed, then the land is held in common by all the heirs."

He could feel that she'd had this conversation many times before with people who knew things he didn't, or who had agendas that she was trying to ward off. Rayne was sorry that he still could not understand. He stood mute at the counter work-ing his face to communicate his attempt.

"Heir property." She said it as if it made everything clear. "Or heirs property."

"Whose heirs?" He figured that any question might elicit some new information that would give him a sense of what he was not getting.

Khalil asked: "Can I go get the rest of my soda?"

"You remember where we parked?"

Khalil's head bobbed up and down. "And I don't need the key, 'cause you didn't lock it."

"Shhhh."

"Oops." Khalil made a naughty smile at the young woman. A slight softening of her angular brown face indicated that the boy had succeeded in breaking through her bureaucratic cloak of invisibility.

"It's all the heirs," she said, elongating the word *ahhhhhhl*. "Those people on that deed, who are they to you?"

"They are my great-grandfather's grandparents."

"Okay. Think like the Genome Project, like that. All the people on this earth who came from them—all them people—that's who owns that land."

"Oh, my Lord." Rayne understood now why she'd been so emphatic. But he thought now it was merely a matter of clarifying. "But my great-grandfather bought them out, as I'm told, years and years ago."

"Okay. For every heir who gives up ownership, we have to have a quitclaim deed, meaning that they acknowledge legally they have no claim to the land." She stopped and looked Rayne up and down, this time with a hint of appreciation and even sexual interest. Rayne noticed the tendril of a tattoo curling up at the back of her neckline. "You Ms. Selma Needham's boy from Philadelphia, aren't you?

"She said you was big. She said you look just like her husband, only darker. And I knew it was you 'cause Americans down here don't wear big ole dreadlocks like them. Only Jamaicans, couple of 'em now and then. She said you got your own company, too."

He smiled weakly. Khalil returned, skipping noisily, banging the door, and sucking the ice dry. "Can I have the rest of your soda, too? You got the *supersize* one. I just got the child's size."

"Sure. Don't let the door go."

"He cute," the woman said, her eyes following Khalil skipping back out.

The door slammed. *Bam*.

"I'm sorry."

"Don't worry. Everybody does it."

"So. We can't all own that one place. I mean it could be thirty, forty people."

"It could be 182. You sound like Ms. Selma. She don't believe it neither. That why she sent you in here? Tell 'er she ain't slick."

"No. It's me. I just didn't understand. But the point is that she can't sell it. Is that correct?"

"I told her that she should go the Center for Heirs' Property Preservation. They know all about it—and they know how to get clear title on the land. But without clear title, you can't will it or sell it, can't. Can't borrow against it either, which is what she wanted to do. Least you can't do it unless all the heirs agree."

"Thanks."

"No, really. You should go see 'em at the Center. 'Cause if one of the heirs wants to sell, lemme tell you, it's South Carolina law that they can force the sale—and y'all will only have ten days to buy out that heir, and then another thirty days to match the best sales offer."

"But if there are 182 of 'em, like you say, then how much can their share be?"

"Hey, look at Hilton Head."

"That isn't heir property?"

"Not anymore, it ain't. Here, I'll give you the number. I gave it to Ms. Needham, and I know she threw it away."

"Okay," Rayne said. "Let me put it in my phone."

"Shame you don't live down here," she said.

CHAPTER 16

"Well, that was the longest trip to McDonald's I ever saw."

"We stopped at the courthouse," Khalil said, getting ready to stuff Rayne's giant drink cup into Selma's trash can. Rayne had stayed outside to finish a conversation with Lillie.

"Unh-unh-unh," she said. "Take it over to the sink, empty all that ice, and then roll up the cup." She watched him. "I didn't say ball it up, I said roll it. You fold it in half lengthwise, and then roll that. My garbage here is no bigger than a pocketbook, and I can't be running up and down emptying it every commercial break."

"I'll empty it," Khalil said, grabbing the liner bag. "I saw the trash can outside. It looks like a Dumpster."

"It is a Dumpster," she called after him. "And bring me back my bag!"

Outside, between the trailer and the old house, Rayne paced a leisurely parabola while he told Lillie about his conversation with his mother, Selma's aging, and the confusing business about the land. The mild March sunshine showed up the disrepair. Early weeds grew thick and luxuriant, so tall around the house and the trailer behind it that had there been a breeze, they would have waved to welcome him. As Aunt Big Tootch used to say about people she disapproved of—including Selma—the weeds had "pushed themselves forward."

Dandelions and chickweed forced through cracks in the asphalt driveway, laid twenty years before but still called "new" by Selma; already tall wild onion and garlic lined the walkway to the back door, as did bushy yellow nut sedge, and something mintlike that had taken over the kitchen garden between nubs of old collards.

Everything Rayne saw needed sweeping, at least, and a coat of paint. The downspout had been wired back into place crooked. Old hog houses across the south field had finally fallen in, and JJ's new chicken wire around the coop was stapled to listing scraps of plywood instead of proper stakes. The whole setup was sloppy. It looked like Selma couldn't keep it going much longer.

In the last good structures to remain standing, however, and in the lay of the fields and what was left of the ingenious system of dams and drains, Rayne felt the presence of King Needham. It never failed. King's phrases came to mind, as if Rayne had heard them himself:

Know your boundaries, boys; what am I talking 'bout?

Before breakfast or after supper, Selma said, the towering King, his son who died in the war, and Jones traced the periphery of the land. In this way, eight or ten acres a day, they maintained each area. They policed the weeds, disrepair, insects, varmints, neighbors. By the end of the week, they'd circled the farm. Bobo remembered King carrying him on these jaunts as a toddler: in his arms, on his shoulders, in a sling over the big mare mule.

Grandma Bett used to say: little by little, hen drink the water.

A day off on Sunday and do it again.

Think with your feet, boys, Bobo quoted him. *Think with your eyes, boys, your ears; taste and see. We gonna notice what other men miss—pay attention, boys!*

It was the only way to keep the land.

Rayne told some of this to Lillie, who listened, it seemed to him, as if she were taking a patient history. "But I thought you didn't want the land."

"I don't. I don't want the goddamned land. And I don't want Selma's money from it. I want Selma to sell it. But she talks double-talk about it, and the county courthouse says it's not possible, and my mother even said she thought it might be more complicated than just selling the land. Yo, all I wanted to do was to bring the kid down and go fishin and eat some corn bread. Shit."

"Listen. My old man and my kid are away for the week. So maybe I could do a little research for you."

"Oh, baby, would you? Keepin these two occupied is about all I can handle. Damn, one needs twenty-four seven activity; the other one needs to sit down. I'd rather build a damn retaining wall in the rain."

"If I find somebody home at the Center you mentioned, you want me to make you an appointment?"

"Baby, baby, please. But aren't you studying?"

"Oh, for sure. Here at home, and then, later, I'm going out to the medical library to join the study group. You'd be amazed how much I can get done—"

"Without us to take care of . . . Go on, you can say it."

"Plus, hey! Who got called back to the shop, because another one of the Eagles asked for scarification and wanted the person who did his teammate? Who's guaranteed a thousand dollars to start? Rocco said he said: 'I want somebody knows what she's doing. I want the nurse!' Hah-hah-hah."

"Which player?"

"You know I don't know. I don't know 'em till they come in. I'm only interested in whether they keloid and whether they tip." She laughed to herself, sighed, and said, "Okay, so I can make an appointment with the Center for any time tomorrow, Thursday, or Friday, if they work on Good Friday, or Saturday. So, now you can go fishing. Hey, did Nana Selma make you your corn bread?"

"She did make us corn bread. That was good."

"And, not that you need to think about it now, but your mother called back to invite us out there to dinner next week."

"Too much too soon, you think?"

"No, why not? I don't know. You tell me."

"Aw, baby, you know I talk about not having any family around . . ."

"And now you got two ladies plus us, and it's too many."

"Black people never satisfied," Rayne said. It was an all-occasion quote they used regularly.

"Hey, Ray, listen, speaking of black people, your mother's husband is white."

"How do you know?"

"She told me about the reappearance of his cancer, and I really urged them to go see my nurse-practitioner mentor."

"You and that mentor."

"She's the best. She's a healer, Rayne. Oncology's her specialty, and she knows healing. It's not just medicine and a cure. She's a *healer*. I don't think you're hearing me on this. You think I'm talking para-science, but healing is more than medicine."

"I'm tryin to stay with you, baby. But what's that have to do with him being white?"

"Oh, right, sorry. 'Cause I started in on how sometimes black men don't want to go to white women for their health care, and I have this other practitioner to follow up, and she's, you know, Blasian, blah-blah-blah, and your mother laughed, and said it wouldn't bother him, because he's white, too."

"Okay. Well, okay. Uh-oh," Rayne said. "I see Selma's sending Khalil out to the truck with the old fishing poles. Looks like it's time to roll. God, I miss you. Why'd you give me that send-off?"

"So you'd miss me," she said.

CHAPTER 17

They headed for the river, but driving the old way proved impossible. Where there had been country roads through farmland alternating with swamp and scrub forest, now there had sprung up the new golf course, two pretentious, plantation-something gated communities, and new corporate headquarters for two foreign companies. They swallowed up rights-of-way, so that the roads ended abruptly. Selma thought she remembered, but finally admitted after the third detour that she could no longer find a way. Here and there, they drove through one-horse towns with names Rayne recalled. Twice, they slowed past a lineup of smallish houses, ranch, saltbox, trailers. Young black men stood in the middle of the road where the centerline must have been painted once.

"This brother must know how to get there," Rayne said, rolling down his window.

"They don't know nothing 'bout nothing but how to sell some drugs and steal," Selma said. "Don't ask them niggers nothin."

Rayne's window was already opening to let in the heavy, gritty bass line underneath rap music from a boom box perched on top of a broken kitchen chair. It was a low-tech country setup for a piece of music that Rayne knew from somewhere, but couldn't place.

"Hey, you a Rasta? Want some ganja?" the young man asked.

Selma said: "Don't put none o' that stuff in this truck, you! This a clean truck. We got chilren in this truck."

"Hey, lady," the man said, palms up. "Y'all stopped to talk to me."

"I'm lookin for the road to the Edisto River. I'm looking for one of the places right where it opens up to the sea. It's like a bay, and there's a place that juts out; it's like, on one side people swim, and on the other they fish. We used to call it Mermaid Landing, I think."

The guy looked at Rayne with heavy-lidded eyes just focused. His cap had slipped back off perfect cornrows done in a tight zigzag. His eyes looked dead.

"Don't worry 'bout it," Rayne said.

"Where you from? New York?"

"I tole you he don't know nothing."

"It's just like a swimming hole." Rayne meant this to end the conversation.

"A what?"

"Roll up the window!" Selma whispered, making a lifting motion with her hand.

"Nothing, man, just a swimming hole."

"Oh, swimmin *hoes*! No, man. We ain't got no fuckin swimmin hoes down here. Hoes down here go on they feet, or preferably on they back." He cracked himself up, and doubled over laughing. "Or on they knees." The other three men lined along the road turned to see what was happening. The rap line ended with "my bitch."

"Jesus!" Selma said. "The boy's settin right here in the back listenin to that filth. Ray, roll up the window, I tell you!"

Rayne couldn't help but think of a crazy comeback: that they used to have mermaids, but now they had drugs instead. He smiled to himself.

"What is you smiling about?" Selma hissed. "That fool is high as a kite."

"Thanks," Rayne said, and drove off.

"Oh, my Lord," Selma said, breathing heavily. "I was sure he was gonna shoot us."

"What was the music sayin?" Khalil ventured.

"No, baby, don't ask no questions right through here, baby," Selma said. She huffed as if they were in an emergency.

"I just wanna ask do he know what they were saying."

Rayne did know the piece. He'd forbidden his demo team from playing it on the job. "Don't interrupt me," the tagline warned, "while I'm beating my bitch." Lillie's Facebook friends had gone into full-cry viral outrage a while back. It was an old piece.

"That's all right, I tell you," Selma said. "We don't need no more confusion."

————

At the intersection of the next little town, on either side of the train tracks, Rayne left Selma and Khalil in the cab with the engine running and the doors locked while he went into a convenience and package store. When he came out, he was carrying a bag of local hot sauce. On the outside of the bag, four old-timers had collaborated on a pencil-drawn map of the area with Mermaid Landing indicated by a large, circled *M*. He also threw five pounds of ice into the ridiculously large cooler he'd found in the old shed, as if they were going to catch a fifty-pound black drum with twenty-year-old line and a number-two hook.

Selma was telling Khalil how to smoke fish, and how they'd kept the fish-smoking tradition in the family all the way from Africa, and that Grandma Bett said that smoked fish kept them alive for the two terrible winters that followed the Civil War.

"The Civil War?" Khalil whispered it to himself incredulously in the backseat. When Rayne looked into the rearview mirror to discipline him with a glare, Khalil grabbed his cheeks, pulled them down, and rolled his eyeballs upward until only the whites showed. An involuntary sneezy laugh escaped Rayne's nose, but he managed to master his face by the time the eyeballs in the mirror returned to peer at him.

"They had some *tur*-ble winters," Selma was saying. "You think down here is all sunshine-palmetto like today, but it could get *bad*."

Rayne gave a stern frown and drove on toward the river, ignoring the bare foot that poked its way into his peripheral vision, waving, no doubt, a naughty reference to the shoeless childhood Selma described.

"Time we get there," Selma said, "it'll be time to turn around and go home. 'Cause lemme tell you, I can't be up cookin no dinner at ten o'clock tonight again, y'all hear me. No wonder I fell out. 'At's too late. I'm havin a hard enough time on my pins as it is. Playin around with you young bucks'll finish me off for sure. I'm already so stiff y'all gonna have to pry me outta here with a can opener . . ."

Rayne started laughing then, and Khalil whooped. Selma herself said, "It's the truth," and then laughed with them. "And it'll take y'all half an hour just to get me set up on the dock. Oh, Lord, did he bring the blanket?"

"I'ma tell you something about the Broadnax field, since we was talking about it before: the old father Broadnax kept hogs there, and it was the sloppiest, filthiest, stinkinest operation you ever saw. Contaminated ev'rybody's water. That's why the whites didn't mind King buyin it, 'cause they knew he'd clean it up.

"Well, some years before we bought it, the little shoats would get out and run over to our place, and we'd make sure to take 'em back; show 'em which one it was, tell 'im where the fence was broke . . . But this one time, we was comin back from fishin at night. Dark, dark, dark, and almost home, come up on this fat little shoat. We knew right away whose it was, and King said, he said, just like this: 'Selma, you think we could can that thing by sunup?'

"And, oh, my Lord. Good thing it was cold, 'cause we had to work so fast . . ." Selma remembered King slaughtering the shoat with the fish knife, the mess of it, dragging it home in the fish buckets, blood enough to slosh as the wagon rocked in the cold, clear, quiet night; stoking up the old stove to boil the thing piecemeal. Faces greasy with condensation, they met the morning by piling manure into the wagon to sop up the blood. It was that night chewing cracklin that King and Selma got the idea to buy the place outright.

———

When they arrived at Mermaid Landing, Rayne and Khalil set Selma in her chair, and wrapped her in two blankets despite what was to them a mild day. Then they arranged their gear and pole. Selma reminded Rayne that the summer he came to live with them was one of the last years that the Philadelphia relatives sent their children to stay July and August. He'd forgotten most everything about that summer except that it began with him anticipating his mother's return and ended with him confronting her abandonment. Now—maybe because he was here, or because he had talked to her and because Lillie was making plans for them to visit his mother in little more than a week's time, or maybe because the flirtatious woman at the courthouse had drawn in his mind a family tree—he recalled them here, those of his own generation, mostly older, who knew the ropes and enjoyed that he didn't. He also remembered Binky, the older girl cousin he'd had a crush on, because the bell-like curl at the end of her laugh sounded like his mother's, and because her presence seemed somehow connected to the mermaids that Jones told him swam in from the sea.

———

Rayne was allowed to ride in the wagon with his Philadelphia cousins. They called him Ray, as Selma did, or Wild Bill Hickok or Samson, because his thick hair had not been cut. All three cousins showed Needham blood: tall and broad-backed, they had the wide-set Needham eyes under arched heavy brows. Also a metallic-edged quality of the voices, so that when they spoke together fast, finishing one another's sentences, their voices hit him with the noisy clatter of cutlery. Their accents sounded familiar, not quite New York, but closer to it than the people here in South Carolina, whom he could only barely understand. It felt like family with them—and it didn't. It made him angry that it didn't.

"When do you go back?" Binky asked him.

She'd just turned twelve. Her breast buds pointed sideways. They fluttered up and down on the rutted wagon road. Rayne wanted to touch them. Instead he shrugged.

"You should probably ride back with us as far as Philadelphia," she said sensibly.

"On the train?"

"No, we're too young to go on the train by ourselves."

"I went on the train by myself."

Binky studied him as if trying to judge his truthfulness, but the fact, on its face, was too bizarre to judge. "We drive," she said.

"Daddy borrows the station wagon from Uncle Amos. There's a seat way at the back that looks out the window. That's where I sit. You can wave to people in the cars behind you. It's pretty big. We could fit you, I think."

"Philadelphia comes before New York?"

Binky nodded.

"I could hide in the trunk. Will you help me?"

"What are you talking about? It's a station wagon. It doesn't have a trunk."

He spoke into her ear. No one else could hear him over the road noise and wind in the open truck bed. "They're trying to keep me here. Granddaddy Bobo's trying to keep me from going home. I swear for God."

She studied him for clues to the mystery. "You're crazy, you know that?"

"If you tell anybody they'll beat me."

"Why would I tell anybody that crazy mess?"

He decided he'd stow away as far as Philadelphia, then get to New York from there. The thought seemed just right. He had a way home.

Rayne remembered the exact moment when he decided to stow away to Philadelphia. He remembered the calm that seeped through him at the thought. He withdrew from the others. The Philadelphia cousins decided that he was strange, as their parents' gossip had already informed them. Why else had his mother shipped him south and disappeared?

The adults put him to fish with the women and girls, while Granddaddy Bobo and the men sat across the wide tongue of land on the saltwater side. Bobo was complimenting Uncle Jones and an older cousin and two hired boys on the fence they'd laid alongside Bill Gunnerson's field. Rayne sat next to the tinkling-voiced twelve-year-old who resembled his mother and envied the boys. So, very slowly, he reeled in his line, stood, and ambled toward the men to get a new piece of worm to skewer on the hook Jones made for him from a pounded nail.

"I helped with the fence," he said, holding out the empty hook.

"So you think you get to use up all the bait?" Granddaddy Bobo shouted in mock amazement. "What're you doing? We supposed to be catchin the fish so we can eat 'em. They feeds *us.* Jones, hey, Jones! Why'on't you 'xplain so he can learn? We been out since four diggin worms. Look here, just cut the damn worm and throw it in. Be easier for everybody."

"Leave the boy alone," Jones said. "He can't help if mermaids take his bait." Jones made a delicate plucking motion. To Rayne he said quietly: "You're gonna have to learn to do this yourself, Ray-Ban. Watch me."

Jones motioned to Rayne. He cut off the makeshift hook and invited the boy to squat next to him over a gray-green tackle box and a hinged lid with neat tray compartments like tiny steps. With his hammer-top fingers, Jones selected a weight, a bobber, and a hook, tied each on the line with a different knot, and guided Ray to do the same. Then Jones closed the squeaky lid and snapped shut one of the rusty clasps.

"Uh-oh," Bobo said. "Now he gonna lose good tackle along with the bait."

"Now lookahere." Jones called Rayne's attention back from his grandfather. But the boy still could not listen. The ocean crashed on rocks, throwing up a clear-white spray that rose straight up, taller than a tree. "Pay attention, Rane-bo, so we don't make no accident."

He removed a tiny cutting board that fitted exactly into a notched groove in the side of the tackle box and took a worm from their dirt-filled, sweetgrass basket. With a small, sharp knife he sliced the worm into halves that writhed as if trying to find each other. He allowed Rayne to try to thread his worm onto his hook. The bloody piece of worm slithered. It wanted its other half. Rayne hooked his own finger by mistake, and Jones congratulated him on not crying.

"That's what you want," Bobo commented from above and behind them, "you *want* it to move."

Jones's fingers guided the worm's moving flesh onto the hook. "See that. It's gotta go *through* 'im."

"Shut up, man. Come 'ere boy, let me show you how to put this worm on so can't nobody snatch 'im offa the hook while you staring out to the sky."

Jones handed him the hook. "Show 'im that." To Bobo he said: "He got it now."

"Lookin for mermaids." One of the cousins, laughing.

"He should be lookin for God," Lil Tootchie said. Since no one stopped her, Lil Tootchie continued: "He should be up in church tomorrow morning thanking God for bringing his little brown butt safely these many miles to the bosom of his family. He should be promising to be good to Selma. What we don't need is no firebug bringing home no trouble. God knows—"

Bobo said: "No, Lil Tootchie, nunh-unh. No church here today. You go to church tomorrow and the preacher will not sit up there talking about fishing. So please don't bring that high and righteous talk to the water's edge today. I didn't come here for that."

"He will talk about fishing. He'll tell these children to expect Jesus to come walkin toward them on the water, not no devilish mermaid . . ."

"I'm telling you what's right. Don't look at me funny," Lil Tootchie said. "I'ma take these children. We could take JJ's boys, too."

"We got our own church, thank you," one of JJ's sons answered quickly.

Rayne wondered out loud: "What's a mermaid?"

CHAPTER 18

I t occurred to Rayne years later that Lil Tootchie and her children had stayed not just that summer but throughout most
of the year. He didn't ask until he was in college, and then
Selma told him that Lil Tootchie's husband drank and knocked
her around. It got so bad that she took the children to Richard
and Big Tootch's house, but the husband followed her there. At
night he'd appear, drunk, shouting into the windows, banging
on the door. Selma told Rayne that Lil Tootchie and the four
children were like prisoners, and Big Tootch's neighbors were
restive.

Could they come down the farm, they asked.

*I didn't say: you sold out your share to Pettiford and lef' me here
by my lonesome. Nope, I say: King say this heir proppity; that's what
it's here for.*

When Lil Tootchie's husband finally sobered up the next
year, he drove down in the same station wagon he'd borrowed
from Amos before. The family behaved formally with one an-

other, but determined to make a go of it. The Husband, which was how Selma referred to him from then on, thanked Selma with a piece of money and a face full of shame for keeping his family for him. She wished them well. The next summer, the children did not return. Selma said she figured that the Husband thought she'd turned his family against him, a job she said he had accomplished his own self by cracking Lil Tootchie's tooth on the bathroom sink.

———

Rayne did not meet Big Tootch until he went to Philadelphia to attend Cheyney University and visited them for holidays. A self-proclaimed truth-teller and Christian woman, Big Tootch was a widow by the time Rayne met her. Like everyone else, she spoke of King in oversize terms, even when it was to bemoan some occasion when he had overridden her poor husband, Richard. When she talked of Selma, however, a hard self-righteousness pinched her round little mouth and set the jaw under her double chin. She wanted Rayne to know that during the Depression it was she who had taught the motherless Selma, daughter of sharecroppers and oyster shuckers, how to wash her privates with soap and to pull that nappy hair back in two rows instead of in a hundred braids like a pickaninny. It had been Big Tootch who had tutored the tongue-tied, stuttering young Selma to speak in public, drilling her, like a traveler to another country, on stock phrases:

May I give you my list, sir, so I don't make any mistakes?

I'm sorry; I can't answer that.

Please give me a moment; sometimes it takes me a minute to say what I mean.

Can I buy some of this?

Can I pay you next week, please?

Big Tootch had taken Selma to church in the first place, and didn't appreciate that King had been too arrogant or political to go. Big Tootch had introduced Selma to the preacher who'd given Bobo his text—might as well say it because the whole family knew: "If the landowner had known the hour at which the thief would come, he would have kept watch." And, Lord, would that he had heeded those words!

These were the things Big Tootch said not only in private but also at Thanksgiving dinner in Philadelphia. Rayne did not appreciate hearing them at table. Hadn't Selma taken in Lil Tootchie and the four grandchildren? Didn't that deserve better than to have her unwashed, sixteen-year-old privates mentioned in her absence over turkey and gravy?

"Just so you know, Aunt Tootch, Nana Selma never talks about your family like this. Never." It was the best he could muster.

To her credit, his favorite cousin, Binky, looked embarrassed and got up to fuss around. "Nana Selma was very good to us," she said.

"How many times you think we gotta thank her for letting *us* come stay on our own land, I'd like to know?" her mother asked.

"I thought that you all sold out to Pettiford."

"How're we gonna sell out to Pettiford? Pettiford don't own the land. We do; that's what make it heir property. We always owned it; always will."

Rayne ignored these pronouncements, as Selma had taught him to do. Selma called the land hers, and told Rayne that one day it would be his. It was why she wanted him to go to college, so that he could see to it, legally, himself.

"She *was* very good to us," Binky repeated quietly as she cleared and motioned for her seething young cousin to help. When they got to the kitchen, she showed him two quarts of peaches Selma had sent with an old itinerant minister, a seventy-year-old Socialist with no church to call his own, who still went up and down the coast every year. Rayne brought down one quart. The two of them opened it for dessert and ate out of the jar, sharing a spoon. Rayne thought and then said aloud the question that never seemed to occur to anyone else: How could a man own land without paying for it?

Binky stopped with her spoon full of peach, halfway to her mouth, trying to figure how to answer her cousin, as quick to anger as he had been as a boy, and still as concerned with impossible questions.

"You used to look at me the same way back then," Rayne said, and to avoid her eyes, he scanned the kitchen. It was littered with Thanksgiving preparation. Rayne muttered that this holiday mess wouldn't be in Selma's kitchen. *She* insisted that they clean as they cooked.

Then Binky laughed, and her whole body moved delightedly with her breath. "Remember when she took us fishing. And they cut your hair?"

Rayne didn't laugh.

"Something else happened on that trip. I'm sorry, I forgot. You fell or something, didn't you?"

———

Out on the green-and-brown banks of the estuary, with the sun shining right through her glittering eyes, Selma said, in a voice that came out of her like a radio: "Patient! That's what the mermaid is. They patient. Time don't mean nothin to a mermaid. They be waiting for bad children all their life, good children, too. Lord, Jones, don't hit one."

Selma looked right into Rayne, her see-through beer-bottle brown eyes exactly the color of her skin, and she laughed. He knew that she was play-acting, but a note of true danger rumbled at the back of her throat.

"Stop scaring the boy."

"You know what used to scare me?" she asked in response.

"Wha?"

"That old song we used to sing."

The older Needham clan answered by breaking into raucous singing:

> *Mermaid make the blood run cold;*
> *Cast it far, drop it deep;*
>
> *Call your name, and read your soul;*
> *Cast it far, drop it deep;*
>
> *Snatch you in or give you gold; at the crossroads, pay the toll;*
> *Pray the Lord my soul to keep.*
>
> *Cast it far, drop it deep.*

Rayne blinked at this choral outburst and the talky aftermath. The landing smelled moist, both swampy and salty, and what had seemed like a lush green background now threatened. He scanned the surface, wishing there was something he could hold on to.

"What's she look like?" Rayne asked.

Jones answered: "Well, it's hard to tell how she'll choose to appear . . . Probably come up greenish-brown like water with green-and-gold scales on the bottom, right under a smooth, bare belly that changes when the light hits 'er, like the inside of a seashell. Probably have green eyes can see right back to the day you was born. Hair'll be thick and black, matted like the beard hanging out of the clam, with ancient money from pirate ships locked in it, catching the last rays of the sun."

"Like Ray's hair," someone said.

"Lookit Ray's face," Bobo shouted. "Boy can see it now, can't you?

"Black nipples with sea water dripping from 'em like diamonds . . ." Bobo continued in his reverie, and although Rayne heard him, and would normally have enjoyed the scandal of his grandfather's language, his attention was grabbed instead by the cousins who took up the teasing: that he had hair like a mermaid, like a nappy old girl, that the mermaids would think he was one of them and grab him in.

"You need to cut your hair, *little girl*."

Rayne had gotten it into his mind that his mother must cut it, and that if he did so without her, he would jinx her return. So he had resisted, and Selma and Bobo had indulged him.

Boy half-crazy, without a doubt, they said, but he got his reasons.

Jones beckoned him with two fingers to encourage him to ignore the kids, but Rayne's oldest cousin, a teenager, reached for the scissors out of the tackle box. Two other cousins tried to grab him and hold him down.

Rayne lowered his head and charged the oldest boy, catching him under the chin while he was still laughing. The scissors clattered onto the rocks. Rayne caught them all off guard, so no one responded quickly, except the boy, who recovered himself enough to roll over when Rayne came at him again, and to let him slide off the landing and into the water.

There was no stopping the bruising slide down until one foot wedged between rocks under a green-white pool of froth.

The boy, Jesus, Jesus, Jones, 's our boy.

Water slammed Rayne's head, flushed his ears, scoured his eyes. More than water. Force. Foaming, frothing force spinning, trying to roll him over and curl his head down into a carbonated death. The green tunnel roared. No light. Spinning tumbling pulling out to sea.

Except for one wedged shoe.

Suddenly, the force was gone, leaving green and white foam to slurp at Rayne's waist and legs and stuck foot. He could not tell nose from mouth, could not breathe in air without water, mucus, choke.

It came again, from behind his head. Oh, God, please, and then the slam and a grip hard, under his arms, a grinding wrenching of his foot, wedged in the rock, wedged as the rod had not been, Jones's arms like trees next to his head, hammer-fingers wedged between his ribs, yanking, tugging, grabbing his thigh, leg, and the foot wouldn't move, so he gave up, a willing sacrifice, and did not know what was him or Jones or ocean.

They carried him to the bank and wrapped him in something rough. They prodded and squeezed him until it seemed that his belly and lungs had yielded up their seawater. He coughed and sputtered and cried. Selma rocked him hard. She was wet, too. She'd waded into the water behind Jones, ready to grab, pull, ready to swim out for him on the off chance that Jones had to let him go. Selma held Rayne's body, already half as big as hers, so tightly in her arms that he could feel the vibration of her voice calling Jesus in his own body. Then: "What is wrong with you? What could possess you? What did you think would happen?"

When his breathing was steady again, he answered, and Selma detected reproach in his swallowed syllables: "Nobody can make me cut my hair."

Selma stopped rocking. She'd suspected his secret super-stition, and she had not wanted to take from him what she'd thought was a harmless hope. But he'd almost gotten himself killed.

Rayne felt a change in her body.

"You wanna know something, boy?" she asked him in deadly earnest and quiet. "Your mother is not comin back. I been soft-pedaling you, and I can see it ain't no favor. She ain't coming back. You hear me? She ain't sending for you. You know what that means? You stayin here, boy. This gonna be home, and you gonna learn to get along.

"Your foolishness today almost took *my* brother away from me. My one brother. I watched the water come up over his head, tryin'a get you out. And my brother is my heart. You hear me? We are not gonna have that."

———

There was nothing he wouldn't have done now to get his mother back. Nothing. He would take back playing with her things. He would eat his every bad word. He would take back playing with the pilot light. He would stay awake all night like a soldier in the storybook and never pee in her bed ever ever again.

"Jesus fuckin Christ, Lonnie. Not again."

No, never, ever again. It be okay if she left him with the lady next door for the afternoon and didn't come back till tomorrow. He wouldn't break her cigarettes, like he did her last one that she put on the table to save, because she wanted it later, and the man said he would leave his for her, but he didn't. That's what you get, Mommy, because you stayed out.

It had taken her a long time to slap him, because she couldn't believe it.

He wouldn't do that again, ever.

———

Bobo had been watching, irritably. He grabbed Rayne from Selma's lap, swaddled him tightly in the blanket, pinning his arms and legs, and flung him over his back. "I'ma get my belt for this little pussy."

"Bobo!" Selma tried to speak over his last words so that the children wouldn't hear, but they did.

"Well, what *you* gonna do?"

Selma motioned for Bobo to come back. She took something from the tackle box. Jones and Lil Tootchie rounded up the other kids. Lil Tootchie said that Rayne was just like his mother, and Jones shushed her. JJ packed the fish and gear. Bobo's massive arms clamped down and pulled Rayne's face into his chest.

"And stop cryin like a baby."

Rayne heard the scissors before he felt them. Jones's sharp, stainless fillet scissors lay cold next to his scalp, and in a few minutes, his big, knotted Afro lay on the ground. Some of it blew into the estuary. He had stopped crying. His head felt cool and light. He smelled fishy like the blades of the scissors.

———

Maybe she couldn't find him now. Maybe he'd grow to be a man and find her himself. But he'd have to do without her and grow up. He told himself until he almost believed it that she loved him. He imagined her crying at night, alone, sorry that she ever let him go.

———

That night, after he'd filleted and frozen the fish, Rayne slept uneasily on the less mildewy mattress in the old house. He gave Khalil asthma medicine just in case, and dreamt that Lillie was in bed with one of the football players she'd tattooed. He saw her lovemaking faces. He heard her sighs and laughs and grunts, and watched the other man's hand holding, grabbing, rubbing handfuls of her hair and flesh, which shone from oil and sweat. They were in some expensive hotel. And she was loving every single, goddamned stroke.

When he awoke with Khalil's leg thrown over him, he was almost sick to his stomach. The image of her chiseled face and open mouth, open legs, full of betrayal and luxurious pleasure, stayed with him. So did the appalling fact that in the dream, he'd been waiting for her at home—her house—with his belt in his hand.

It was nearly dawn. Rayne slid out of bed, into his clothes, and escaped the little bedroom in the little house. A mild chill braced the dark-blue air that promised a fruitful spring. He walked the edges of the land, tracing the boundaries, hoping that five or six miles, half walked, half run, would restore him to himself.

Rayne remembered that Bobo used to do this sometimes. He never should have stopped.

CHAPTER 19

illie sent him a text at 6:30 a.m. telling him that his appointment for the Center was scheduled for that afternoon at 3:00 p.m. The text said specifically: *Bring all docs: deeds, wills, quitclaims(?) AND bring Nana. They say fam must be down. Period.*

But after a drive into Charleston for brunch and a stop to photocopy the documents in the strongbox, Selma did not want, as Rayne put it casually, "to stop in at the Center and see whether they could give us some tips."

She knew what they had to say, thank you very much, and she'd watched the video on television, and lots of people had seen to it that she attended the information session they gave at church. She did not want to be lectured again by young black lawyers, could be her grandchildren, who had never pulled a plow or strung a hand of tobacco in their lives. No, thank you.

Rayne had expected resistance, but he hadn't thought that she'd be so well acquainted with the Center. They'd done a good job of marketing, he thought. He tried saying that he'd stop in and get their material and have a brief talk with anyone who was there. Khalil added that he'd be willing to stay in the car with Selma.

"Thanks, Lil Man, but I don't need no babysitter. 'Specially not if my grandson will just take me home.

"Look, Ray, you see it fixin to rain. I'd like, if possible, to keep from getting drenched and catchin my death. Besides, I been lookin forward to Maundy Thursday service. We go home now, I got time for a little nap to gather my strength to stay out late. That be nice." Selma's tone varied through her little speech from arch to piqued, to hurt, to pleading, to reasonable. "I do think Maundy Thursday really is my favorite service of the year. Look like every year something tries to keep me from enjoyin it."

Rayne sneaked a side look at the woman who had sat propped on Mermaid Landing the day before and caught two mullets and a small black drum fish, which she planned to fry tomorrow. Her hands, with their big knuckles and lone gold wedding band, were folded in her lap. Her bottom lip was drawn up in a tight line of determination. She looked directly ahead, taking notice of as many signs as she could see that told them they were going into North Charleston, instead of south and west toward home.

In fact, she continued, if she'd known that Rayne had had ulterior motives, she would not have gone to brunch at all. She had food in her fridge. And she could have started on Easter dinner. Then he and Khalil could have come out on their own on their personal errands. At any rate, Selma wished that Rayne had talked to her if he was planning to make this move. Because she had things to tell him.

He parked in one of the four spaces behind the tiny corner office building in a modest section of town.

"If they such experts on real estate," Selma wondered to no one in particular, "why couldn't they manage better headquarters for themselves?"

Rayne left the keys in the ignition, telling her to cut on the engine if she and Khalil got cold.

"Oh, Lord, are you planning to stay in that long? Last year Maundy Thursday, JJ's pesky truck broke down."

"No, last year Jones took you. I talked to him that night."

"Well, are we gonna have to go directly from here to the church? So we just rush in, like firemen?"

"Nana, we got four hours!" Rayne said. He could not keep the exasperation out of his voice.

"Old people take a long time to do everythin, honey. I'm sorry. I cant just zip here and there anymore."

"*I'm* sorry, Nana. This here won't take more'n fifteen-twenty minutes."

As Rayne opened the door, Selma indicated to him to take his keys out of the ignition. "Keys hangin like that just make us a target for carjacks. And this ain't Charleston. This right here is North Charleston. Yeah, he smash the window, jump in, drive off with us hollerin bloody murder, don't make no difference . . . boy in the back. Here, gimme them keys. I'll hol' 'em."

Rayne could not think of anything to do in the moment to help Selma feel less hurt and threatened. He reached over and patted her hands that clasped the keys.

"I'm going to take in the documents," he said. "Just the copies, not the originals," which sat behind her feet in the strong-box. Selma sniffed.

Inside, the young receptionist gave Rayne their brochure, a DVD of the documentary Selma said she'd seen, and a Dixie cup of water. She herself had lived outside of Philadelphia. They talked mid-Atlantic landmarks until the Center's director came through the little door in the thin wall that marked the waiting area, where Rayne felt like a hulking, too-large presence. He ducked his head in the doorway and followed her back to her office.

The director greeted him with precise diction, wide experience, and total control of the facts. She checked Rayne out quickly, he could tell, with a fast scan of the dreadlocks, work boots, and eastern accent. She asked where he'd been to college and what he'd studied. Then she looked out the window at Selma, who sat staring straight ahead in the truck while Khalil played with his video game in the back. She smiled. "Your son?" she asked.

He nodded.

Then the director confirmed, in clearer language, just what the courthouse clerk had said. But she put the laws into context. William Tecumseh Sherman had given low-country land to ex-slaves. If the original owners bore eighteen live children, then the land was divided eighteen times, and each of those heirs' children and grandchildren owned a proportional segment of their parents' part. So the shares could become very small.

Then, heir property's vulnerability was this: any heir—or anyone who bought out an heir, say, a developer—could go to a judge and force a sale. The family had ten days in which to buy out the shareholder who wanted to sell, and then, if he would not sell, another month before a general sale. A poor extended family that was scraping by on the heir property would be up against the developer's investors. Time and again, the investors offered more money than the family could match.

"We see a lot of cases like your great-grandmother's," the director said, parting the blinds to look again at Selma's implacable profile. "I mean, it's human nature: one member or one branch of the family stays on the land, pays the taxes, keeps up the buildings and grounds, and will not bring in other heirs, because they cannot believe that these people a thousand miles away who never speak to them own as much of a share as they do . . ."

"She says that both my great-grandfather's brothers gave up their claims."

"Yeah," she said, lips tight, eyes compassionate. She nodded, uninterested, Rayne was sure, in the many tiny, conflicting details he'd been compiling. "I don't mean to diminish the uniqueness of your situation, but merely to let you know that many times what seem like insurmountable family dynamics actually can be problem-solved."

Rayne shook his head. Selma didn't want to be "problem-solved." She did not think that there was a problem or that she was it. Almost involuntarily he shook his head. "I don't live here with my great-grandmother," he said. "I live in Philadelphia. So do a lot of our family members. This family you talk about really hasn't been close."

"Sure, sure," she said. "That happens. But I can tell you, in some cases, where there is a family member willing to work, this has proved an amazing opportunity to transform, or even to rebuild, a family. Usually that change agent is the person who seeks us out." She smiled at him. "Think about it."

"Lady, I am not your 'change agent.' You're lookin at my great-grandmother. Look at that face. As far as Mrs. Selma Need-ham is concerned, she is the Little Red Hen. Nobody helped her cut the wheat or grind the flour or bake the bread . . ."

"So no one else may eat the bread? But you can hear what that does, can't you? Everyone goes hungry. Including her, and, correct me if I'm wrong, but that's not really what she wants. I'm telling you, all you have to do is to be the catalyst. Often there are wonderful human resources among the family that have been overlooked. In other words, your leadership is likely to be needed as a spark. You may not have to carry the whole burden alone, which is what it looks like, I know, from this side.

"You say you studied business."

"Yeah, but I do construction now."

"Still business. Listen. Some families have formed limited liability partnerships so that anyone who wants to sell can only sell to the partnership," she said cheerily, as if this made it easier.

"One family created a partnership and then they themselves developed the hotel resort—and the whole family shares the profits."

"Like an Indian tribe."

"Exactly. The man who put that deal together is a great guy, and he loves to talk to other families about how to do it. I can get you his contact information if you'd like to talk to him."

"Thank you," Rayne said, although he felt irritated to hear about this paragon of family organizing. He stood. He could see that the truck was idling outside. She must have turned on the heat, he thought. Or maybe she'd let Khalil do it. He was sitting behind the wheel pretending to drive. They were talking, which was a good sign.

The director, meanwhile, had scanned Rayne's documents and separated them into two piles. "What seems to have happened is that your great-great-grandfather left something that is written. I doubt it would pass the legal tests for a will. But it is pretty doggone close: your great-grandfather King Needham states that he and his brother Richard have paid their brother Amos for his third, and Amos has written a letter that gives up his claims to his portion. It's not a proper quitclaim deed, but it does corroborate their statement. So far, so good.

"What's troubling: actually, a couple of things are troubling. One is that this document with a list of heirs is typically the kind of thing that developers create, that is, unless your family has been doing this research."

"No. I just got that from a girl at the county courthouse."

"Oh, dear. Well, you'll notice that it lists someone named Pettiford, and the only reason that stuck out to me is that there's a Pettiford who represents that district in the state legislature. I know that because he has worked to bring us in for workshops with his constituents. Are you all related?"

"No, I don't think so," Rayne said, trying to remember the many facts Selma had tried to tell him his first night back. "But what do I know? The chick at the courthouse tells me that there's one heir property piece and one piece my great-grandfather bought. I think that maybe Nana borrowed against the land they bought in order to pay taxes on the heir property."

"Here. I can see that. Look, here's the settlement: it's a sale of land by M. T. Broadnax to your relative at the end of the Depression. Wow, how did he swing that? It looks like Pettiford witnessed the signing. I also see that on the deed of sale—oh, this is interesting—the reclamation clause has been crossed out: this was a standard clause that was used when an African-American bought from a white; it allowed what were called the 'rightful heirs' ten years' reclamation."

"What does that mean?"

"It means that in the rare cases when black people bought land from whites, the white heirs were given ten years to demand the land back."

"And that's crossed out?"

"Yes, crossed out and initialed. Twice. Your great-grandfather had to have more than ordinary pull to get that."

"And we get ten days?"

"It's a total of forty now. We've done some very energetic advocacy to make that change. Doesn't seem like much, but it gives families time to organize."

"What does Pettiford's name as witness to the Broadnax sale have to do with his name on the heir property document?"

"Well, you see, I don't know. One doesn't explain the other," she said, "but sometimes a white family would be involved if there was an old kinship tie, or the remnant of a relationship from slavery times, or when people's lands or water were interconnected. Sometimes you need to tease out these things, but, frankly, sometimes it's really none of our business.

"More important, especially if she's borrowed from them, and is strapped for cash, you've got to get her some company in handling this."

"You know, between my great-uncle and I, we have the money she borrowed. I know it's a lot when you don't have any coming in, but she knows that we can scrape this together. I don't get it."

"If you're the Little Red Hen for fifty years, Mr. Needham, and someone comes and says, why don't we plant barley and open a microbrewery, maybe you might not jump at the chance.

"But let me put it this way," she said, pulling up a mini-blind to look out at Selma and Khalil: "Fifty years ago, as a people, we owned fourteen million acres, Mr. Needham. Now, we own little more than a million. My sense is that you're telling me that you'd rather sell and be done with it. And then we'll own even less."

"*We* don't live here, ma'am. I live in Philadelphia."

"Real estate can be thought of as a commodity or in other ways. The old people had a collective way of thinking about this land."

"I know, I know. Like when she always says that whenever anybody needs it, it's here. I mean, that's how I came to grow up here. But there's no collective now. It's just her."

She smiled. "It might not hurt to talk to some of your other family members. Your great-grandmother may not feel as if they are entitled to have a say, but the law says that they do, and if you're not united, all her years of work can easily slip away. Probably will.

"Here," she said, pulling on her jacket, "come out the back door. I'll walk out with you."

"She does not want to talk. So you know. Nothin personal."

"I'll just pay my respects," the director said. It was an old-school, back-home exchange, very correct. He didn't know why he'd tried to talk her out of it. If she didn't "pay her respects," Selma would never listen to anything she'd told Rayne.

At the truck, she knocked on the passenger's window and said in a warm, but professional, voice: "Mrs. Needham?"

Selma started and stared at her. Khalil pushed the button from his driver's side door console to lower her window.

"Mrs. Needham," the director said with her pretty bow mouth and enunciation, "your grandson has told me about you, and I just wanted to pay my respects and thank you for all you've done. People such as yourself have held our community together. You're our heroes here at the Center, and I just wanted to come out and meet you myself."

"Well, that's very kind of you," Selma said stiffly. "I really didn't need to come, but my great-grandson here has a mind of his own. Which you want, really, in a grown man."

"And he has your interests and your family's at heart. I can tell you, in my job, I don't always see that, so I'm so pleased when I meet families like yours."

Rayne nodded his thanks and opened the driver's door. "Jump in the back, Lil Man," he said to Khalil.

"We do family counseling referrals if you need it," she said.

"Yeah, we need it."

"No, thank you," Selma said. She looked straight ahead and rolled up her window as if to deter a panhandler.

CHAPTER 20

◑◐

They did not speak as Rayne drove out of North Charleston through construction and badly marked detours. At the sight of a KFC, Rayne started to change lanes, saying that he'd buy a bucket of chicken to keep in the house. Selma suggested that they stop instead at Piggly Wiggly, whose fried chicken she preferred; and might she have a piece or two to keep in her fridge? He could also pick up milk, bread, and fruit to have in the house for Khalil, who had not eaten a piece of fruit since they'd been here, and coleslaw to go with the fish tomorrow for Good Friday—*if* all this running around hadn't made her too tired to cook; and *if* the sky didn't open up and drench them all so that they'd catch their deaths.

Khalil laughed at the name Piggly Wiggly until his sides hurt, so Rayne did not take him inside the store. When Rayne returned, he loaded his three bags into the backseat. Khalil ate an apple and an orange and a handful of grapes. "Now, see? See? Tell Mom."

Once they were on the road, the cloud cover thickened. It turned grayer and cooler. Sprays of forsythia in the median and on the roadsides stood out in bright, happy relief against the darkening day. Khalil announced that he felt as if he had lived his whole life in a truck, and then promptly fell asleep.

"When you finish reading all your package from those people, I still need to talk business with you."

Rayne tried to find a tone that would communicate resolve as well as care. "Listen, Nana, I need you to know that if I think I ought to learn more about something, I'm going to do it. It's no disrespect to you. It's like when I do a job: the electrician may explain something to me, but I may have to go and study it on my own, or read about it, or ask someone else. It doesn't mean that *he* doesn't know what he's talking about; it's that I may need to hear it differently. Or hear it or read it ten or fifteen times till I can fit it into my whole picture."

"I know that," she said.

"'Member how when I finished college and you wanted me to go to law school—"

"Unh-hunh. I knew you was gonna say that. Sometimes I wonder why they all dead and I'm still here. I'm just trying to do my best."

"Me, too."

"Things I know about, nobody want to hear anymore."

"That's not true."

"I'n't it? What do I know that you want to learn about from me?"

"I want to learn more about our family."

"Ask Jones. He can tell you without getting cranky."

Rayne threw back his head and laughed.

"What's so funny? I mean it. Every time I start with them people up there in Philadelphia, they just act the fool. Every time. Lord knows, *they* don't wanna hear anything I got to tell.

"Here's something *I* wanna know," she said. "You tell me: Why don't young people get married anymore? Since we all speaking our mind today—" She looked into the backseat to make sure Khalil was sleeping. Then she whispered: "You got the boy callin you Daddy; now he call me Nana, and I'm fallin in love with him. You and the mother send telephone messages fifty a hundred times a day . . ."

Rayne's phone vibrated once, to signify a text message.

"There she is again, probably askin how it went, and did the old lady act up." Selma leaned sideways, as if talking into the phone on Rayne's belt. "And the answer is yes, she did. Can she hear that? Or do I have to write the letter with my thumbs?" She held up one hand and thumped her thumb up and down.

Something in the movement seemed wrong to Rayne. "Nana," he said, "are you wearing your seat belt?"

"No, matter of fac', I ain't wearin this damn seat belt. Yesterday, it like to cut off my windpipe. I'm holding it here for pretend to be a good example for the boy."

Rayne looked down to her left hand, which was indeed holding the buckle next to the latch plate.

"It binds me. Come on, Ray, just drive; don't worry me about this devilish belt. What is you gonna do? Come round here and latch me in?"

Rayne pulled the truck onto the shoulder, put it into park, got out, and walked around the back to her door. He opened it and adjusted the seat belt housing down to the lower setting. "Try it now," he said.

The belt, which had angled past her ear, settled across her shoulder and collarbone. Selma humphed as she fastened the lock.

Before he got back into the car, Rayne peered through the long row of tall cypresses that screened a wide lawn, perhaps five hundred feet deep, and a fake Tuscan villa up a long driveway of crushed seashells. Next to the road, a stone wall covered with yellow jessamine perfumed the ditch. This could have been heir property, he thought.

After a mile or so, Selma said: "You could do contracting down here. They buildin. I don't care how much they bellyache about the economy; every day the Lord sends they build places like you just saw. You could build your own home outta brick or anything you want. You wouldn't pay a dime in rent. No mortgage. Just taxes. Onlies thing you gotta keep up is the taxes."

Rayne did not respond, although for the first time he also did not retort the obvious: that he had a life and a business in Philadelphia. After another few miles, he said: "You asked why my generation doesn't marry. I'm not sure. But most of us haven't seen a lot of good ones. Good marriages, I mean. We've seen a lot of bad ones."

"You seen me."

"But, Nana, I never saw you married. That was before my time."

Her hand, freed from its duty of holding the seat belt, but still cold and stiff, patted his fist on the shift. "We're goin to church tonight, right?"

"Yep."

"You want a marriage that will last; you want one that will help you; you wanna drive out the demons and run 'em over the cliff into the sea?"

"Yeah." He laughed a little. "Sure. All that. That be good. I'll go for that."

"So, when you come tonight, pray for it."

It was a funny phrase coming from Selma, who had always quoted King that God wasn't Santa Claus. She'd stopped attending the church King had helped build in the twenties with ten dollars and a thousand feet of lumber he'd hauled with his own wagon. They'd used the church for years to do everything they needed to do away from whites' observation. A Philadelphia recruiter, also a minister and a friend of King's sister and brother-in-law, used to come talk about jobs in the North. When one of the white town councilmen found out, there was trouble.

It occurred to Rayne that the Philadelphia recruiter dustup might be another clue to King's land saga. Rayne asked Selma about him.

"Well, the recruiters was stealing away people, so the white folks thought, who otherwise would've stayed on the land. So, when they heard this one was comin, I don't know how, and they let the preacher know they were not particular about him recruitin from church.

"So the preacher wouldn't let 'im in church; so we had 'im to our place. Railroad wanted them. Some factories did, too. They'd give 'em a free train ticket and a job."

"Did any whites ever come visit Great-Granddaddy King?"

"No, not directly. But Pettiford warned 'im. He had supported him in the Broadnax sale, 'cause he said that dirty hog operation was ruining his water, too, so the others just dealt with it. But Pettiford warned him to be careful bringing in agitators." Selma sighed. "I miss that old church."

The clouds that had been gathering closed out the last bit of sky and dropped a sudden blue-gray rain down around them. Rayne turned on everything: the wipers, headlights, heat, and defrost. The cab felt intimate and safe. Rayne and Selma had earned the moment, it felt like.

"I guess you could say my parents had a good marriage," she went on. "It was a hard life, but from what I remember and from what Jones tells me, it was a good marriage. Although sometimes I think it was just that they had it so hard, people had cheated them and treated them so bad, that they couldn't afford to argue. Plus, women really had no choice but to get along. When somebody told my daddy there was a colored man a couple counties up who had a good place, and paid fair—that was King—he just up and came. She came with 'im, what else was she gonna do, and she dragged us, used to be six of us chil'ren.

"And when the influenza came, and my mother went down, the little kids all was sick in the bed with 'er, Daddy made Jones and me sleep outside to try to keep us from catchin it. I'll never forget, it were rain like this. We was outside, and King's first wife and baby was sick with it, too, and after he saw to them King took us into the barn and made us up a pallet there.

"And my daddy said to us—they all in there sick, and he left for twenty minutes to come check on us—he said, 'Say a friend come to you round midnight from a long journey, and you don't have no food to offer him. So you go to your friend down the road and ask him for bread to feed the traveler. And, naturally, that friend is sleep in bed, and his children are sleep, and he don't want to get up and bother about it. So he holler down, tell you go away.

"Daddy told us, 'Now, here's what Jesus said: He said, "I say unto you, Though he will not rise up and give him, because he is his friend, yet because of his *persistence* will he rise and give him as many as he need . . . Ask and it shall be given."'

"Daddy told for us to pray for mother and the babies, and all I knew was Jonesey went and got an old apple from the horse's bucket and bit out the worm and all the rot in the middle around the seeds and fed me from his hand, and finally I went to sleep.

"But later, after Daddy died, too, and it was just me and Jones, I remembered what Daddy said. You know what I prayed for? I prayed for King.

"Every night, from the time I was nine years old, and he taught me the times table, I told God that I was asking in the name of Jesus, and that I'd ask every day and every night for the rest of my life.

"On my twelfth birthday, Mr. King Needham sent his son Junior over to give me two chickens of my own to raise.

"And less than five years later, he married me. King Needham married the skinny little Scattergood gal from the shack. He bought me a beautiful dress, and they threw a little party after. And you'd think he'd married the black Queen of Sheba the way he talked to me so gentle and carried me into the house over the threshold in front of all his relations.

"He told me I was smart. He told me I was beautiful."

Rayne had slowed to just below the speed limit, and drove almost reverently onto their old road, so familiar, and new in light of Selma's persistent will and love, whose remnants he had felt until now as constraints rather than freedom.

———

Selma walked over the threshold in her mind now, back into their bedroom. Mr. King, as she'd called him all her life, never touched her until the first night. When it came time, he pulled her into him, and kissed her, mouth open and smiling. He kissed his way into her, rumbling low in his chest with delight. *Taste good.* Then he laid her down on his bed like an offering unto himself, that's what she felt like, and ran his big hands lightly over her tight skin.

Call my name.

Mr. King.

No Mister now, baby.

King? I can't call you that.

She laughed into the darkness, conscious of her appeal, feeling her breasts shiver under his rough hand with its missing fingers. But when he stood to slough off his clothes and his shoulders blotted out the moonlight, her girlish desire turned to fear.

Maybe I ain't big enough for you.
You big enough, girl, if you want it.
I'm scared.
If you don't want it, I could wait.
I been wantin it since I were little.
Don't tell me that. Oh, Lord.
I dreamed I was lying up in this bed. Ev'ry night, I dreamed it.
Oh, Jesus. Stop sayin that, girl.
I snuck up and looked in the window.
Well, then, you big enough now.

He made love to her twice on their wedding night, as gently as he could, he said, given how long he'd waited and how young and sweet she was. Then he fell asleep. Still tingling and tender, every inch of her awake, she ran her hand along the contour of his huge, pale body, holding her palm just half an inch over his torso to feel his warmth and the coiled-up energy in his chest. One flesh. This was the blessing she'd prayed for.

Her real life had begun.

CHAPTER 21

S t. Anthony's Episcopal Church echoed loudly as heavy metal folding chairs, each equipped with a padded metal kneeler to be used by the person behind, scraped the stone floor. Selma had explained that the Maundy Thursday service included a foot-washing ritual, and Khalil was looking forward to seeing old people take off their shoes and a preacher kneel down and wash their feet: "stinky feet," he said enough times from the backseat to prompt Rayne to turn around and order that he not speak in church.

And silence was appropriate. People went to the altar bare-foot, and sat in special chairs. The priest knelt in front of the first half-dozen comers; after that he sat on a low stool. He slipped their feet into a white china basin and poured warm water over them from a matching white pitcher. Next to him was a pile of white towels, and another pitcher. The church was dim.

Rayne found himself listening to the sound of the water, pouring, splashing loudly onto the ceramic surface, and softly onto people's skin. He remembered Selma's words about her persistent prayers for a marriage to King.

Petitioning God for favors seemed childish to Rayne. And yet, Selma's earnestness had its own truth. She told him once that in years past she had failed to pray for Bobo, but now that he was in prison, she prayed for him every day. She figured he needed it more. And she had never failed to pray, she said, for Rayne.

Selma used her cane to navigate her way to the front of the church alone. Rayne heard the water splash over her feet, and thought that the sound of water could be its own prayer. The priest took time to dry Selma's feet carefully, and to slip on her socks and the Velcro-clasped black orthopedic shoes that she had shined that morning.

As a boy, Rayne had imagined himself married one day. He'd seen himself as a man, driving a truck, coming home from somewhere to a woman and children who would be delighted to see him. He'd taken such a future for granted until he went away to Philadelphia to college and entered into a series of complicated relationships, none of them close to the easy and natural picture he'd imagined. Until Lillie. But he knew the undercurrents in himself, riptides of rage that had never surfaced, but threatened. Both he and Lillie had chosen wrong before. How could they trust themselves?

After the foot washing, people from the congregation came up to read at a table illuminated by a semicircle of candles. After each person read, he or she would snuff a candle, and Rayne felt an unaccountable sadness spreading through him. Khalil gave evidence of boredom, but also a reverence that helped to enforce the dictum of silence. "Maundy," they learned, came from *mandatum,* the commandment Jesus gave to his disciples after washing their feet: to love one another.

Then, after the readings, with only one white candle burning, the priest and the acolytes began to strip the altar. They took away altar cloths, embroidered chair pads and kneelers, the palms, carpets, candles. Soon, members of the congregation went up to help. Before Rayne realized, Khalil had stood and slipped out into the aisle. He was the only child in attendance besides the acolytes. The priest, a medium-height dark brown man with a Jamaican accent, bowed to Khalil, who reciprocated with his eyes wide. Then the priest reached around his neck, took off his embroidered red stole, and handed it to him. Khalil followed the others into a sacristy off to the side of the main sanctuary to hand the stole to one of the waiting adults.

The service ended without a benediction. Parishioners filed out quietly, while Rayne and Selma waited in their pew for Khalil to return. The place no longer seemed cold, only reserved, like Selma when they worked together and did not talk. It gave him room for his own mind to float up out of him, and then to return.

Now his mind returned bringing an image of Lillie and Khalil taking each and every old farm implement out of the old flue-curing barn and placing it somewhere safe until the place stood starkly empty. Rayne saw himself go into the empty barn in search of a plow yoke that was so heavy that only Rayne could shoulder it, as his great-grandfather had. But it was gone. They had opened the front and back doors. Air swept through, and light. The old flue-cure barn was revealed to be a well-built structure, too good to be wasted as a storage bin. Lillie came to him and kissed him, and there in the darkened church he felt an unexpected desire that made him close his eyes and smile.

"You not gonna go see where the boy went?" Selma whispered.

"No," Rayne said. "He's fine. I'll go get your wheelchair."

"Not to the truck. You're not gone leave me here alone."

"No, it's right at the back of the church, 'member?"

Khalil came skipping from the entrance to the side of the

altar, swinging an Easter basket and obviously chewing candy as Rayne wheeled the chair from the rear. With a jump and a pivot, Khalil threw himself into the chair. Rayne tilted him back for a spin that spilled candy onto the floor. Rayne stopped the chair where Selma stood holding the pew with her left hand and pointing at the candy a few rows back. Khalil dove onto all fours to find dusty yellow Peeps and shiny foil eggs that rolled, wobbly, under the kneelers.

In the truck, Khalil told them all about the scented sacristy, where he'd met a teenage acolyte who showed him the brass instrument they used to light incense and swung live coals during Easter service. Then the ladies in the sacristy reached into a closet and gave him an early Easter basket. He did not say that they'd told him to wait until Easter to eat the candy. "What did you do while you were waiting for me?"

"I did what you're supposed to do in church: I prayed."

Selma studied him in the dark. "Did you really?"

"I think so," he said.

"Well, in case you didn't, I prayed for you, too."

CHAPTER 22

◦⃜◦

That night after Khalil went to sleep, Selma wrapped her coat over her bathrobe and used her walker on the gravel and rough field between her trailer and the old house, because she had to talk to Rayne. It was about the land, and it was complicated, and she'd been at fault. He was right to want to check up on her, she said. She only wished that he'd appeared a couple of generations earlier. He made her a cup of tea with milk and sugar, and he lit King's box stove to warm her stiff joints.

Selma knew all about the heir property laws, and she agreed with most of the people of her generation that holding land in common gave families a value that individual ownership could not provide. The problem was that this particular family had *not* worked together. Amos had left first, after their father Rome had come at him with a buggy whip. Selma was not saying that that was right, but it was hard to explain how things were then. "If you didn't make a crop, you didn't eat. There weren't no Social Security. There weren't no *nothing*. You wanted to eat—"

Rayne finished her statement. "You worked."

"And if you didn't pay your taxes, they took the land."

Since she'd been on the property alone, she'd borrowed against the Broadnax land, she'd told him that; but he did not know how much. He figured that she did not have the money to pay it back. And although she wanted to sell Broadnax to finance the heir property, he'd been hatching an idea to do a search of the family, write them, and lay out the scenario. Human nature being what it was, he figured that some of them would agree to sign a quitclaim; some would want to be paid a token; and some others might want to help.

Rayne hoped that Selma would agree that the Broadnax ownership was in fact more stable than the heir property. He figured they could move the house and trailer for her, and that for a few years while they determined how to convert the heirs' property into cash, he and Jones could manage the taxes and the fee for someone to come in and help her for as long as she could stay by herself. But first he'd have to attend to Selma's story, especially since the documents were not straightforward.

Selma continued: over the objections of King's brother Richard, King insisted on sending Amos a share of the farm proceeds until Amos made good in Philadelphia. Because Amos had principles and a good heart, when he got on his feet up North, he wrote his equivalent of a quitclaim letter. In a way, Selma said, it was a shame, because Amos was King's favorite brother and, between Amos and Richard, the harder worker and the more honest man.

Although King and Richard could read and write, neither of them took the letter to the courthouse or had a formal quitclaim deed drawn up. The people who ran the courthouse did not appreciate landowning blacks. Coming in to do too much legal stuff attracted attention. And when they started paying attention to a black man's land and his paperwork, bad things happened. So, King and Richard kept the letter, and stopped sending Amos payments, although from time to time, one of his children would come for a summer, work, get paid, and live in one of the old shacks by the eight peach trees and two dwarf apples they called the Orchard.

Then, after King died, Richard and Big Tootch lost heart. King had protected everyone, and without him, they were scared. Selma tried to get Richard to work with her to keep the land together. She hired JJ and they put in some crops, and she made a schedule for paying Richard some little something at least, but he told her that he had already signed a long-term lease with Pettiford.

"What kind of long-term lease?"

"I don't know. That's all Richard told me: it was a fifty-year lease he signed with his half of the land."

"But that's what the Center is telling us, Nana; it's not his half and King's half. It's still all the descendents of, who was it, Ma Bett and Rome? Those were Grandma Bett's parents."

"Well, see, I don't know nobody else."

"And I think that's a problem."

"I can't tell you what I don't know. But you ain't finished hearing what I do know."

"Sorry, Nana. Go on. But why Pettiford? Why'd Richard go to him? Why did you?"

Pettiford had been the white man who backed King when he'd bought the Broadnax land years before, and then he'd been a godsend, Selma said, after King died. He'd run interference for her with the county, helped her file paperwork, and stood between her and Broadnax's son, Fairlie, who had come back to the county, saying King had stolen his father's land and wanting it back.

Now, Selma said, Pettiford's grandson owned the golf course next to them. The Needham heir property that Richard leased to them for fifty years was now part of the golf course. So, Selma figured that when fifty years was up, she'd go to Pettiford and see what kind of deal she could make with him. That was last year. How could she forget?

Fifty years. Rayne could not believe that she'd have such a tickler file memory. Fifty years. She hadn't seen any lease document, of course, because Richard had never consulted her. Luckily, the old grandfather Pettiford said that his one concern was to make sure that no bad development went up next to his land, and then next to his grandson's golf course. So, Selma proposed that JJ and his family continue to live in Richard's house, and he and a small crew could work on the golf course and continue to farm King's land. Pettiford said fine, fine. Selma wanted to write something up, and he said he'd get his grandson to do it.

"But after I didn't hear from the devilish grandson, I called him, and he's sayin there is no such thing as a lease on heir property, and that Richard sold the share to his grandfather, and now the Pettifords own that share, just the same as we do."

Selma's eyes darted across the floor, as if she were checking all the places she'd searched over the years for the strongbox that was supposed to hold in it the documents that would protect the land, as she had vowed to do—and prayed to be allowed to do—for fifty years. "I took care of Richard's children," she said. "Richard and Tootch lef' me here, Ray. They sold out and lef' me here and never told me."

"You think it was a lease or a sale?"

Rayne recalled the Center director telling him that a Pettiford was listed among the owners. He felt as he had when he'd agreed to partner with a large builder to bid for a job that required a certified black-owned company, and then, when they got the bid, and administrations changed, the owner found a loophole—and dropped RayneDance Construction through it. Rayne had turned down other, smaller jobs, because this one was to keep them working for a year. So he had no big job, and no smaller ones to fill in. He wondered whether the Pettifords could force a sale; whether they could have done so for fifty years.

"And what about the loan on the Broadnax land?"

"What about it?"

"Nana, it's me. It's Ray." He turned away from her to feed thin, short logs into the box stove.

"You oiled the door?"

"Yeah."

"Nice it don't squeak." She watched the fire catch again. "Why'n't you leave it open?" She took in the heat and cheer before she spoke again. "Over the years, when I need a little loan, I'd get it from Pettiford rather than go to a bank, because they want collateral, and the only collateral I got is Broadnax and the heir property. So, better the devil I know than the one I don't."

"So, you've kept a running tab with him?"

She did not answer, but also did not dispute it. "And then people from the Center came to church. And by the way, Pettiford's son, the father of the golf course guy, he's in the State House. He's supposed to be such a big friend of the blacks here that he's the one brought the preservation people to our church to talk to us.

"So after that I went to Pettiford, the legislator. Made an appointment and had JJ carry me over to his office on Friday, when they come back from Columbia. I asked 'im: Did we have a lease or not? He told me, say: 'As you know . . .' And I interrupted him, and say: 'I don't know anything, 'cept how to work the land and take care of it and mind my business and pay taxes. And work for his father.' That's what I said. 'That's all I know, and look like it's not enough.'

"And so he stop the BS and say to me that there never was no lease arrangement possible with just one heir. Any lease, everybody had to agree to in writing. The only thing one heir could do was sell. He told me that. And then he admitted that the South Carolina lawmakers wrote it that way so that it would be that much easier for black people to lose the land than to keep it. And people like his father and himself, he said, tried to be good neighbors despite all that. And his father had tried very hard to be a good neighbor, especially after my husband had died, et cetera, et cetera."

"But he didn't give it back."

"King *told me*." Her watery eyes spilled tears down either side of her nose, and she talked faster. "He said, 'Anything happen to me, keep your eye on Richard.' He said, 'Anything happen to me, call Amos, 'cause Amos got a mind like a steel trap, and he don't take nothin offa nobody, which is why he couldn't live with his stepfather Slim, who was a bully.'"

"I thought it was his father who beat him."

"Nah. Bett said. Said it were that ol' Slim. He thought he'd be all set up. Amos wouldn't have it."

"So, it's us family and the Pettifords. Are we related?"

"I ain't."

Rayne thought through the new facts. Jokingly, he said: "So we should get some of the golf course revenues."

"Shhh. Don't say nothing. That's why I can't tell Tootch and them people in Philadelphia. They'll think: 'Oh, now we can get some more money offa this land that their daddy already done sold down the river.' Lil Tootchie and that deadbeat husband of hers look for any handout there is. And the minute they start talking like that, the Pettiford grandson could force a sale."

"'Cause he's a shareholder just like any Needham."

"'Cause they wrote the law." Selma poured herself the rest of the tea. "Yes."

"Or he could demand the full payment of the loan on the Broadnax land, and in a month's time"—he whistled—"it's over."

"That's why I wanted you to become a lawyer."

Rayne got up and cracked the window. Between the fire and the real estate tangle, he'd begun to sweat. He tied back his heavy hair.

"Not too much, Ray, I was just gettin warm," Selma said. "You cut off that hair, you won't be so hot."

Rayne did not answer. He went into the bedroom where the sleeping Khalil sprawled sideways on the mattress, and changed from his flannel shirt into a RayneDance Construction T-shirt. Something occurred to him.

"So, Nana, how much do you owe on the Broadnax land? I wish we'd stop calling it by his damn name; getting on my nerves to have his name in my mouth."

Selma smiled, glad to have someone with whom to share the news that she could hardly stand to think about, and to hear him growl and stomp around the house, making the floorboards groan, like his great-grandfather, who also refused to refer to the land by its former owner's name. *I bought it,* he said. *It's Needham land. What does old scary-cat Richard call this? My "King"dom. Damn right.*

"I owe eight thousand dollars."

"Well, that's not the end of the world. You got any paperwork on that?"

She shrugged. "Not like you and your new Heirs Property Center friends want. I figured that probably I'd sell it to him someday, and we'd just take it off the sale price."

"Jones knows about this?"

"Mostly. Some."

"What's he say?"

"He said talk to you. He told me to tell you. So I wouldn't die and leave you with a mess."

"How about you just don't die for a while?"

"I been holdin on to this for fifty years. I need some help."

Rayne sighed loudly. "I've gotta go home tomorrow after dinner."

Selma said: "I know, I know. You got to work, and the boy's got school."

"And it'll take me a while to wrap my mind around this."

"Well, it's just between us now."

"No, it is not. It's us and all the heirs and the whole goddamn Pettiford family. Sorry, Nana. You *know* that." But when Rayne smiled into Selma's beer-bottle eyes to soften his words, he could see that, having handed over the very old mess, she didn't know that. She knew that she'd carried this alone, or nearly so, for more than fifty years. She'd contained the damage as best she could and kept the land. What she knew, he saw when she smiled back at him, was that she'd given over stewardship to the only person she thought worthy and capable. What she knew was that, lawyer or not, he'd find a way.

To him it felt like a way out of no way, the ownership as fragile as each step Selma took: dragging her walker through gravel; going up the trailer steps backward on her bottom, and pulling herself up with both hands wrapped around the railing, over the threshold, using two hands on the doorjamb, and then cooking lemon–poppy seed pound cakes from her wheelchair to sell to B&Bs on Hilton Head. If everything remained exactly, precisely the same, and if she never made a mistake, the system would keep working. But if a screw came loose on the threshold, or a pebble rolled onto the bottom step, everything could change in an instant.

When the phone rang that night, it was Jones, calling on Easter eve to wish them a happy Easter, in order not to miss them at church or interrupt the ham dinner he knew would follow directly. In answer to Jones's usual opening, which Rayne could

hear from across the table: "Hey, little sis, how's my girl?" Selma
answered: "Oh, I'm here by the grace of God—and bein careful."

The tension in Selma's face relaxed, and by the time she
passed the phone to Rayne, she appeared positively happy.
Jones surprised Rayne by saying that he'd be at a horse farm
outside Philadelphia the next week, and would love to meet
up. Jared had insisted he get a cell phone, so he gave Rayne the
number and promised to call with exact details in a day or two.

"Well, Ray, I hate for you to leave," Selma said, standing, bent
over, rubbing first one hip and then the other.

"I'm not gone yet."

She accepted the coat he held behind her, slipping on first
one arm and then the other. "I should just say: 'That's the way
of the world.'"

"No, let's just enjoy the last swig of tea and the fire, and our
little walk across the driveway."

She obliged by turning her cup up to her head. "Don't it do
you good to hear Jones? That's just how I feel when I'm down
here and you call. Just like that. My Big Ole Ray of Sunshine,
I say . . ."

They washed the cups. A light rain was falling again, so
Rayne told Selma to wait while he got his golf umbrella from
the truck. When he returned, instead of stepping out, she motioned him in. "You think you can get *to* all of 'em? We haven't
spoken to some of 'em in years. You can get to Bobo, but what
about the others? I mean, where Amos's children are I don't
know. And what if Bett wasn't the only child to survive?"

"I stay in touch with Binky. She's great, actually."

Selma looked past him and said: "Fairlie Broadnax moved
back here after he didn't make it up in Ohio. His father had died,
and he come here expecting to inherit the fifteen acres his father
had sold to King a few months earlier. What Fairlie thought he
could do with fifteen acres, and not being a farmer, I can't tell

you. And I can't tell you what they said or didn't say to him to explain it.

"I do know that King paid the old man in cash. And I know that Fairlie's own brother Butch carried Broadnax to the bank to deposit the money. So how can Fairlie not have known?

"But everything was legal. Even when he went to the county courthouse trying to find some loophole, they told him there was none. How I know that is that Pettiford told King, and he told him to keep top eye open."

That's when King got the strongbox, Selma said, because he knew that the same white people who were glad to see Old Broadnax's sloppy hog operation cleaned up would just as quickly turn when the prodigal son appeared: poor Fairlie, the firstborn cheated out of his homecoming by that big, arrogant red nigger, which was how they saw him. *He saw it coming,* Selma said.

And he was arrogant; so what? The whole family was, right down from Grandma Bett, who would always quote Paul's letter to the Romans, which she called his letter to Rome, using her husband's name: *"In Christ you are not slaves, but sons, and if sons, then heirs."*

That's what this heirs property had been all about, Selma said. Nobody cared anymore about the land, and they moved away, just like nobody cared anymore about getting married. And what did they have? Rootless children, floating around, like the Needhams would've had . . .

"Without you," he said before they stepped out. "I know that, Nana. They got little monkeys in the zoo just roll up and die without their mothers. I know you saved my life."

She patted his arm. "Well, you wa'n't no monkey, which is good."

They laughed, and he walked her to her trailer in the rain. When they got to her steps, they stopped while she collected the energy to mount them going forward, not on her bottom, as she would have done had she been alone. She talked, as if to postpone the physical challenge. "This time tomorrow," she said, "you'll be back with your girl."

"Yeah, that'll be nice," he said.

"Do me a favor, Ray. I don't know how else to say it: if y'all make a baby, please get married. Please don't just have 'em and then he gotta run all over the world tryin to find you, and I can't get to see 'im without going through some Chinee girl I don't even know."

"She's half Philippine and half black, and we are *not* making babies. Okay. *No* babies."

Selma didn't answer as she climbed the steps, which were too narrow for them to take together. He walked behind and held the umbrella over her as best he could. Rain came into his face. In the tiny trailer porch light, she became a shadow.

Inside the trailer, once they'd stripped her wet coat and sat her back into her wheelchair, Rayne wiped his eyes with the bottom of his T-shirt and bent to kiss Selma good night.

"Why not?"

"Why not what?"

"Come on, Ray?" She reached up and pulled one of his locks. "Ding dong. Why you *not* making no babies? Why not? That's why you young. I bet them drug boys out in the road makin babies. Whatchoo gonna do? Wait till y'all too old, like all these white people on TV?"

"Good night, Nana."

"I'm not always wrong, you know."

"I do know that."

"Good."

———

Rather than go inside, he walked the boundaries again. Somewhere, a burning field was being rained out, and the charred, wet smell came to him on the wind; or maybe he was remembering. He navigated clumps of dirt pushed up by JJ's early, haphazard plowing, and under the rainy sky, the wet fences guided his tentative steps. He wondered again, as he had at first manhood: How could it be that a man could own earth without paying for it? He shook his head in the dark. He had not been raised to be an heir. Eight thousand dollars of loan he could handle; the motherless and bitter Bobo in jail, he could visit; less, rather than more, was his default setting. In their few recent conversations, Jewell had signified something similar. And Lillie: Was this the more that she wanted, the push he'd felt and resisted? On this land, they'd been talking, but not living, the spirit of adoption for generations: *If sons, then heirs.*

This laying down of the balls of his feet on the earth, and breathing deeply of burned-out ambition and yellow jessamine; this aching for fertility and laughter and love; now that he'd found his mother, could he accept the complicated inheritance of being her son?

Fear and rain dripped down his collar. What had seemed so solid could slip away with the filing of a document. Then they'd have ten days to try to buy off the owner of a golf course and his state rep father and paternalistic ninety-year-old grandfather. Thirty days more to outbid them.

Standing in the east field, near the golf course, where he could smell the fertilizers, he called Lillie. "Hey, baby," he said in greeting, "everything down here is, like, it's pretty fucked up."

"Hey, Ray, listen," she answered quietly. "I'm over here at Temika's house. Her baby's just back from oncology."

"God, I forgot."

"The baby's taking treatments like a champ. Temika, too. You want me to call you in a little bit, so we can talk?"

222 • LORENE CARY

"No. You hang with your friend. I'll talk to you when I get home."

"Well, here," she said, "I'll go in the other room, and you can talk to me now."

"Naw, that's all right. Goddamn, how's a two-year-old get cancer?"

"Born with it. They're lucky they found out. But they're trying to be normal. So she's doing my hair."

"That's nice."

"'Cause I gotta wear it up in the hospital. Plus, we thought we'd do something special for you. And, listen, if the baby's hair all falls out, we might just cut ours, like, in solidarity."

"Are you cutting it now?"

"You sound different. No, I'm not cutting it yet."

"Good. So I can come home and mess it up."

"I hope so."

———

Every few days that summer before he died, King Needham checked his fences, because alert was not good enough. Bobo told Rayne these things. When Rayne was a boy, he told him, and then he told him again later, in that stark room where prisoners and families "met." Bobo told him because he himself had not watched carefully enough . . . Vigilance had to be a running song of attention. It should have been both vocation and amusement.

"Come on, boys, best repair today gets a pie." King'd say crazy stuff like that. Like, "No, I ain't jokin. Custard pie. I'll make it my damn self . . . Second peach bough down in a month, i'n't? Come on, boys, wha's she need? Talking to you in Tree. Wha's she saying? Lookit all the fruit: too much, too small; lookit the leaves. Do she have to throw all 'er limbs on the ground fore somebody will have the heart to prune 'er back? Not too hard . . . We take these old ones. Here. Here. And

here. Clean cuts. And tar the stumps. Don't leave 'er raw. Not now. After she fruits.

"Jonesey, how's our mule?"

————

Rayne wanted to lie down on a clean, dry bed and curl his body around Lillie. He wanted to smell her freshly washed hair and feel the soles of her feet on his shins. And yes, he realized with some chagrin, he did want to make a baby with her. He wanted to watch her grow big and feel it jump under his hands when he pulled her close. Of course he did. How had he not admitted to himself how much he wanted life to run through him?

CHAPTER 23

On Easter morning, they drove to church early so that Selma could get seated without trouble. Outside the church, the teenage acolyte whom Khalil had met on Thursday motioned to him to come to the side door where they were lighting the incense. Rayne let Khalil climb out of the truck and shouted to the acolyte: "You'll send 'im in to us before the service?"

In the chilly breeze the acolyte's white vestments blew wide. They looked as if they might lift off and float away. "Oh, yes, sir. Mos' def. We're done in five minutes. I'll send 'im back to the ushers in the narthex."

Selma turned to Rayne. "That boy don't know a narthex from a hole in the wall."

"I keep telling you, Nana, it's just a church, and he's been here before. Besides, he hasn't been around any kids this whole week."

"Fine," she said.

She seemed agitated. Rayne attributed it to the number of people thronging in now, dressed, fussy, many, like him, essentially unchurched and not sure what to do. Knowing this, they'd decided that she'd stay in her wheelchair throughout, rather than park it at the rear of the church and let her venture to walk in. Rayne unpacked at the loading zone in front of the church. He helped her into the chair and gave her her pocketbook before attaching the footrests and pushing her up the ramp and to the row where a pew had been removed to make room for wheelchairs.

"Does Cornbread know where to come?" She'd begun to give Khalil nicknames: Cornbread, K-boy, Muffin-man.

"Yeah, hold on." Rayne asked one of the ushers to look out for his son, and then asked for two folding chairs so that they could sit next to Selma. For the next ten minutes, Rayne followed one person and then another looking for the chairs, which he brought, only to find two other companions for handicapped worshippers asking the same thing. When he began to move his truck from the loading zone, he saw in his rearview mirror Khalil running behind him. Rayne stopped in the narrow street, drawing beeped horns and gesticulations from the cars behind him. When Khalil caught up, he clambered into the truck and laid himself sideways on the seat. He smelled like incense, and he was wheezing.

"Asthma?"

Khalil nodded.

"Shit. Sorry." Rayne studied the boy for clues. "Did that running get you?"

"Nah, I run way more than that at school. It's not bad. I can wait. I went into the little room with them with the charcoal and the incense, and they let me help twirl it around to get it going. I think maybe I breathed in too much."

Rayne gave Khalil a piggyback to the church. It was nearly

full. The ushers were beside themselves. Selma was looking around. Rayne nodded, pointed her out to Khalil. He bent down to Khalil, speaking next to his ear, hair falling heavily next to their faces. He pushed it back, and Khalil held a lock from getting into his eye: "Look, Lil Man," he said. "Here's what you do. You go sit next to Nana Selma, okay, right there in the chair with her pocketbook. I'm going home for your inhalers."

"Can I come?"

"No, I really need you to stay with Nana. Tell 'er I'll be back in forty minutes."

Rayne watched Khalil walk to her just ahead of the procession, and whisper the plan. He smiled at an usher, a trim grandmotherly lady in a gray-and-pink pantsuit who called him back. She was reaching into her pocketbook.

"Here," she said, "for when you come back in here." She handed him an elastic. He'd never used one, but he grinned and slipped it onto his locks at the base of his neck. Then, laughing, he loped to the truck.

Lillie was calling. "Hey, babe," Rayne answered.

"Everything all right?"

"Mostly. Khalil's got some wheezing this morning, just started up, so I'm on my way back to the house for his inhalers. Should be back there in half an hour."

Lillie did not answer.

"Listen, baby, he started wheezing no more than ten minutes ago, and I'll have him taken care of fast as I can."

"I called because I realized that it was this day last year when he had his first attack. So I had a hunch. Which is why I called. He'll be okay. If you catch it in the first hour or so, you can usually get on top of it."

"Yeah, well, I'll do that."

"I can hear the truck burnin up the road. Thanks, Mr. Rayne. You got my little guy covered, I'm mighty grateful."

"How grateful you gonna be?"

She laughed. "Just come on home and see. But first you've got to bring my son back from all that damned fresh country air."

"You know it could be. All kinds of allergens that he probably hasn't encountered before. Not to mention the house really does have mold problems. That's what I'm thinking it may be."

"Could be an anniversary. Something he's intuited."

"From where?"

"Us, or his grandparents. It's folk wisdom."

"I don't know. Maybe too folksy for me."

"Yeah, my nursing mentor, too. She said not to say stuff like that in my oral exam. I think holistic, and they think, like, hocus-pocus . . . You tell Nana Selma about your mother?"

"No, I haven't, and I feel bad about it. But we've been talking about her land situation, and it's complicated. So that's been plenty."

"Can you sell it?"

"Short answer?"

"Yeah, for now, short answer."

"No."

"Wow." She sucked her teeth. "Wow. Okay. After church, you'll eat and come home? . . . And bring Khalil."

"Right away. I'd like to see me try to come home alone."

"On second thought, why don't you take a nap first?"

———

They did. After dinner in the old house, and another dose of meds for Khalil, Selma suggested that man and boy stretch out on the bed while she washed up dishes. In an hour and a half, when Rayne woke, brushed his teeth, and carried their bags to the car, Selma had packed individual bags of chips, apples, lemon–poppy seed cake, and ham sandwiches made from dinner rolls into the cooler underneath two Ziploc bags of ice cubes. She'd saved and rinsed four of their original water bottles, and refilled them: two with milk, two with water. And, in a Ziploc bag, one small, round corn bread for Khalil to take to school for lunch the next week.

Khalil's breathing had returned nearly to normal, and Rayne felt less of his usual anxiety about leaving. For one thing, he'd be talking to her more about the property. And for another, he'd promised to visit every month, one weekend out of four. He had no idea how he'd do it; but when he said to tell him what she really wanted that's what she'd asked. At least he would no longer feel guilty about not being there.

For her part, Selma waved from her trailer window, exhausted, but more at peace than she'd been in a year. She'd transferred some of the weight of the place, and of figuring out what to do, and it made her lighter. It took generations to build, she thought, and only a moment to tear down.

It was nice this year to have Easter with Rayne and the lovely new boy. And although she didn't talk about it much to anyone, it was especially good to have their company on this weekend. Easter was early this year, so she hadn't been alone on the anniversary of the day that Bobo and Jewell had both left her and the land twenty-five years before.

She opened the strongbox again, even though she could not stand to read any of the papers. But she had found King's first wedding band, which he put away when he'd married Selma. She figured it would probably fit Rayne.

CHAPTER 24

W
hen Jones stepped into Lillie's little house, he and
Rayne filled the room. Lillie and Khalil stepped back.
The two men embraced and shouted. They jumped
up and down together, reared back on their heels, eyed each
other, and hugged again and again. Thin, dark, as tall as Rayne,
with a bald head and a tiny gold stud in one ear, Jones looked,
as Khalil later said, like a black Mr. Clean, old, but nowhere near
his eighty-three years.

"Keep workin out of doors, man," he said in answer to Rayne's
question: How to stay young? "Don't stop, and whatsoever you
do, don't go in the house and sit down. That shit'll kill ya."

"Down at the old place, I found myself walking most every
night."

"You know why: 'cause King's mindin the damn fences,
wantin company. My sister wouldn't have it any other way. How
is she? Tell me the truth, Ray-Ban. How she doin? She don't
sound so strong."

"Ray-Ban?" Khalil asked.

"Yes, Ray-Ban. And what shall I call you, Lil Man?"

"Oh, my God!" Khalil said. "That's what he calls me!" He pointed at Rayne.

Jones squatted down to look Khalil in the eye, and asked quietly: "And what do you call my Ray-Ban?"

Khalil shrugged.

"Well, while we were down South, he called me Dad," Rayne said, "which was nice."

Lillie started to speak, first to Khalil then to Rayne, but she stopped when Rayne threaded his arm around her waist.

"See, this is what happens when Uncle Jones comes around. He makes you feel a little more courageous."

"Is that so?" Jones said, picking Khalil up in his one arm and tucking the other under.

Khalil shook his head yes. Then he proceeded to give Jones a report on Selma's physical welfare. He described how she worked from her wheelchair and walker in the kitchen and how she pulled in an eight-pound fish after sitting bundled in the cold. "Uncle Jones, Nana Selma is *tough*."

Jones sat down and balanced Khalil on his ropy thigh. "Boy, you don't know the half of it. One day I'll tell you just how tough she's been in her life. But I bet you're pretty tough, too, if you're the kind of young person to notice such a thing."

Because it was a school night, and in order to give Rayne and his uncle privacy, Lillie excused herself and Khalil to go upstairs for his bath, which he took by himself while she reviewed the report he'd had to write about his vacation. After that, they visited Tomorrow-Land, which was their ten-minute review of the next day's schedule. Then bedtime, where Lillie read to Khalil, and then, when she fell asleep midsentence, Khalil read to himself.

———

When they left, Rayne told Jones how things stood. Jones slammed the table with his hand when he heard about Pettiford's name listed among the heirs and his grandson as Selma's erstwhile banker. "She put such a store by that damned Pettiford. Damnit. I was gonna take care of the taxes, by the way, but she said she had the damn money!"

"She's a proud woman."

"Proud? Jesus." Jones stood, pacing just a few steps in the narrow parlor. "You know, you're a grown man now, and it looks like it's on you to handle the heir shit. I've got the damned eight thousand dollars to pay them back, and can do the taxes if she needs it, or we can do it together, if you want. You're her heart."

"Uncle Jones, what am I gonna do with fifty-five acres of South Carolina backcountry? Not to mention the Needhams: a whole family of people who think light skin is a skill set." It was his stock phrase for them. "Why do I want to go find these people?"

Jones threw his head back and laughed. "But listen, Ray, before you write it off, lemme tell you some more about it."

Jones told Rayne that the reason he was able to work with racehorses was not because of his experience with their mares or mules or nana goats, but because King had taught him to aspire to best practices. They didn't call it that back then, Jones said, but that's what King searched for.

King took Jones as a teenager to the agricultural expansion meetings for the same reason that he carried him to North Carolina twice to see a colored doctor: because he wanted him to understand that in matters of vital knowledge there existed higher authorities than county white folks. In the first talk that Jones remembers, a skinny Agriculture Department representative, a half-lame man with thick glasses, exhorted farmers to rotate crops.

"Gentlemen," he said to the colored men in the Baptist

Church. "I hold here a leaflet, and I'll leave some for you to take to your homes and read carefully. It's called 'What Is a Peanut?,' written by one of your own, Dr. Carver."

King sent Jones to read it aloud to black farmers who couldn't read. *Ver' interestin.*

A few farmers asked him to read it two or three times. Some made him come back and read it to their children and workers, so that the whole crew could discuss crop rotation. Mostly, however, they admired his reading.

King took him to hear another Ag-man who begged farmers to refresh the soil with soybeans one year and peanuts the next for an infusion of "peanut nitroglycerine." On the third year they could go back to cotton. King, Richard, and three other colored farmers did the experiment with one field each, and produced bumper cotton crops, right after the bad boll weevil years, that were the envy of the county.

"You could see when they set bolls how big and fat they were. The bolls broke open so full and fluffy, they looked like the cotton people talked about back in slavery days, back when they said a tiny little woman could pick three hundred pounds a day."

So strong was the subsequent white interest in this rotation miracle that the chamber of commerce requested a visit from the Agricultural Adjustment Administrator each year. He visited black and white farmers separately. Although the colored farms were poor, and half the black people in the rooms owned not one hectare, they questioned him vigorously and debated loudly among themselves when he finished.

The year before King died, however, the Ag-man made only one appointment—at the town hall. The meeting was supposed to be free and open to anyone. They had had what they used to call "dirty days," with airborne topsoil clouding the sky like in photos of the dust storms that drove people out of Oklahoma and Kansas.

"Crop rotation was the best thing the Ag-man could say to them. He'd been telling them *every* year. Always quoted the old 1899 National Soil Survey; I swear he said it like that, like people call on the King James Bible: 'The 1899 National Soil Survey tells us, gentlemen, the Egyptians did it, the Romans, the Indians. What better authority?'

"King liked to repeat that. Some of the soil guys tried to tell farmers about soil bodies and soluble salts. Most of them men, black and white, couldn't read their own names—and here they come displayin irrigation blueprints. One guy told us when we chopped cotton, we should leave in half the weeds to help hold the topsoil. Those men would look at him like he had two heads.

"But King's favorite, the tall, skinny one, he just kept saying that if they could do just one thing that would do the most good—'for your families, men, and for America!,' that's how he talked, like an old radio announcer—it would be: crop rotation!

"And, by the way," Jones said, "he stopped at our place every year to see what King had done. He'd gimp out his old Studebaker and start to shoutin. 'Soybeans—soybeans! Look at you standing in clumps like schoolboys in the yard!' He just stood there talking to 'em."

Jones took the Ag-man around on the little hay wagon so that he could see the peanuts, sweet potatoes, and pecan trees. Of course there wasn't much market for them. Which the big white farmers knew. If everybody grew sweet potatoes, everybody'd go broke.

"But that white man almost cried when they turned on the Town Road and saw Selma's three little goats on Needham's hill. It meant that someone was listening to his diatribe about the most efficient use of hillsides in animal husbandry versus the waste of hog management. And he saw what we'd started to do with Broadnax's nasty-ass hog operation."

Rayne had been listening with fading attention. As a contractor, he found interest in the land management, but what Jones was telling him—that King sought out and practiced crop rotation as well as mentorship—these were things that Rayne already knew. "You're telling me why this land should not be sold. That what you're telling me?"

"Yeah, I am. I know, it's all the way uptown to come back downtown, but humor me. For years, I have only been able to talk to Jared about this, and he doesn't know the players. He doesn't know the land and the town hall and the crazy package store at the bottom of the Church Road.

"Listen, then we drove right behind the Ag-man to the town hall meeting. Outside, Fairlie Broadnax barred the door to King and a handful of others. King was trying to assess the mood of the white men milling around. Broadnax had just come back to town, and everybody knew him to be a son of a bitch, but had they given him any authority there?"

As Jones remembered, it was old man Pettiford who came out and suggested gently that they should leave—he had no objections, but not everyone was so neighborly as we'd all hope. He said stuff like that. So King backed off. For one thing, he'd had the factory recruiter from Philadelphia come through recently, and for another thing, he was just getting ready to take his son to report to the army. It was breaking his heart to do it, and Jones thought that he'd lost some of his usual confidence. Jones remembered walking away and hearing Broadnax say: "Don't look like he needs no advice, 'cause he's the nigger knows everything there is to know, 'cept how to be careful."

Rayne felt blood pumping in his temples. "Why you tell me this shit, Jones?"

"Because I can't stand keeping all these damn secrets. And we had nothing to go on, and I only knew what I saw."

"What did you see?"

"I saw King go to Fairlie and offer him the land back for what King paid his father, plus improvements. That was a big concession, because he believed that you should never sell land. And they'd worked awfully hard on that nasty ten or fifteen acres. He figured that it was better to sell, though, if Fairlie was going to keep sniffing around and agitating.

"So, before Junior goes into the army, he makes it his mission to finish off the Broadnax field, which you couldn't farm worth a damn, because it was full of tree stumps that Old Broadnax never dug out. And we all work on it like dogs, just to be with Junior before he goes, and we're thinking that this'll help sell it and get Fairlie off his back. Even Bobo came out and helped at, like, five years old or something. He was big like you and King, and by this time, he was a real trooper. He could fetch and carry.

"Funny the things you remember. I remember that Bobo got brown as a nut. And I remember that the Ag-man arranged for King to be sent seed and instructions to try fava beans as a winter cover crop.

"And we all asked: 'How you cook 'em?' and finally Selma and me went to the library and found out: Just like any beans. Dry 'em. Store 'em, and boil 'em.

"Funny. They was so big . . .

"The field was almost done when it was time for Junior to go. By then Fairlie had rejected King's offer to buy back the Broadnax field. He sent word that since King had cheated his father, he owed it to him to restore the property free of charge. King just ignored him.

"Then, he went to Columbia for Junior to report, and I worked on the stumps in the field, and some of them were sitting right next to the holes they'd come out of. And Fairlie's daughter came into the field. I'm supposing her father told her that it was their homestead, and she got herself caught under-neath one of the stumps, and Selma and I went into town to get someone to help." He made a big sigh.

"Where was Bobo?" Rayne asked. "Where was he?"

"With King. King took 'im with 'im. He went along, because they were going to stop and buy chicks for Selma. They would get different strains and mate 'em to get their own hybrids. And Bobo was gonna get some of his own to raise. They were gonna be his first little business."

"Uncle Jones, what did you see?"

"Early the morning he came back, I saw the truck on fire. I saw the smoke, actually, from where I was comin out of the barn. I saw the smoke. So I started running.

"And I heard a shot. When you get all the way down to the road, it turns, and you can't see the field for the stand of oaks there, and I tried to cut through, and Greenie, this little white man who bought eggs from us, Greenie hears me, and he comes crashing through the timber there, pushing me and tellin me to go back, and I start to push past him—I can hear the fire and men ahead of me—and he looks up over my shoulder, and right then somebody gives me a gun butt or sompin like that on the side of the head." Jones points to the uneven scar on his temple. "When I woke up, I was on a train north.

"And when I called my sister a couple days later, she told me that King was dead."

"What happened to Greenie?"

"Selma said he left. He had family somewhere. Never came back."

Lillie had returned and was sitting on the mission bench where they dumped backpacks and bags on the wall by the ves-tibule. "Selma stayed," she said simply.

Jones nodded. "Yep. Since I was up here, I came to find Amos. He'd made good here. He was King's favorite. When I told him King was dead, he stood on his steps on Girard Avenue and cried like a baby.

"Then him and Mary went down to get Selma. Three times, she unlatched the car door and tried to roll herself out onto the road. So after the third time, they just turned around and took 'er back. I mean, what else you gonna do? Keep driving and let her roll out on the highway and kill 'erself?

"Richard and Mary was the shocker. They left, and my little sister's been there ever since."

Lillie came to sit next to Rayne on the couch and suggested that Jones should come with them to Bucks County the next night.

"For what?" Jones asked. "I was gonna go back, but I'm good for another day if you need me."

"Well, if I'm supposed to start contacting this family . . ."

"Who?"

"My mother."

CHAPTER 25

They were late because of the weather. Jack Thompson sat on the window seat—his oxygen tubing extension barely reached—watching ice drops rain from the sky. To save his breath for company, he snapped his fingers when Rayne's truck turned into the semicircular driveway.

Jewell jumped into the air an inch or two as she stepped away from the lemon vinaigrette she was whipping, having decided to add a tablespoon of zest to keep her hands busy. She ran across the room in her new mules, bought for the occasion, and checked her face in the mirror as she went, noting, although there was nothing she could do about it, the forked line of tension between her eyebrows. Eyebrowns, Lonnie used to call them, back when every eyebrow in her life and his was, in fact, black or brown. Outside, in the cold, they were chatting as they came out of the cab, slamming doors. Lillie and Jones saw her, but stood back to let Rayne go first.

He handed his umbrella to Lillie and reached his hand out to

Jewell's. They studied each other's hands and face in the yellow porch light before Rayne opened his free arm to beckon her into his chest. Lillie thought she saw Jewell looking for something; some back-of-the-hand was what she appeared to expect, but instead she stepped into the empty space in Rayne's large arms that seemed to have been waiting for her. Lillie observed each movement, because she believed that this relationship had to be found, even if only to be rejected, for Rayne to turn back to her and Khalil and welcome them in closer. She wouldn't tell him, directly, but it was why she'd volunteered to find an address, even after her girlfriend Temika warned her of the risks.

"Whoa," Rayne said. He felt his mother shaking her head against his coat. He memorized the feeling, so that it would be there for him later.

"On the train," she said, "you put your head against me." Jewell hated herself for bringing up that moment of betrayal, but it was all she could think of, and how their roles were reversed: that she had been bigger, and had held him and gone away, and that now he, the son, was so much larger than she, and holding her, stepping into her life, her home, filling her with hope, as the visiting nurse sometimes said, where she hadn't known she was hopeless.

"Oh, God, I'm so sorry. There is nothing I can say," she said into his chest.

"No," he said. "Me neither."

It was a few minutes before Jewell turned to Lillie and thanked her for her help. When she saw Jones, she made a little yelp and then cried.

"Yo, you didn't cry for me," Rayne said, teasing.

"That's because you're not eighty years old," Jones said.

"You're not either," Jewell said. "Look at you; it's impossible."

"Seventy's the new fifty," Jones said. "Hey, baby. I'm holdin on to that one."

"So what's that make you?"

"Alive!" Jones said. "Vertical. Still here!" He laughed into the house and met Jack, who stood, shook their hands, and asked them to forgive his oxygen tubing.

"Man," Jones said. "This is *your* house. I'm glad you let a crude old cuss like me come in. I told Rayne last night: I work with animals, man, and it doesn't do my manners any good at all."

Then Jack hugged Lillie, whose big hair got caught in the hinge of his glasses, although for a moment, they couldn't figure out whether it was the glasses or the tubing. Once untangled, Jack sat heavily into his long chair.

Rayne couldn't help laughing, which gave the rest permission. To his mother he said: "How well did you prepare your husband? Like add water and get instant black rels?"

Lillie had brought him a gift bag full of vitamins and supplements, which she began to unpack.

"These are special African-American family supplements?" Jack ventured quietly.

"Yes," Lillie said. "And you're gonna need all of 'em!"

She brought him salve that she said eased the dryness in the nose that Jewell had mentioned on the phone, and later she wanted to check his oxygen machine. For laughs, she'd also brought a foot glove on which were marked acupressure massage points to help various parts of the body, including lungs and heart.

"We've been needing a nurse in the family," Jack said. He smiled and closed his eyes.

Lillie said: "For something specific?"

"Mexico."

"Jack!" Jewell heard him from across the room where she was making drinks for Jones and Ray.

"It's better than when I was doing tattoos," Lillie said. "People would just go into their wallets and pull out some drawing on a piece of lined paper they'd had since ninth grade. And I'm like, 'Are you serious? This piece of crap you did before you had facial hair?' What do you expect I'm gonna say: 'I've never seen artistic creation like this before in my entire life? Pull up your sleeve?'

"But Mexico. I mean Mexico makes sense."

Jones said: "Tonight, man. I'ma call Jared and tell 'im to book us something. Tomorrow morning: let y'all go home and pick up the kid . . ."

Rayne said: "I guess she feels at home."

"A tattoo," Jack said thoughtfully. "Gee. I don't have an image ready to go."

"You could get a heart with my name in it," Jewell said.

"Or you could get this new thing the football players are doing, man," Rayne said, with an edge of sharpness in his voice. "Scarification."

Lillie hadn't told Rayne that the player had come back to the shop every night that week for a complicated image that he wanted punctuated, or skin-embroidered, she called it, with scarification. He'd paid $1,500 each night; out of which she got $1,000 times five. He paid in cash and she put the money in her drawer just slightly anxious, meaning to tell Rayne but forgetting. The player had indeed behaved seductively, asked her out, and brought a signed football for Khalil, which she also had not revealed.

"Scarification I already have," Jack said. "I got it last time, fifteen years ago."

"Do *not* show it!" Jewell said. "Talk about pulling up your shirt. He'll just do it anywhere."

"It's a whopper," Jack said.

"Hey, you want us to look at it, we'll look at it," Jones said.

"You want to go to Mexico?" Lillie asked.

Jack smiled and nodded. "Very silly to think I could pull it off. Jewell humored me as far as possible. We've gone every Easter for years. So, I've been thinking about it, of course."

"You didn't see the Passion, did you?"

Jack nodded.

"My mother went to one in the Philippines, and she always talked about it like . . . a mystery. What was it like for you?" Lillie asked.

"Well, now she's done it," Jewell said.

"We walked miles behind someone who considered it the greatest honor of his life to play Jesus."

"Play Jesus?" Jones asked.

Jack closed his eyes again as if to resee the scene. He spoke quietly. "We all walked behind him while he carried the cross. Hundreds and hundreds, in a thousand different stages of belief, from people who had ground glass into their backs and were flagellating themselves to tourists like us with bottled water.

"You know, you know what is going to happen, but you almost cannot believe it." He stopped to collect the memories and to catch his breath.

Jewell continued for him. "And then, we carry on, carry on. You just walk and walk until you're exhausted, but you cannot stop. I don't quite know what Jack was thinking we'd do this time. But it's inexorable. It's as if once you start, the thing must be accomplished. Almost everyone around you was crying, and they were saying things and praying in Spanish. It was *so hot,* and hundreds of us, thousands, keep walking. Half of them were barefoot. Some were sick. People were always sick. One man's feet started to bleed.

"Jesus was up ahead of us. That was the first look of him I'd caught, and I'll never forget it. Damned if he wasn't dragging the cross. It was so hot, and I knew his feet were bleeding, and probably his hands, too, and he kept going, and we just trailed along with the crying women and dizzy from the sun."

"And you know what happened?" Jack said. "I found my-self feeling, like, a crazy love for the man. I loved him like you should love your parents and your brother and sister. Most of us don't, but at that moment, I did. My parents had not been good people." He stopped and looked around. "I'm afraid that I've gotten started down this road before I realized what bad taste it's in. But I'm telling you that the only other time I knew love like this that I was sure of was for Jewell. And then I didn't know it, except that I knew I wanted to keep feeling it."

"They didn't, um, really crucify him, did they, speaking of big love?" Jones asked.

"Yeah, they did," Jack answered. "Every year. Last week, I lay here and thought about it."

"They didn't . . . nail his hands?" Jones asked more specifi-cally. He was drinking Kentucky bourbon, making appreciative nods to Jewell after every tiny sip.

"They nailed his hands and his feet."

"Crazy-ass Mexicans!"

"Filipinos do it, too," Lillie said.

"Hey, don't want to leave them out. Crazy-ass Filipinos. Did you see this thing happen?"

"Yeah. Yeah, we saw it," Jack said. "Everything I felt that day I'm putting into this tattoo design. Ancient people thought you could learn from the harmony of design. That's it, see, we're try-ing to achieve harmony and balance."

Lillie looked at Rayne with panic. "You do have a tattoo design?"

"He's trying to help restore the balance," Jewell said. "So am I. So are you. That's why we think you'll agree when you see the design he's done. And when people see this on his body, it will go into them along with their awe . . ."

"I don't think I'm worthy," Jack said, and then stifled a laugh in order not to choke himself.

"You two had me going for a minute," Jones said. "I'm not drinking any more of this Kentucky shit."

"And I thought, oh, no, right after I said all those mean things about people's designs," Lillie said.

She thought about the football player's long, elegant spine. The cross stayed straight. It folded into his back and folded out. The crossbar gave just a hint of its terrible weight. She'd hung a crown of thorns over the center, and driven nails into the ends, just where the feet would be. But the cross was empty. The body had been taken away. The flesh involved was the player's, a smooth sacrifice, beaded up into wood grain by the scarification. He'd expressed a desire for her to agree to put into the crown of thorn's tiny scars, traces of his mother's ashes that he claimed to have outside in his Hummer. She'd declined.

In a way, Lillie thought, it was good that he'd gone over the line with her. She had decided to stop scarification sooner rather than later. No need to bother Rayne about it. She could simply stop now.

CHAPTER 26

A t the end of the evening, when Rayne gave Jewell a summary of the heir property laws and what he thought were their options in light of Selma's advanced age, they were surprised to hear her say vehemently: "You can't sell it."

"I know it seems ridiculous," she said, clearing the plates, "considering that I've been nowhere in sight. But think about it, Selma raised the whole family, and we owe her."

"We owe it to her to take care of her and see that she's safe and warm," Rayne said. "But do we owe it to her to hold on to the land? And, I hate to say it, but this has been working on me since you said it, Uncle Jones: How can I wrap my mind around the fact that King may have been murdered and Selma's just livin with the fact. I can't get past that."

"Jones, you think Broadnax did it, that he got a group together and ambushed King?" Lillie asked it, point-blank.

"I have no proof."

"Except that when you got close some white guy knocked

245

you upside your head and threw you on a train," Rayne said.

"Well, somebody hit me. Since I didn't see 'im, I can't say for sure he was white. But whoe'er it was put money into my hand, too. The hundred-dollar bill I gave you when you started your business? That's what was in my hand when I came to."

"Oh, shit, Jones. Jesus. That was what they put in your hand?" Rayne stood and walked from one end of the room to the other. Jones had called it "King's last gift" to him, and had given it to Rayne when he'd first started out with a twenty-year-old truck, five sledgehammers, and a crew of three ex-cons and the girlfriend of one of them, who could pull a day's work and read for them—McDonald's menus, directions, road signs. The bill had blessed the business. Rayne had framed it and hung it in his apartment, only taking it down when he moved in with Lillie.

He walked into the cold sun parlor and looked out into the mid-Atlantic forest encircling the semicircular lawn. "Fuck!"

Jones followed him into the cold, dark room. Rayne turned and started to ask: "Why didn't you . . . ?"

In the dark, Jones's face took on a masklike stillness. He spoke with sudden quiet fury. "Why didn't I what? Take my black self back down there in the 1940s and track down his killers?

"You tell me. I don't think you fuckin take me seriously. The one black man who had ever been able to protect me was dead. I couldn't even look at his barn without bawling. And the war was on, and I thought I could get away from death at home by going to war. How was I to know? I was a kid. So I go to the army and continue pretending to be straight, and they make me a man, which means more goddamn death. And when I went down and saw my brokenhearted sister and our little shack, it was all I could do to visit, and help her for a season, but she wouldn't leave; she wouldn't fuckin leave, Rayne, and I couldn't stay.

"You see that damn wintry mix comin down? Can you make it stop? If you go out there and stand out in the weather all night and freeze to death by the side of the road, will that make it stop? Go on, try it."

"I'm sorry, Jones," Rayne said.

"And I ain't even related. I'm not an heir. You're the heir and you wanna sell the place. You want to get rid of it, and you haven't even tried being an heir. Try it, buddy. See how you like it. There's a lotta ways to man up."

Rayne had been so busy tiptoeing around where he and his mother might hit trip wires of rage that he'd been careless with Jones. "Uncle Jones, man, I said I'm sorry."

"I'm sorry, Ray. But I just come up here and sit in the nice place drinkin Henry McKenna, and I guess I don't want to be second-guessed. I said I'ma pay off the loan."

"We'll work together on the loan."

"No, I said I'd pay for it. You got kids. I don't have any kids."

Jewell had come to the door of the sun parlor.

"We can help. We don't have kids either."

"Yeah, you do," Rayne said.

"Oh, my Lord."

"No more talking by Jewelly tonight," Jack said to Lillie. The two of them had stayed in the room, but could hear.

"No, you save your money," Jones said. "You may have to help some other way. Can we get back to the light? I feel like I been in the dark all my life."

When they returned, Jack, who'd been lying in his long chair with his eyes closed, said quietly: "You know, I've been wondering whether or not maybe this Pettiford might have bought Richard's share in order to keep Broadnax out. In the tobacco industry, I remember seeing that sometimes."

"What do you mean?" asked Lillie. The others hadn't paid him much attention.

"This is a white man thinking he's protecting black people. Listen: these various states' laws—they were all different, and all just as ossifyingly complicated. What they had in common, though, was that they were made to keep black farmers from getting equal treatment. Schools, loans, lands, water, inheritance, anything you could legislate. You read these cases, and you can see the pattern.

"And sometimes, you'd find that the rare white farmer would sign for a black person, or go to the bank and take out money to loan him. Sometimes, they put their names on the deed—you follow me?—and then take out a separate loan on the black farmer's land. The problem, of course, came with inheritance. When the white father died, his son may not have had the same tender feelings."

"I'm glad you all are here, because it makes me mad just thinking about it," Jones said. His cell phone rang. The ringtone was the sound of a horse's neigh. "Jared got me this damned thing," he said, taking it out of his pocket and squinting at the number. "Of course, I don't know why I'm looking, because no-body calls me on it but him. He might be callin about this very thing, because I asked him to look up for me about the devilish Broadnax . . ."

"Uncle Jones, answer the phone!" Lillie shouted, and laughed. They all laughed. They needed it.

"Don't worry. It doesn't go to voice mail until the seventh ring, 'cause I can't be jumping that fast."

"Gimme the phone," Rayne said. "I'll answer it."

"No, then I gotta explain why my big, strong, muscular nephew is carrying around my phone." As soon as Jones heard Jared's voice, his long, tense-mask face eased. It was the first time Jones had revealed himself before them. Until now he'd been theoretically gay. Now, he unfurled his long body and ambled into the kitchen, a relaxed man talking to his longtime lover.

Rayne turned to his mother: "You ever seen Jones tight before?"

"Never," she said.

Jones snapped the phone closed and returned to them, his eyes wide. "Hey, Jared sends his love."

Rayne said mischievously: "We don't know Jared."

"He knows you. And he's home working on your ungrateful black behalf. I asked him to check for me. His niece is a librarian. Listen, Fairlie Broadnax disappeared twenty-five years ago."

"Where?"

"Our town. In Gunnerson. Jared said that the paper there ran a missing-person article—you can look it up—that said that he had come back from Cincinnati and was living with his brother's family, and family members said that he had separated from his wife of many years and disappeared within a few weeks of coming to stay."

"Say anything about the daughter?"

"Not a word."

"When was it, again?" Jewell asked. And when Jones told her, she touched Rayne's arm. "That's right when we left."

"Why?" Rayne heard something in his mother's voice, and wished they were not in the room together, with people around them, but on the phone, where he could simply concentrate on the voice and on asking questions that seemed to cause as well as quell the seismic rumblings inside him. We, he was about to say, meaning him and her: "Why did we leave?"

She hesitated for a long time before answering. "Your grandfather beat me. I had one child out of wedlock, and I was seeing a boy who wanted to make movies. Like Oscar Micheaux. And I let him take pictures of me, and Daddy told me to stop seeing him, and then he found us out after dark together, and he beat me. It was pretty bad. So I decided that we had to leave."

"I didn't know."

"No," she said. "You wouldn't." She got up and cleared the

table. Lillie helped. There was dessert, too. Lemon–poppy seed cake from Selma's recipe.

Rayne excused himself to replenish the inside basket of wood for the fireplace. He needed the outdoors. It was real there, with the ice crystals dropping into his hair and onto his neck. So Broadnax had gone back to Gunnerson and then disappeared. And Jones had no proof, and Bobo, who had always said that he was imprisoned for the wrong thing, had driven his own daughter, stunningly beautiful but poorly educated and immature, off the land.

So nothing was clear. He turned his face toward the sky to feel the icy pricks on his cheeks. Whatever cold-case fantasies he'd had for twenty-four hours were just that: fantasies. And foolish. He felt as if he needed swaddling to keep his limbs from flailing.

And then, as if she'd read his thoughts, Lillie stepped up behind him and reached her hands around his waist. She leaned her head into his back.

"We want retribution," she said, "but it doesn't help, really."

"Besides, I don't even know for sure who did what. I wish I knew what happened."

"What would that do for you?"

"Make me stop looking for ghosts."

Against the foggy gray-black sky the deeper, blacker forest traced a silhouette of animated trees. They moved as if they'd called up the wind on purpose.

"Maybe you don't want to know," Lillie said.

"No, I do. I want to know. I feel like I'm fuckin haunted by this now."

"Well, if it's a haunting, talk to it. Open up."

"You're a nutcase."

"It's true: brown and crunchy, all organic, raised by ancestor-worshipping Pentecostal Catholics. What else could I be? But I'm not the one haunted. You the one twitchin in your sleep."

"Really?"

"I told you that."

"Khalil said on this drive that he felt like he'd been drivin in the truck his whole life. And when he said it, I thought: that's where I've been. It's like I couldn't get out of the goddamned truck. Drivin, drivin, drivin. Fuckin driven."

"You want 'em in?"

"I don't know what you're saying. Why do you say this shit and it's like another language?"

"Invite 'em in, I said. King, the wife who had Bobo and died of the flu, the baby, the son who got killed in the war, old Ma Bett and the slave master's son, Grandma Bett, Rome, all of 'em. Light the incense—you do know what I'm sayin, but you don't wanna hear it—light the incense and ask 'em to come to you."

"Stop it."

She came out into the open in front of him, with her hair sparkling from the ice and rain. She whispered to the sky, but so that Rayne could hear her: "He wants to know. He's open. He's ready. I'll stay with him. I'll hold him here. Give it to 'im."

"Okay. That's enough. Come on, come on, come on."

"Come on, your own self. You don't want me to be flaky and para-fucking-normal, but lemme tell you, when you were gone, the whole house was quiet. Not full of all them ghosts you be bringin with you. It was like it was before."

"Why black people can't just die?"

"Go ahead and laugh," she said, wet and cold now, watching him for any opening.

"Did I lose my mother's dog?"

"Oh, God, call 'im. I'm supposed to be letting him out for a pee. You're trying to distract me, and it worked." She called. "Jewell said that he won't run off in the rain, but how do I know?"

Rayne listened for the dog, but could not hear him over the

wind and pelting bits of ice, the creaky trees and thin, staccato twigs banging against one another. "No, really, I think you lost my mother's dog. I'm trying to get in touch with my family, and you lose my mother's canine companion."

"Shut up."

Rayne whistled for the dog and pulled her to him. "Remind me not to rile old Jones again, will you?"

"I don't think he holds a grudge. In fact, I think he's the best one to rile." Lillie made kissy noises. "Here, doggie."

Rayne kissed her in answer. "And remind me not to get jealous about your Eagles."

"You shouldn't be. But don't worry. I'm not doing any more of those tattoos or scarifications. It was starting to get like a cult."

"'Cause of me, old stick-in-the-mud jealous construction worker. That's not a reason to stop. You like it; you're artistic; it makes you some change."

"I'm gonna be a nurse. I've wanted to be a nurse since I was a kid. You're helping me do that. I don't need to prick holes in people's skin and inject dye into them anymore."

"You think we can make this work?" He bent over and grabbed the backs of her thighs as a sign for her to jump up and straddle him. Her hair with its familiar heavy crimps was blowing up into his face.

"You really gonna cut this?"

"Call the dog," she said while she scooched up and down gently on his abdomen.

"Stop," he said, "you're getting me hard."

"You're so easy," she said.

"Shit, now I gotta go back in like this."

"We're gonna talk about that heir property some more. That'll chill you down."

"It's working already," he muttered. He whistled for the dog. "Come on, damnit," he said quietly, walking to the door. "Inside."

The dog bounded to the back porch and began pawing. Lillie got ready to open the door, "How'd you do that?"

"Like this." Rayne put her down and motioned to the dog with his hand and a snorting sound. "Hey, dog, get back," he said.

"Oh, now you're the Dog Whisperer. That dog doesn't know what you're talking about," Lillie said.

"Oh, yes, he does. My granddaddy showed me," said Rayne. "Now go ahead and open the door." Rayne squatted to pick up an armload of wood. The dog did not move. "Go 'head."

Lillie opened the door and stepped in. Rayne crossed behind her, and then nodded to the dog to follow.

"We are getting a dog," Lillie said. "Khalil needs to learn this."

Inside, Jack was sitting up on the side of his chair. Before Rayne could put down the wood, he said, "The old man Pettiford, he's still alive? Still got his marbles?"

"I guess," Rayne said. "Jack, you in here thinking like a lawyer."

"I am a lawyer, and glad still to be able to think."

"I don't know about Pettiford myself," Rayne said, "but Selma talked about him as if he were . . . viable." He knelt down and laid the short logs in the metal tray, then stood two upright over the fire to make it draw.

Jack said: "You do that just like your mother."

"Selma taught us . . . and his son is a state rep, and the grandson, who's a little older than I am, is the one who's built the golf course."

Jack said: "Well, they have an interest in the land, of course, but how much of the father's district is black? Could he afford a big, ugly news campaign about taking heir property away from a seventy-something African-American widow, et cetera? Think about it."

"It's South Carolina."

"Yeah, but the black voters there can pay attention. We know that . . . Well, in any event, the approach would be first to decide whether or not you want Amos's kids to file another, more recent, quitclaim. If they are good people, it might be better, actually, to have more hands to the wheel."

"Second," Jewell said, "to decide what to do about Richard's and Big Tootch's clan."

"They sold out."

"Their father sold, but if this comes to a court fight, or a fight in the press, do you want these people with you or against you?"

"Jack," Rayne said, "you wouldn't say that if you knew Lil Tootchie."

"Give 'im more black family supplements."

"And then, listen, hey," Jack said softly, "I've talked too much. But before I go to bed—I'm so sorry to spoil the party—do you have any other lawyers in the family?"

"Other lawyers in the family?" Lillie said, laughing.

"He *is* family. Hey, you're not spoiling the party, man. I told you we're in your home," Jones said. "You have been a gracious host, despite your touchy new relatives bringing a crazy deal to your doorstep."

"Richard's granddaughter, my favorite cousin, Binky, is a judge."

"See," Jones said, "we told you not to count Richard's clan out. They need to make amends."

Rayne sucked his teeth. "No, you're so right, Jones. If they are out and we keep 'em out, they'll hate us. If we invite them in, as if it's not an invitation, but expected, it means the possibility of . . ."

"Redemption." Jack smiled at Jewell. "Better and better." Jack closed his eyes to think for a minute. "Does this Binky have a proper first name? Maybe she and I should make a conference call to the state rep. Double-team 'im. I might still know a few good old boys to call—if you want me to." He grinned weakly. "I haven't threatened anyone in a long time. I'm thinking it could have healing properties. Nurse Lillie, what do you think?"

Lillie said that she wanted to examine the water reservoir on his oxygen machine. Jack invited her to inspect to her heart's content. They went into the bedroom together. As she suspected, it was empty. She showed him how to refill it with distilled water and told him that she'd tell Jewell, too. That should give him a little moisture to keep the skin in the nostrils from drying too much. She didn't say it, but they could crack and bleed.

"So you did all the Mexican crucifixion pilgrimages; you're a Christian, I guess," she asked.

Jack gave a half smile. "You know how some Jews say that they're culturally Jewish; well, I think that I'm culturally Christian."

Such a thought had never occurred to her. Lillie had been about to say something to him about prayer and comfort. Now she did not know how to respond.

"You're wondering whether that's enough to face death with."

"I wasn't going to say that."

"Well. You should if you're going to be a nurse. Because this is about life and death, isn't it? Everything we've been talking about tonight. Jonesey in the army, killing Japanese; somebody here killing King, whom Jones probably loved as much as his sister did. My wife running away from them all, trying to kill herself. Her father doing God knows what, spending half his life in prison. And me with cancer, breathing through a tube . . .

"Christianity is obsessed by death. I'm a cultural Christian, because given the pervasiveness of death in life, a dead-human-turned-eternal-advocate does seem like an appropriate response."

"That's pretty sad." Lillie wondered whether she'd heard him right about Jewell.

"This helps—this seeing Jewell find a new family. This is very good. When we were younger, we couldn't find a way to do family. She and I were like damaged houseplants. We repotted ourselves in each other."

"Do you feel as if you're healing?"

"Well, Christianity will tell you that physical healing is often beside the point. But a little lawyer work may help." He sat heavily on his side of the bed and pointed to the tiny fridge they'd sandwiched in the bookcase. "Without work, I feel kind of . . . superfluous."

Lillie could see what an effort the evening had been for him.

"Maybe you'll draw me up a hit of morphine. I'm allowed some before bed. It does wonders. It's that or a sledgehammer."

Lillie pulled up the tiny eyedropper, figuring that he'd use three CCs. "This right?"

He nodded and tipped his chin up to let her slip the eyedropper under his tongue.

She could see the muscles around his eyes loosen in about thirty seconds.

"Thanks," he said. "I can undress myself. At least I still can for the time being."

As she left he said: "The worst thing about dying is that nobody needs you anymore. Jewell has needed me in these last weeks. It was nice to be needed, even just a little, tonight."

————

Despite Jack's entreaties for them to stay, Rayne went out and turned on the truck to let the defroster start to work while they collected their coats and said good-byes. He followed his mother to the guest bedroom, where she'd hung them on hooks on the backs of the doors. Jewell told her son how grateful she was that Lillie fielded her calls while he was in Gunnerson.

"Talking to Lillie makes me think," she said, choosing her words carefully.

"Think what?"

"When you look at it just in terms of facts," Jewell said, "you've found someone who has some of the same circumstances I had when I had you: she's a single mother with a son, and she's made the right decisions for them. For him, is really what I mean."

"Yep, she's good."

"She's mature. She's still got plenty of youthful energy and all, but it takes maturity to think of the child first, to live your life with him in mind first. I admire her for that. And I admire you for finding her. Most people just repeat.

"You could've found another me. There's no shortage of them. Us. You've made a wise choice. Choices, really."

"Choices." Rayne had been only halfway listening. When she began to describe herself leaving him, his mind wandered. His jaw and gut tightened. The purr in her voice rubbed up against him too softly. He found himself wanting to roughen the surface of their interaction. Given the jagged edges of their past, sometimes he couldn't believe her now. "Do you pass for white?" The sentence said itself through his lips. He heard himself and approved.

She'd prepared three or four different answers, all prevaricating, all partly true. In America, people assume race, and unless she quizzed down each clerk at Macy's and then corrected them, in fact, she passed, de facto. But this was not what he was asking.

"I did pass. It started happening sometimes in New York, and I didn't stop it. Then I married Jack. Jack knew from the start. Because he's white, he didn't understand what a big deal it was for me to step over. So we lived in white suburbs, and the lawyers in his department were all white, and his club was white. I told a few people, but only when I got close, and I didn't get close to too many people. It's been mostly the two of us. I didn't join the NAACP or anything. Out in the world, yeah, I let it happen."

"Because Bobo beat you? To get away from Selma? To get rid of me?"

"No, Rayne. I left you because I was a rotten mother and I couldn't make myself do better, and I would have ruined you. Selma wouldn't have. She didn't."

"We're talking tonight about heir property. It's true that after Daddy ran off that boy and beat me there in the barn, and then dragged me into the house through the mud . . . I mean, I didn't want to inherit any of it. Really, I wanted a different history."

It was bad luck for her to have had Bobo as a father, Rayne thought, because Bobo saved his particular distrust of the world for women and white people. So she fixed him, Rayne thought. "Bobo has converted to Islam now," Rayne said, following his own train of thought. "He changed his name to Abdul-Ghaffar."

"Ghaffar? I suppose it means something."

"He's been promoted to a lower-security section of the prison, and he raises dogs for the blind and war vets with PTSD. When he said that, I thought: *he's* like somebody with PTSD; this'll be like therapy for him. And it is. The dogs do anything he says. He's shown me all kinds of things with them."

"Good for him." It was a cool, formal acknowledgment, the best she could do. What she was thinking was: how perfect that he now had a creature to control. And that Ghaffar was a ridiculous name, like something out of Disney. Why, she wondered, weren't any of them satisfied to be themselves? "And you no longer use Alonzo? Or Lonnie? Too babyish?"

"That was your name for me."

"And you hated it?"

"No, Jewell. Mom. I didn't hate it. I saved it. For you."

CHAPTER 27

Rayne drove back to the city over icy Bucks County two-lane roads with names like Mill Road and Alms House Lane. They wound around the hills and creeks with slopes and sharp turns under very few dim streetlights. The four-wheel drive kicked in, but so, too, did Rayne's hyperalertness. Helped by Lillie, his thinking tonight was both magical and analytical. The haunting continued. The whispery sense of a shadow just out of sight, at the edge of his peripheral vision. Not a presence, but presence. He turned on his high beams. Tree limbs had come down in the wind and with the weight of the ice. He felt guided around them.

To drain off nervous energy, he let himself think of how to convert the budget-and-timeline proposal for a nursery school renovation into a PDF with print large enough to read, but small enough to fit onto an 8½-by-11 sheet. A startled deer launched itself up and over the road, from one banked, slippery hillside to the other, almost high enough, it seemed to Rayne, to have cleared the truck if need be. He went back to his technical problem solving. They'd wasted three days in failed e-mailing, because his powerful timeline software for the Mac would not read on the director's slow old PC. Her fax machine sent terrible copies, and she had tried to tape the two halves of long pages, but lost what little data had not been blurred with too much ink.

After the deer crossing, Rayne decided to go simple and old school: stop trying to e-mail the proposal or put it on the cloud and instead take the file to Staples, have them print it out on a large sheet, as if it were a small poster, and then hand-deliver it. He calculated the time they'd already spent messing with e-mail and fax. Two hours for him, one and a half for her, and he multiplied it times twelve dollars an hour, had they had a secretary, or two hundred and fifty, if he'd been able to spend his time installing a photovoltaic cell. He'd also print a large drawing of the playroom in color and back it with foam and stand it on an easel. That way, every person who walked in would see it and get excited. She could take it to her board.

Lillie sat in the back. When she reached over the seat and patted his shoulder, he touched her gloved hand. Maybe he'd ask Lillie to deliver the timelines on her way back from Jefferson Hospital. Last time she'd done something like that for him, she'd sealed the deal by adding a classy little gift bag with a RayneDance baseball cap and two bottles of Fiji water thrown in. Simple. But it never would have occurred to him. Not to mention the pert lift in her walk, the very black almond eyes.

"I'm so glad Khalil stayed over with Joshua and Coleman."

"Yeah."

"It's a good thing to know that your kid is safe. None of them had that feeling. Your folks. Except with Selma. You realize that?"

"And Selma had it with King until they killed him."

His mind answered with the family refrain: *That's the way of the world.* And here he was, back in the cab of a truck. It occurred to him that he should add a few choice truck parts to Khalil's Climbing Wall. *Duh.*

Jones adjusted his body in his sleep and jammed his knee into the dashboard. "Shit." Eyes closed, he touched the glove compartment with his long fingers and seemed to lie back, having measured the dimensions of his enclosure. Then, touching his fingers to the latch, he said: "King used to keep a gun in his glove box. In the house he had that shotgun that Bobo took with 'im, but he also stored a little pistol in the glove box. Forget what kind."

"Jones, you'll spend the night with us."

"Oh, yes, oh, yes. Jared already read me the riot act. I know I'm old and half-drunk. 'S that damn Henry McKenna. I only drank it 'cause I knew you were driving."

———

Once they were home, the wind picked up, and the trees in the alley scratched at the brick walls. Rayne thought he heard the horse stomp in the barn across the alley. He wondered what Jones would say about how the animal was kept.

Still damp from her shower, Lillie came to the bed and straddled him. "Whoa. Whoa. Have I been sleep? What's goin on?"

"Want a little bit?" Mouth, touch, wet.

"Lips," he said.

They'd brushed their teeth, but she still tasted faintly of the coffee they drank in the truck on the way home. It was a morning taste. He touched her wet neck and arms and breasts, quizzically. It was nighttime, not dawn, after all. He couldn't figure out where he was.

"Don't take much to throw some people off."

"Told you. Old Stick-in-the-Mud."

"Come on, Old Stick."

He clicked his tongue. "What's happened to you? You're like you used to be again."

"I'm finishing nursing school. I'm not scared to death of losing my house . . . You've been good to my kid. While you were away I had a talk with myself. Time to stop preparing to live. Like the Chinese fortune said." She felt her throat tightening, and her eyes filling with tears. "I don't know what you're doing, but you have brought your family with you, and you keep trying to stay apart, but you can't. You're repeating something, and I don't know what it is, but I'm afraid of it. You got Khalil and me with you, and now we're in it, too."

Rayne pulled the covers over her body. "Oh, baby. You been scared?"

"I didn't even know how scared I've been. It's all in here." She touched her hands to her body, starting at the head, touching her temples and throat, her heart, her stomach, and groin. His hand followed hers. They were warm on her cool, damp skin. "Tonight I asked Jack what he believes in. You know what he told me? He told me that he's a 'cultural Christian.' What is that? It's fifty-fifty for him with this monster chemo they're doing, and, like, what is his backup plan?"

"My mother is his backup plan," he said close, talking mouth on hers, nibble, talk, taste coffee, morning, wake-up call, go to sleep. "You're mine." He bent his knees behind her back to cradle her.

Support. How could his mother have supported anyone early on if she was trying to kill herself? Why had Jack told Lillie alone? Why did they keep secrets? She lay back against Rayne's thighs, hoisted herself up and eased herself down onto him. "There. Shhh. Don't move."

"I gotta move."

Deeper. Open up some more.

Rayne breathed in her yearning. Their wants had not been the same. Naturally. *That's the way of the world.*

Tonight they are.

Tonight, Lillie agreed to keep him company as he rolled back toward his birth and beyond it to his great-great-grandmother Bett, whose pushing forward got her and Rome the soggy washland that nobody thought could be farmed, but they farmed it anyway; and past her to the Africans whom Selma talked about as if there had been just one black Adam and Eve who arrived and gave birth to their blessing and curses, whether or not deserved, because deserving is beside the point, but survival required. She held on to him as he turned into an estuary, a channel—she suggested it, after all: "Invite them in." She held on to this big, solid man who built floors and ceilings and walls to give him the strength to become essence, a willing vessel, a swinging door that could open and close as he breathed. Her mother told her that there are more things in heaven and earth than we dream of.

———

She feels it tonight. She will stay close to him.

He falls asleep when he comes. A trapdoor opens down to a basement he hasn't visited in a long time. Now he'll know why.

CHAPTER 28

ᕐᕗ

The men smoke, sip, and watch one another, soon to be initiated into a secret society. Some already belong. Some wonder. Some know.

Fairlie Broadnax walks around the trees as if to evaluate them. He is as self-important as a terrier on a rat hunt. Chuff, chuff. Mitchell has lived next to King for years, watched his big, red, arrogant self planting, harvesting, storing up, draining, improving, rotating crops. King built a fence to keep Mitchell's cows out of his corn. Some nerve. Mitchell wants Fairlie to fuck off tryin to boss everybody.

———

Selma's first thought on waking is of King. She chews a cracker that she left for herself on purpose on the table next to the bed. It helps a little. She counts the days from her last period. It's too soon to tell for sure. She's counted this far before plus five days, had this sicky feeling—then nothing. This time she's sicky and hungry. Her nipples itch. She won't say anything until she's past the second missed cycle. Twenty-one and twenty-one plus five for the missed period will be forty-seven: exactly his age.

She distracts herself from too much hoping by remembering the current mess. She wishes that there had been some way to get word to him, so he could be thinking what to do on the way home. She thinks of Amos and Mary in Philadelphia. Maybe they should just pack up and go bunk with them for a while. Hire out?

She can hear his voice: *Well, you know, BabyGirl, if we move, we lose.*

They've had trouble before. Soon after he married her, his dogs took after a white drifter who wandered into the tobacco shed. Folks in town went crazy, said it could have been any of them, got up a party to come stand outside the door and demand that he give up the dogs to them.

He didn't give his dogs over to anyone. But he did put them down. It almost killed him. Everyone adjusted, went on living, like they'd been doing together for years. Happened every ten years or so, he said. The scum bubbled up to the top; they skimmed some off and let the rest roil back into the pot. If he left, they'd lose it all. That was a given.

After her chores, Selma begins to bake applesauce bread from the earliest of those lopsided apples on the Goat Hill ridge, so that she can take a loaf to that Broadnax family as soon as King gets home. Maybe he'll want to go, too. She knows he hated the father, but he makes things work. He won't sidestep whatever mess is coming. He'll walk straight through it.

———

At quarter to seven, Richard tells Big Tootch that he doesn't like waiting for King to get back. He doesn't like the feel of things, so he'll take the mare mule overland on the back path to intercept King south of town and talk to him before he comes through.

"I don't want him to drive in here unprepared," he says. "I want him to know about what happened on the Broadnax field before he gets in here."

"All right. Maybe I'll check on Selma later."

"You go ahead. Kids be all right. Put Little Richard in charge, and tell 'em I'll be back directly."

Jones is glad to hear from Big Tootch that Richard has gone ahead. Relieved, he leaves the house to chop cotton. Knowing that Selma has company and Richard is on the road, he stays only half on guard.

———

King leaves Columbus earlier than he expected. He never sleeps well alone, so when he awakens early, he figures he might as well get going. He's told Selma he'll be back by eight. Closer to seven means he can pull a full morning before midday dinner, then catch a nap and get in a few more hours with Jones while it's still light. He'll leave the removal of the stumps until the next day, when he's fresh. Then, too, he'll need to hire someone to work with him the rest of this month. Jones is a trooper, but Junior, the 230-pound son he's just given to the U.S. Army, was a workhorse.

King has bought a crate of funny-named hybrid chicks for Selma. Folks in Columbus raved about disease resistance and heavy laying. Selma makes a nice piece of change with her egg-and-butter business. She'll be surprised. And this will be a good start at some piggy-bank money for Bobo.

He gives Bobo a chick to play with in the truck to keep him quiet. The boy has behaved as well as he ever did, flattered to be admired by the recruiters, shown off by Junior, petted by the military wives in evidence at the margins. In the truck, he plays with the chick and then asks for a story. Together they recount "That's the Way of the World." King gives him corn bread and jam that he paid the woman they stayed with to pack for them, then water out of one of the mason jars they brought for the purpose. The corn bread is not Selma's and neither is the jam; even the water tastes rusty. They talk about their own sweet well back home. They stop by the woods so that the boy can pee into the ditch. It is still dark. He and the chick go to sleep.

Except for the boy's easy breathing, King feels very alone. Junior's gratitude has been so thorough that King understands that his son will never return to the land. Neither of King's children was a farmer, the others have died, and Selma, for all her nubile health and strength, has not brought one to term. King chews a little tobacco to help him stay awake. But in the dark truck cab, fatigue settles into him. Junior waved good-bye, and King's heart sank. King does not allow himself to imagine Junior's not coming back. He'll come back from the war, King thinks, but not to this land. You had to admire the boy for trying so hard. For someone who didn't really want to farm, he was a marvel: smart, steady, flexible, strong; he has played the role of the son a farmer prays for. King already misses his easy company.

Just before dawn, King stops to relieve himself and wakes Bobo to make him go, too. He removes the chick, still alive, somehow, from the sleeping boy's hand. He'll tell Selma that these little chickens can survive any damn thing.

It looks to him in the half-light as if he has only eleven chicks, not a dozen, after he's replaced the one, but he will not take time by the side of the dark road to check. Instead, as he drives, the missing chick plays in his head idly, like the end of a joke his stepfather used to tell, but that never seemed funny to him as a child, perhaps because he knew only the punch line.

—*So I asked: What the hell happened to those chickens?*

—*He told me: they flew the coop.*

Such a silly phrase. Chickens don't. That's why we call 'em chicken, he said, amusing himself. He guesses that that was what was supposed to be funny.

———

Mitchell knows Needham's truck a ways off. When he sees it turn the bend, he drives his own truck into the middle of the road to block it.

"Here he comes."

"Okay. We home." Fairlie says it to no one in particular. He notices that Mitchell is trying to take the lead. That irks him, like everything else. With his own rope no less.

King sees Mitchell's truck in the road and takes in the scene. The boy is awake. Fairlie Broadnax striding up to Mitchell's truck. Clementine, Potts, Strayhorn, the hateful ex-mayor James. James, Potts, and Mitchell, of course, came with the group who harassed King about the dogs ten years ago. That's what they do. Broadnax is different. King slows the car just enough so that he can decide whether he has room to wheel it there or can reverse up the road out of their running distance and then spin around.

He sees Greenie Nightingale, though, and hesitates. What is Greenie doing here? He thinks that maybe he'll give Greenie one of the chicks after whatever this fracas will be. God knows Greenie doesn't have a pot to piss in. At that moment, Pickerelle's car drives up behind him. Fairlie is running toward him, Butch Broadnax next. They are unarmed.

King throws open the passenger door, and in as firm and calm a voice as he can, says quietly to Bobo: "I want you to get out and run home. You know the way from here? Across the field, up the nanny goat hill. Run straight there. Tell Nana Selma I'll be along."

"Can I take my chick?"

"Not now. I want you to run. Go home. Fast."

Then he shouts in a bass that reverberates through Bobo's body: "The boy's goin home now!"

The field freezes while he runs, afraid now, hearing King's hard voice, clipped. This is not what King thought at first. He smells their fear and his own. Like hogs start to squeal when you take one out to slaughter. They know the difference.

Go home. Fast. Go home. Fast. Go home. Fast. Go home. Fast. Go home. Fast.

Maybe he's too suspicious. Although any black man who's not must be crazy. It makes him smile. While the men watch, King uses his position, leaned over toward the passenger door, to grab for his pistol in the glove box, but for the first time in years he has locked it, just for this trip, to make sure that the boy can't get at it accidentally. Jesus. They are almost on him, excited, because it has happened so fast, because they weren't ready yet, because the boy running out of the truck has sealed the deal.

As they run to him, they say: *We just wanna talk, Needham. Step out here and talk for a minute. Needham?* They believe themselves.

King has slipped the keys from one hand to the other and turned the knob on the glove box toward the unlocked position. Strayhorn and Clementine have planned to speak. The price he's asking for the Broadnax field is too high. The Old Broadnax did not realize he'd signed a bill of sale without the ten-year return clause. That was a very bad move. Unreasonable, and now Fairlie's back, and disinherited. That's what they'd say.

And Butch had planned to say that he would've done something about it except that the old man didn't tell him anything until it was done. Until he was taking the old sharecrop house off to put on their land. Which, by rights, he should have gotten the hog houses, too.

Strayhorn and Clementine try to keep Fairlie back, because he's so hotheaded. He hasn't lived here in Gunnerson with King and his people. Fairlie's been away, and they know how to talk to King. He may be an arrogant son of a bitch, but he'll back down, and everything will go on. You can't make a living with everybody at one another's throat all the time. They know towns like that. Gunnerson's not that kind of town.

But Fairlie and Butch push past them and try to throw both doors open. King is laid out sideways.

King kicks at them with his feet as hard as he can, visualizing the fields next to him, where to run. He pulls at the glove box, but the door does not open.

Greenie is shouting something from behind.

Which way can he go?

What does he know that they don't?

What does he know that can save him, except that the wind blows backward and they, too, are breathing in the ashes of their children? His grandson with crinkly half-moon eyes will not be safe unless he interposes his body between these men and the future.

Broadnax shouts.

They take the kicks in their bellies from his big feet, stronger than any that have ever dared assault them. Greenie thought they were only going to talk. He calls to King to stop now, while there's still time.

Potts is knocked down, backward, and Clem steps in to take his place. Four of them try to push the feet toward the other door, which Fairlie is smashing into his head. Once, twice, three times. He's come up so hard and the head and shoulders have taken a lot of punishment. Take the hit. Pulled off a mule, knocked off the dray, pushed against the barn wall by the bull when the cow was in heat. Take the hit. There's pain somewhere; do not take notice. What works? He coils his body to spring again. It responds slowly. His hands still work fine.

Fairlie is the first to see when the glove box falls open that it holds a small pistol. He didn't expect it; he didn't expect the strong hand that jabs out across the cab to reach for it. Fairlie is terrified now. "He's got a gun!" He keeps ramming the door. "Jesus, Butch, grab 'is hand."

Butch does grab the hand, and it pulls him into the window, slamming Butch's weight into the door, making it slam even harder into King's head and shoulders. From behind them a tire iron appears. The first time it misses King's head, catches King's and Butch's arms, intertwined, and breaks the window glass. The men scream at Butch to let go, because he's in the way, but he cannot, because King drags his arm over the glass, skin, flesh, muscle, ligament, laid back to the bone.

"Goddamnit, somebody help him," Fairlie screams. His brother is in shock. His open mouth does not even yell. "Gimme the tire iron, Greenie!"

Greenie delivers, but falls, and Strayhorn steps on him. Greenie rolls to the side sick with it all, begging God's forgiveness. They never even talked to King like Fairlie said they would. Greenie knows he shouldn't have come. He needs another drink. He crawls toward the stand of oaks, hoping that the woods will open up and swallow him.

It is hard, backbreaking work to subdue King Needham. He is a dangerous animal, a black snake that can strike when you think you've got him, after you've bashed him with the shovel, cut off his tail. The fangs are still poison. The muscles can still contract on their own. Put your eye out, bite you or something. Butch will never have the use of that arm again. Strayhorn's knee is damaged. Fairlie's got the shakes. Thank God the big red Negro was laid out when they started, not sitting, not standing on his own two feet. Jesus. He is an animal. It's like trying to stop a bull with your bare hands.

Martin Mitchell has gone crazy. He's on the driver's side by the feet. He runs around and grabs the tire iron from Greenie, who's rolling on the ground like a goddamned little girl. He raises the tire iron in his hand and the others stand clear of him, because he is swinging wild, hitting the hood, the car door, hitting Needham's legs, shattering the windows, and grabbing through the window at the great, flailing, dangerous, bloodied body. King tore up Butch's arm. Mitchell cuts up his own arm. It bleeds onto the car door and down his side. He lets out war yells like an Indian.

"Shut up, Mitch," Clem yells.

Mitchell opens his mouth, spreading wide the brown stumps of jagged teeth. He roars into Clem's face like boys roar at the cat. *Raaahhhhhr!*

King can only recoil and propel himself one way or the other. They'll smash either way. He has to get out, because otherwise they'll kill him here in the cab of his own truck. He has to get out, past the berry bushes, where the creek ran. It's mud-and-stone now. He knows it well, and they'll lose their footing. He could get up to Selma's mare. No, the mare is gone. He thinks of her new chicks.

He has to keep thinking. The pain is coming down now, blunt and terrible, to distract him, but he must keep thinking to stay alive. He has to get out of the cab. He has to sit up or else shoot out feet first. He tries to push out with his feet, but something keeps bashing from that end. He kicks and the door gives way, but then they push in again. Now they are trying to grab his arms, because he's managed to thrash away from the head bangings. They are pulling open the door, and he crouches to spring. But someone has tied his legs. Now they are pulling. He draws his knees up as far as he can and shoots his legs out. One man falls down. He can hear him. It's an opening. With legs together, he kicks again. The rope loosens. It's wrapped, but not tied. A few more and he'll pull his arms back from protecting his head and spring out onto his feet. He'll get only one or two more kicks.

Mitchell has given three men the rope to pull tight around Needham's legs. It's hard to get the rope underneath. Potts yells: "Wrap it!"

Clementine dives down and takes a hit to the face. King's boots break his jaw. Clementine rolls to the side. This time they leave him be. Potts calls for Greenie to help, but Greenie has disappeared. The rope finally encircles the legs.

"Pull!" Mitchell hollers. He raises the tire iron. King falls back, then springs, feet touching the ground, legs straight. They almost lose him. Mitchell smashes at air. He bashes the running board. He wounds himself. But he doesn't stop until he hears bone crack in the legs. King howls a low strangling snarl like a bear and starts to slump back into the truck. Can't go down; he knows it.

He must be finished off before he strikes again.

———

Because the air is disturbed and the animals are restive, stamping, frightened, Jones runs back to the dry stone wall where he'd first heard, then seen, the girl's dog, and then the girl. He looks over the wall and sees the cars. He sees the Ford, and he sees them bunched like ants on either side of a caterpillar. He sees the smoke. Jones jumps the stone wall and runs down the hill. He trips and tumbles, rolls to a stop, gets up, and runs on. He runs across the field of stumps and holes, into the road and halfway up the next field, by the creek bed, and next to the woods.

———

Greenie, crawling into the woods: *You shouldn't have done it, Big Boy.* Whatever it was to make the men so angry. Because blame is better than nothing, better than this.

Jones does not think as he runs between them. He jumps onto the grille of the truck and onto the hood, colored boy among white men, so afraid that he isn't afraid anymore, past fear, walking on coals with soul bared, naked as the mermaid, mounting the hot metal hood barefoot to make them stop, make them hear him, distract them for a moment from this thing that cannot happen. He looks around, so insane with fear that he cannot recognize their faces, but only sees Greenie Nightingale curled up in a ball by the woods. No one would believe—no one but Jared—how out of his mind he was to see King like that. If they'd asked him who was there, what would he have said? *King was there. King was still there.*

"*I* found the girl. *I* found her. He wa'n't even here!" Jones shouts.

Stunned at the insane conceit, they stop beating King, whose face is smashed, like an Easter egg, if you believe in Resurrection, which they do, and whose lower body is broken.

King hears Jones's voice. Jones hears King's thoughts.

Don't let Selma see.

King's thinking has bled into pain beyond his imagining, as sharp and long and blunt, as varied as possible, simultaneous and everywhere. Jones's voice slices through and what is left of King's tongue explodes inside his head.

please please mama please mama please
jesus make it stop please please god

Butch knocks Jones off the hood of the car with his one good arm. Jones feels the fall resonate through his thin body in waves. Then someone kicks him in his side and back. He cries like a baby. He cries for Selma and then for the mother he's never known. Jones doesn't know who does it, but someone hits him in the back of the head so hard that he thinks he has died with King, which is the best he can hope for.

He holds out his hand to the man who raised him and asks him to carry him in his arms. King carried him once, when he fell and the ground knocked him out. Jones had felt the power of each thigh pumping up the hill. They'll die together and have company. They'll die easy as long as Selma doesn't see.

———

She doesn't. She and Big Tootch are baking loaves of applesauce cake for the silly damn Broadnax girl who fell into the hole and for King, because he likes applesauce cake with cinnamon, and for Richard and Big Tootch's children. As a treat.

———

And because Bobo gets lost in the cornfield, which has grown enough in just three days to look different to him, after eight minutes he finds himself in Richard and Big Tootch's field, tries to backtrack and ends up at Mitchell's cows before he can find the fence he recognizes. *Go home. Fast.*

He tried to go too fast and got lost in the oaks. He knows what he is: he is a dumb little shit. Now he settles down and walks deliberately, determined not to get lost again. Wishing he took the chick.

———

At the end, they kill him there in the Ford. Fairlie, who is the only one experienced with a pistol, shoots King with his own gun. Pickerelle watches the scene. It was crudely done for certain. The men are bruised, bloodied, stiff from their labor. Pickerelle thinks to himself that had he known King would have beat them up this badly, he would have recruited a doctor. Butch needs a doctor something awful. Strayhorn leans against the car, bent over. They are out of breath and shaking. He is too heavy to drag out of the truck. Pickerelle hands Broadnax a gallon of gasoline from the trunk of his car, and motions toward King's truck with his chin.

At the end of the road, Pettiford drives past, then reverses to peer down the road. The truck catches on fire, and the injured men limp away from it. Pickerelle grabs the boy Jones and drags him to the road.

"Jesus Christ, what have they done?" Pettiford asks Pickerelle.

"It was a terrible accident," Pickerelle says. "Can you put the kid on a train?"

"No," Pettiford says.

"You're a pain in the ass, Ross," Pickerelle says.

"It's your mess," he said to the judge. "You and your boys can clean it up." Then, on second thought, he looks at Jones and the desperate men and opens the back door of his car. No telling what else they might do. "Put him in."

Pettiford will never forget the sight of the truck burning. And chicks hopping around on the ground behind it.

Though unconscious, Jones hears the fire. Later, it's what he remembers.

Selma smells the rubber smoke and burning flesh, and steps outside. Here comes Bobo, trudging alone. Richard rides up on the mare mule. He and Big Tootch hold her back from going over the hillside. He puts her and Big Tootch onto the mare mule and sends them to his house for the car. Selma breaks away from them and runs toward the orchard hill. Bobo sees her and follows. At the top, she looks down on the Ford, in flames, and then men standing 'round, smoking.

They hear her when she screams.

―――――

Jones awakens the next day on a freight car, surprised to be alive. Someone has paid his fare to Philadelphia. In his pocket has been stuffed a hundred-dollar bill. He tries to tell people in Philadelphia what has happened. They tell him that those things don't happen anymore.

―――――

Rayne awakens before dawn.

He has curled his body around Lillie's. They are naked, but safe.

The wind blows from the south and the branches continue to scratch on the window.

He will be given only this one dream.

His pillow is soaked with tears and snot. The smell of smoke clings to his nostrils. They have breathed in King. He is lodged in their cells. He trickles through the groundwater. There will be no cold case for the heirs. No triumph. Only the land if they can hold on to it. And life abundant, if they choose.

He moves Lillie's hair out of his face. She'll cut it soon to keep Temika's kid company. Maybe it will help the child heal.

CHAPTER 29

I nmates controlled almost nothing at Graterford prison. They could not determine who drove up to the facility to see them, certainly, but they did have some control over who was prohibited. Until Jewell could convince her father that she'd reunited with Rayne, until Rayne confirmed the fact in writing, Bobo would not put his daughter onto his approved list of visitors. But after four weeks and four letters she arrived at the facility, which hulked on the yellow-green and pink Pennsylvania spring landscape like a cursed castle: big and impenetrable, so set apart that she almost expected it to disappear and swallow her up once she had driven onto the parking lot.

She called Jack once she'd turned off the engine. "Okay, sweetie," she said. "I'm here. Now, I'm going to turn off the cell phone and put it into my bag and lock the bag in the trunk."

"That's fine. Thanks for reminding me. I won't be calling, though, 'cause Lillie's acupuncture lady's coming again at nine-thirty."

"The black Korean?"

"Yes, she's marvelous. Blasian, I'm told, is the argot: black and Asian. I asked Nurse Barb to come so they can meet."

"Okay, no more talking. Love you."

She'd arrived just before visiting hours began at 9:00 a.m., as the website advised, wearing approved clothing, bringing no contraband, just a disposable bag with a small loaf cake, and carrying her Pennsylvania driver's license and car registration information, change, and keys in her jacket pocket.

Then Jewell had parked on the wrong side of the parking lot. She walked to the wrong doors, then went back to the main entrance and took a number. By now she was no longer early. She was called sooner than some others, however, and they gave her bad looks as she walked past them, back through the metal detector to another building, up a staircase, and reported there. She asked whether she'd be allowed to bring her father the food she'd made for him. The other visitors tripped their tongues and rolled their eyes. In the maximum-security visiting room, the only food allowed had to be bought from the vending machines and eaten there. She was going to the OSU, where rules were different, according to the prison website, but the regulations were so stringent, and so perfectly followed, it seemed to her, that she had to ask. She didn't want pound cake thrown into the trash. The guard repeated that she should get to the OSU and talk to the officer there.

Bobo appeared fifteen minutes later, a big gray man: gray-and-black hair cropped close, a gray rim around his drooping brown eyes, and deep lines from those eyes down to a hard, gray-stubble chin. On his hulking Needham body, he wore a gray correctional institution suit. He led a sleek young German shepherd, which he put on a down-stay before he acknowledged Jewell.

"Still gorgeous, I see," he said. "You didn't tell me that in your letter. What are you now, like, fifty?" There was no smile, but also none of the old malice. No one else had come into the visiting area yet. The stark and battered waiting room echoed.

They were allowed to embrace here, but they did not. "Forty-seven. I run now," she said rather nonsensically. Hair dye, she thought. "And you've stayed very fit."

"Well, look where I am. And I train dogs now. It's the best job in here, and Blue—don't tell the others—Blue is the best dog so far. Aren't you, Blue?" he asked in a gentle voice.

The dog's ears moved with intelligent attention. Its eyes registered Bobo's every movement, but it did not change position. "Good boy," Bobo said, acknowledging the dog's temptation to get up, and its internal discipline.

They talked about Bobo's move to the OSU unit, where he had more privacy, a real bathroom, and a microwave. "So, the physical realm," as he referred to his living conditions, "has greatly improved. Socially, the OSU is more like a rooming house, or a halfway house, I guess you could say. The men here have worked to get here. Up there," he said, inclining his head toward the main buildings, "you've got what this one chaplain calls 'the festival of dysfunction.'" He shook his head. "You know the old movies with synchronized swimming? Well, in there, you've got synchronized issues. Coordinated craziness. My spiritual guide's been in here for twenty years, and he's the most peaceful man you'll ever meet. I said I wanted to be like that, and he'd tell me to do this and that, and I'd just say: you couldn't get sane in the middle of a nuthouse.

"And he would just look at me and say that line that Richard Pryor said Jim Brown would say to him when he was smoking like a thousand dollars of crack a day. He'd say to 'im: *'Whatchoo gonna do?'*

"Usually Abdul Mohammed don't make jokes. He's, like, a real serious cat."

Jewell translated: Abdul Mohammed was humorless. Who else, she thought, would have helped Bobo come up with the name Ghaffar?

"Like I said, he's, like, a real serious dude, but he'd just walk by and whisper it—*Whatchoo gonna do?*—and crack himself up. He reached out to a lotta guys, but if you're busy throwing yourself a pity party or a rage-fest, there is no answer. You just stuck.

"But I thank God, whom I choose to call Allah, the all-merciful, because He let me see that Abdul Mohammed had something these other dudes didn't have."

Given that mentorship over five years, conversion to Islam had been the end, not the beginning, of a gradual transformation. Rayne had been a big part of his change. "I say that Abdul Mohammed schooled me, but Rayne made me able to be redeemed. He did. After he came back North, even when he was in college—no car; I don't know how he did it—the boy came to us here faithfully once a month. I used to say, 'like a bitch gets a period.'"

"Wow."

"I know. Now, I say, he came as regular as the phases of the moon. That son of yours is a marvel. Ain't nothing he can't do."

"I want to thank you for helping to raise him."

Bobo humphed. "Selma's the one."

"Oh! Speaking of Selma: I brought you some of her lemon–poppy seed pound cake."

"Hers?"

"No, her recipe."

"You seen 'er?"

"No, although Lonnie—Rayne—and Jones said that she's gotten weaker."

He used the hand sanitizer she offered, then ate a slice of the cake. "Wow," he said, closing his eyes. "Don't they say that taste is, like, the strongest sense? Takes you right back.

"Rayne's something else, ain't he? No thanks to us."

Jewell didn't like his brand of honesty, which seemed somehow to slap her harder than it did him, but then, she reminded herself, she was looking for fault. "And he's having to face this heir property stuff really without much help from the family. He's going to have to organize us, I'm afraid, if we're not to lose the land."

"Anybody gotta handle this business, he the one to do it."

"But he shouldn't have to do it alone. I owe it to him to help," Jewell said, as much to herself as to her father.

"Good. Maybe that's your job. Good thing he found you."

"And he's just learning that King's death was not accidental."

Bobo took his eyes from her face and back to the dog. Blue noticed the shift in Bobo's attention. Jewell, who'd kept dogs for years, had never seen such exquisite attunement. Abdul-Ghaffar stood and walked the dog around the room. With a hand movement he had the dog sit in a far corner. Then he turned his back on the dog, walked to Jewell, and squatted down to face her eye to eye. "I've become an adherent to the teachings of the prophet Mohammed."

"Yes. I looked up your name. Abdul-Ghaffar, servant of the Forgiver."

"I have been forgiven. That's a wonderful thing to know. But it's a more difficult thing to live up to. Do you know what I mean?"

Jewell looked between him and the dog, who leaned from one front leg to the other in anticipation, then, as if recovering its dignity, stayed freeze-frame still. "Yeah. I think I do." She wished that they could embrace as she'd embraced Rayne, and begin to let love soak into dried, cracked openings. But they stayed still. She stayed as still as the dog and spoke through specific and articulate lips, which, to their credit, did not want to spit or curse anymore. "Rayne was wanting to open up a cold case investigation. If he can find Broadnax alive somewhere."

"Come 'ere."

Jewell almost missed it, the tiny plume of Bobo's voice tossed lightly into the air, higher and softer than she'd ever heard. Low, carefully, stealthily, Blue came and sat where Abdul-Ghaffar's pointed finger indicated, next to him. Bobo stayed on one knee, his face close to Jewell's. His was the same bitter-smelling breath, as if his insides were burning up.

"Tell him," he said almost as quietly as he'd spoken to the dog, "that that won't be necessary. Tell him that there's no more Broadnax to find. You hear me what I'm sayin?"

"That's what I figured."

"Good, you figured it."

"It was this time of year, wasn't it? Not King, but what we're talking about."

"Yeah, it was."

"The night you caught me in the flue-cure barn with that boy from Los Angeles?"

"Yeah."

"It wasn't about me, then, really. That last couple weeks, all those nights." He knew what she meant; the nights he sat outside on the land, in different places, but often on the Broadnax land, blending in with the shadows, cradling King's shotgun in his lap. He'd told her he was going to make sure that she didn't bring any more boys onto the land to make any new babies. The man from Los Angeles who made movies had come over from Charleston to photograph her when Bobo was away, driving his 18-wheeler somewhere—Ohio, Illinois, New York—and Selma was working. Now Jewell knew that she had been his excuse. Like the article said, Broadnax had come back into town, and Bobo must have known that he'd be unable to keep himself from coming onto the land he thought should be his. This is what Jewell had figured out, and what she came here today to have her father confirm. It occurred to her that she should have come for forgiveness or to forgive. But at least she was here.

"I've worked my way to the OSU, and soon I'll be eligible for parole. You know what I'm in for? Rayne tell you? Not for anything that happened in late March twenty-five years ago. So I'm not wanting to stay on this track. But because Allah is all-merciful, I do have the option of praying every day. People all over the world pray every day, all day, for all kinds of things. I didn't know that before. So I lived in a world without prayer. Anything can happen in that world. Do you understand me?"

"Yes."

"I also pray for forgiveness for beating you that night. I really hadn't expected to find you outdoors. I had a-uh—a lot more to do that night. And I packed out a load to go cross-country, you hear me what I'm sayin—and my nerves were beyond shot. I found you there, and I lost it.

"It's the best amends I could do for you to try to help raise your son. You understand. I screwed that up, too—and damned if the kid doesn't come visit every month. All-merciful, I'm telling you."

He moved his glasses up and down and sighed as he sat heavily in a chair beside her, and called the dog to come between his knees for gentle rubbing.

"These dogs go to the blind, you know, and they go to vets with posttraumatic stress. I love each of these dogs, and then I give 'em up." He smiled at her. "It's the only thing I've ever done right in my whole life."

Jewell stood. "If I give you the rest of this cake, can you take it with you?"

"If you leave it here on the chair, my man Mr. Gregory over here and I can finish it off before I go back. How about that?"

He opened his arm wide and held her to his gray cotton chest. It was the same movement that Rayne had made. She rested against him, and let the one help her embrace the other. He spoke into her perfumed mahogany hair. "You tell my boy Rayne that if there's anything had to be done, I already did it. Okay? Tell 'im stay clean. That other thing is over."

"I will."

"And look, I'm sorry. You hear me? 'S all I can say."

————

When Jewell came home, Jack was asleep. She lay sideways in his hospital bed to be close to him, and when she awoke, he was tracing the curving hairline on her temple, breathing each breath like a countdown.

"He killed Broadnax, Jack."

"You had already figured that out, Jewelly. Which is why he lost it and beat you so badly."

"He'd already killed him, I'm pretty sure, and I must have been very close to the body."

"What do you think he did with him, with it, the body?"

"I think he stuffed him in his eighteen-wheeler. It was right there, a tenth of a mile away, on the road, packed for, I don't know, somewhere."

"And dumped him somewhere far away?"

"He must have."

"So they could never find the body. God, that's chilling. No wonder you wanted to get away."

They lay together, listening to each other's breath.

"Is it justice?" she asked.

"Maybe."

Jewell lay back, thinking of the stark prison with the bales of razor wire and the family members she saw driving in on her way out of the parking lot. She thought of the exquisite black eyebrows of the dog Blue shifting articulately at each of her father's sighs. "He thinks that it was his duty to do it, and his business alone and his crime and his punishment. All these years of being tortured.

"But we *all* paid for it. We *all* paid. He does not get it. Lonnie paid, too. He doesn't even know that he's been paying, I'm sure."

"I hate to sound like the white guy," Jack said, "but . . ."

"You're feeling sympathy for the devil."

"Some." Jack took as deep a breath as he could. They were getting shallower, as if some tiny character from an Edgar Allan Poe story were bricking up the walls of his lungs, brick by tiny brick. "The dead guy's family paid, too. I'm sure they've paid dearly."

CHAPTER 30

J udge Hortense Needham-Reece, Rayne's favorite cousin, Binky, made the date for the conference call to bring in help for Rayne.

"It's heir property," she told him, "and despite what one overworked, overwhelmed, and undervalued stubborn old lady may think, Cousin Rayne, the heirs really must work together. And can, Ray. I mean, that's the good news." She suggested the initial members of a family leadership council that included members from the three brothers' branches, plus Jones, acting for Selma. They'd include all the generations but not bring in, to start, her mother, Big Tootch, who tended, let's face it, to argue with everyone, or old Uncle Amos, who couldn't hear. Binky also insisted on inviting to the leadership an upbeat Methodist minister, Ivy Ivans. She was the child of Amos's old age, born to his neighbor lady live-in after Aunt Mary's death.

"She's pretty proactive," Binky told Rayne. "Kind of a loose cannon, but these are black people you're related to—even your mother—and you need clergy involved. Trust me."

Selma disagreed until Ivy appeared at her trailer door the next week, on Monday, her day off, alone. She was a Needham, all right, with the heavy, arched brows and precise bow lips that seemed to open and close on their own. She wore her black hair clipped very short.

"Well, how'd you get down here?"

Ivy reported matter-of-factly that she'd flown to Savannah that morning, and driven to Gunnerson to meet the aunt about whom her father had told her so many stories. She wondered if Selma would have a private prayer service with her right at that moment, for the family for whom King had so richly provided, for the land that Selma had preserved from his ancestors and for his heirs, including those, like Ivy, who had been invited back into the family. She wanted Selma's blessing on her, and on the family's proceedings.

Selma commented that she didn't know what the Negroes were up to, because they didn't tell her anything, and she wasn't interested besides, unless someone said they were going to pay the taxes. And the water and sewer.

Ivy had brought decaf coffee, crumb cake, and orange juice. They drank the coffee while Selma enumerated her bills, and told which ones Rayne was already paying, and how she couldn't ask him for more.

Ivy pulled out a small white stole, which she draped around her neck, and her Bible and a Communion set. "Will it be all right?"

"Sure," Selma said. "I never turn down Communion."

Ivy read from Paul's letter to the Romans: they had not received the spirit of slavery and fear, but the spirit of adoption—and thanked God that Selma had lived that spirit in the Needham family.

Selma nodded.

And, Ivy went on, because they were not slaves, but children, and if children, then heirs of God, through Christ, with whom they suffered, and in whom they would be glorified. She took out the little silver plate and chalice, the size of a liqueur glass, and wine and said a shortened Communion mass, quietly, but with reverence. Selma mouthed some of the words with her, ate the wafer, and drank the grape juice. At the end of the service, Selma said: "Sounds like Easter."

Then they were silent. Selma felt a not unpleasant but deep-purple sadness. She was content to taste the grape juice and the last trace of gummy wafer on her tongue and watch the younger woman polish her miniature chalice and paten and pack them up into her brown leather box.

Then Ivy said to her: "Amos never married my mother, Aunt Selma. But my oldest sister brought me into the family through the spirit of adoption. When she did, she told me about you, how you adopted Uncle Bobo after his mother died, and then this little cousin Rayne I'd never met. Anita told me that that's the sort of family we should have. She said that that's what Uncle King died for."

"Nobody ever come down here from Philadelphia and took note of it before."

"It takes people time, sometimes, to do what's right, Aunt Selma. But I think a reunion here this summer—"

"Oh, no. Oh, no. Where am I gonna put all them Negroes? Troopin around the place. I barely get JJ to put in a little crop, and I'm tryin to get a better orchard established over on the Broadnax field before Pettiford's grandson steal it away from me."

"What if I tell you that some of these people can help with that?"

"Well, where has they been? And how they gonna help? You

290 • LORENE CARY

show me one who can transplant a pecan tree, other than my Ray."

"Could I do a Thanksgiving service here, then? Whoever comes, comes? They would bring their tents if they want to camp out; they bring their own food. And we have a service for the family . . ."

Selma's eyes brimmed behind her reading glasses, which she'd put on for their Bible reading. She withdrew her hands from Ivy's to reach for her handkerchief in her sleeve. "What you could do," she said, "is say a funeral for my husband. A memorial service I guess it would be by now. None of them ever came to bury him. Well, we couldn't really. Didn't really have anything left to bury."

Ivy tried to understand what she meant. It seemed incomprehensible that the man would have died and not been properly buried. "Aunt Selma, did your church have a service for him then? I mean, even without remains we can say the burial service."

"The Reverend did a little something for me. But there was so much confusion. And everyone was afraid. And then Richard and Tootch were leaving. They sold out to Pettiford, so I tol 'em don't bother."

"Oh, Aunt Selma."

"Yep. I did. And I've been sorry. He was Richard's brother, too. 'Course your father offered to come. He always were decent like that.

"But you could do a service for King. And any wanna come pray here, on his land, that'd be all right with me."

Ivy took Selma's hands back into hers. The old lady sat so proudly, and so alone. Ivy finished reading:

"Who shall separate us from the love of Christ? Shall tribulation, or distress, or persecution, or famine, or nakedness, or peril, or sword? . . . Nay, in all these things we are more than conquerors through him that loved us. For I am persuaded, that neither death, nor life, nor angels, nor principalities, nor powers, nor things present, nor things to come, nor height, nor depth, nor any other creature, shall be able to separate us from the love of God, which is in Christ Jesus our Lord."

"Except, really," Selma said. "Those people ain't comin down here for no memorial service. Nice of you, but they won't come."

Ivy thought for a minute and sent a text to Rayne. "How about doing the wedding in Gunnerson?"

Thirty minutes later, Rayne texted back: *lillie sez yes.*

———

On the appointed day for the phone conference, Binky reported that she'd talked to Pettiford, the grandson, who had made some blustery remarks at first. He'd built the golf course with a lot of hard work; he'd hired a pro; he had two companies giving careful consideration to a new tournament there, which would bolster the entire county's economy. His grandfather had been a great benefactor to so many people, and it was the Needham clan itself that had given his grandfather a stake in the heir property, after all his help. Plus they'd loaned them money over the years, interest-free, as far as he could see. So, to continue his grandfather's tradition of benevolence, maybe he could swap the heir property claim for the Old Broadnax farm, for which he had better use than Mrs. Selma.

Binky told her family that she'd just called him the night before, a Friday, and scheduled the conference call for Saturday morning to make sure that he would not have any business days' head start on them in case he tried to force a sale. Now that he'd been alerted, they had to move fast.

Ivy asked whether Rayne and Selma could sneak in a visit to the grandfather before the week was out.

Rayne had work left over from the week before, because of bad rain. "I don't know," he said. "I've got jobs this week. It takes all day to drive . . . You really gotta get Nana Selma on board . . ."

"Well, think of it like this," Binky said in her warning judge voice, "as the Center for Historic Preservation has told us, they can probably line up more dollars for purchase than we can, and they can likely do it faster. And they can argue land value at, I don't know, a couple million."

"Oh, my goodness." A few members said it at once. Rayne was sorry that Binky had injected the big number. It inflamed some and put fear into others.

Ivy spoke over the six-line mumble: "I say we zip Auntie Selma over to the old Pettiford's nursing home. She told me which one it is—it's an Episcopal facility; I've talked with the chaplain there—"

"Already?"

"Yeah—and present Mr. Pettiford with two checks: one for the eight thousand dollars Selma still owes him for the loan, plus interest—Uncle Jones, you say that's ready to go?"

"Yep, just say the word." Jones and Jared listened together on the old Bell Telephone console with a speakerphone feature that Jared claimed was better than the more modern versions. They raised their eyebrows together, satisfied that this group was making a move on a situation that had worried Jones for years.

"Great!" Ivy said. "Okay, and also a check for $2,614.98, which represents the five hundred dollars Pettiford paid Richard and Mary in 1942 for their 'share' of the land, plus two-point-five percent interest for sixty-seven years since 1942."

Rayne laughed into the phone. He'd thought that the minister would come along to provide moral persuasion. No one else was laughing. "Sorry."

"I was thinking ten percent," Jewell said. "That's what it would have made in stocks, you could argue." Jack was reclining next to her. He pulled down the corners of his mouth, shook his head gently, and mimed no. Jewell swiveled the receiver up over her head. "Too much?" she mouthed.

He nodded.

She handed him the telephone and went to the kitchen to get another extension, so that they could both listen.

"This is Rick in New York, Richard's grandson." Rick was a year away from retiring as a community outreach officer for a communications company. He introduced himself each time he spoke in a rounded soft-belly of a voice that sounded perpetually satisfied. He kept an eye on the story they were creating, and the spin. "I was thinking of lowballing them at three percent, making the case that that's what a savings account would have averaged over the years. But Ivy, how in the heck did you get it down to two-point-five? How do you justify that? The downturn in the economy? That's just recent."

"Victory bonds were three percent at the beginning of World War Two, Rick. My parishioner, a very funny man named Jubilee, almost got hit by a car, and that was all he talked about for weeks, was finding his Victory bonds," Ivy said.

"Jubilee?" Jewell asked. "Jubilee? Funny little short man?"

"Yeah," Ivy said. "Don't tell me you know him. Mr. Jubilee knows *everybody*."

"I'm the one who almost hit him."

The conference line made its quiet crackle and hum. Then Ivy spoke: "You're the crazy white lady?"

Jewell laughed along with the others. "How does one answer that?"

"Hah!" Ivy laughed loudly over the comments others were making. "You are the crazy white woman looking for her family!"

"I didn't say all that."

"Well, he's been prayin for you to find 'em ever since. He had some crazy name for you: Pearl or Ruby—"

"Those are jewels. He was trying to remember Jewell, I bet."

"Well, I guess we can take you off the prayer list now, since we found you. Oh, Lord. Mr. Jubilee strikes again."

"Uh, this is Rick. Very funny twist. Very funny, and I love the three percent war bonds thing, but, sorry to be so, uh, goal-oriented, but how did you get it down to two-point-five percent?"

"Oh, Rick!"

Binky couldn't help herself.

"No, he's right. Okay, Rick: turning, turning, we come down right."

Jack put down his phone extension altogether, having laughed so hard that he was having trouble breathing.

Ivy continued: "So, here's the little cheapie part: in 1942, the feds put a cap of two-point-five percent on government issues. I'm guessing they were just spending money hand over foot. So, anyway, since this money we're talking about changed hands in 1942, I thought we'd play by World War Two rules."

"This is Rick again. Ivy, that's brilliant. I don't know if it's Christian, strictly speaking, but it's brilliant."

Jack whispered: "See if anybody's got frequent-flier miles so Rayne can jump on the plane. And then he'd take Selma to the nursing home, so he'll need a rental car, too."

Binky volunteered her husband's miles and promised to send out an e-mail to collect others so that they could travel on demand a few times that spring. Rayne thanked them and looked at Lillie, on the cordless extension, who rolled her eyes and nodded that she'd make the ticket arrangements.

"But is the old man still making his own business arrangements?" Rayne asked. "I mean, say we go in there and drop a few thousand on him, and find out that he can't sign his name, or the grandson has power of attorney, and then we've bullied some old guy who was nice to the colored people. Makes me want to hit somebody."

Binky answered: "Now, Rayne, we know you're a big, strong man. No need to hit people."

"Especially not in the nursing home," Ivy said.

"This is Rick. But he's absolutely right about how it will look if he goes in trying to get some old guy to accept, what, like, ten thousand dollars for a parcel worth much more?"

"It's eight thousand in repayment for the loan, not for land," Louis said. He ran a small accounting business that did payrolls for beauty shops and day cares. "The twenty-six-hundred-dollar repayment of a five-hundred-dollar heir property share is not payment for land, because I think you could argue—Cousin Binky, you're the judge; Jack's the lawyer—that they got the share fraudulently."

"How fraudulently?" Rayne asked.

"Because if Pettiford was in the chamber of commerce and on the bank board back then, then he certainly knew that if there was no will, then they all owned it together, and that clearly, it was acting in pretty bad faith to buy into a share without telling the other principal owners, in this case the widow of the family patriarch."

Jones made some noises. "Well," he said. "Well, here's the other thing about that: he's gonna say that the only reason he bought it in the first place was to keep Richard from selling to Broadnax, because Richard was desperate to get out, and he'd sell to anyone. Sorry, Binky, Rick; don't none of this sound good. 'Cause Broadnax was tryin to find a way in to steal the land back then."

"This is Rick. No offense taken, Uncle Jones. My dad actually told us that that was the one thing he wished he could take back. My concern is that I know he tried once, and the old man wouldn't take his money back."

"Shit," Rayne breathed. "Sorry, guys."

"Well, that was a long time ago, and the circumstances are different now," Binky said. "Jack, are you on the line?"

"Yeah."

"Today's not a real strong day for Jack, everybody," Jewell said. "So he's trying not to talk a lot." But Friday was a good day, Jewell said, and Jack called an old U.S. congressman whom he had worked with on years of tobacco industry legislation and asked whether he knew and could get Jack a priority phone meeting with Pettiford the father, the state representative. And the congressman's people had arranged a Monday-afternoon phone call during lunchtime, which was when Binky said she could join in.

For now, they'd leave the grandson alone and go over his head.

Ivy ended the call with what she called the shortest and most necessary prayer for all family business: "Fear not!"

———

When Jack Thompson and Judge Hortense Needham-Reese came onto the Monday lunch call together, Pettiford's first question was whether Jack had mentioned this heir property business to the congressman.

"Well, I had to give him just a heads-up," Jack said suavely.

"But Representative Pettiford," Binky said with assurance, as if they were already good pals, "Jack and I have been double-teaming this whole effort, and I can tell you that he's just been as discreet as you'd want. We in the Needham family are really only recently working together in these new ways, and I'm just sorry I never had a chance to see Jack at work in a courtroom."

"May we tape this conversation?" Jack asked in a low voice just this side of a growl.

"Of course. I had nothing to do with any of this," Pettiford said.

"And if your family just sends us a notarized quitclaim, then it'll stay that way."

"I hope you haven't worried my father with this. This kind of thing gets him awfully agitated."

"Well, I believe that Mrs. Selma Needham has gone to visit him personally. But she tells me that she's an old family friend. She has cared for him, too, right? She says that your father was very good to her family."

"He's awfully fragile."

"I'll tell you what, I've learned that our older relatives have a steel in their spines that we mustn't fail to recognize," Binky said. "And our younger relatives sometimes need to be reined in."

"What are you talking about?"

"Representative Pettiford, Mrs. Needham is taking a check to your father that comprises the whole of the loan your son made to her, including whatever interest they agreed upon. But you ought to know that he was trying to cut a deal . . ."

"When?"

"This morning. Old folks are better in the morning."

Binky heard Jack's breath run out. She took up the thread. "The deal your grandson was trying to cut, Mr. Pettiford, was to get Mrs. Needham to turn over the entire parcel to him in exchange for his forgiving an eight-thousand-dollar debt."

"I'm sure he didn't mean exactly that."

"Yes, I'm sure he did. And there was just a hint of a threat, Mr. Pettiford, that he might force a sale of the heir property if she refused."

"We could have handled this without the visit. I wish you'd come straight to me."

"We have." Jack was using his emergency oxygen tank instead of his machine to keep down background noise. Now and then, he took the phone away from his mouth to keep from breathing too heavily into the receiver. Jewell had turned up the oxygen as far as it would go. He could hear that Binky was about to say something, but he cut in with a snarl, as much as he could muster. "I don't know what exactly happened to King Needham, but your father does, Mr. Pettiford, and so does Mrs. Needham's brother. He was there."

Binky continued, "It was enough to make my mom and dad cut and run. They were grateful that Mr. Pettiford paid them five hundred dollars to get started in a new and less threatening place, but believe me, they had no idea that they were endangering the entire parcel of heir property by selling him what they thought was theirs. We think that your father knew these things, Mr. Pettiford. If there had been no threat, then she would not have needed 'looking after,' as your family has called it."

"She's a very capable woman," Jack said.

"Why, certainly she is, but back then, there were a lot of people, frankly, who had no scruples about just finessing African-American widows and some of the illiterate people out of their land," Pettiford said. Then, catching himself, he added, "Of course I hardly need to tell you all that."

"Well, it still happens, Mr. Pettiford. I'm just letting you know that we believe she's being finessed now. And the other heirs—I mean, our conversation with your son did not reassure the judge at all. That's why we've called you directly before we do anything else. Because we know that your family doesn't need to finesse this family out of its property today."

"I resent that word, and I really resent the direction of this conversation. I resent your trying to muscle my father. My daddy was a great help to their family, Mr. Thompson, and he always thought of what he did for the family you represent as a gift."

"It's my family, Mr. Pettiford, through my wife. Let's think of it as a loan. Five hundred dollars invested in 1942. The children of Richard Needham figure that if you'd invested that in 1942 war bonds, you'd have about twenty-six hundred in the bank now."

"That's ridiculous. Do you know what the land is worth today?"

"The heirs are not selling the land, Mr. Pettiford. They're repaying a loan, with interest and gratitude. Are you the one to sign the quitclaim? Does your father do his own business or are you power of attorney? Can we have the quitclaim messengered over to you today? Binky, we can do that, can't we?"

"I can do it before court goes back into session if we stop talking about it and get off the phone in the next ten minutes."

"Look, wait till I'm back in Gunnerson. Don't send it here to my capital office."

"We'd hate to have to wait. Once these things are out . . ."

"I'll be there Friday. I see people there every Friday."

"And you'll talk to your son, so nothing changes between now and then?"

"You take care of your family; I'll handle mine."

"We'll enclose a FedEx envelope."

"Now, that's to my Gunnerson office."

"I'll make sure to let the congressman know what a help you've been," Jack said smoothly. "He's a great guy, isn't he?"

————

Jewell called Rayne. "You driving?"

"The rental car."

"Where's Selma?"

"Here, next to me."

"She feel like talking?"

"I don't think so. Let's just say we did what we went there to do. We left the check. And he has a whiteboard next to his bed, so I wrote that we'd been there and left the check. Then we told the nursing staff. Every damn body in the place knows. No more secret."

Selma sighed heavily.

"How'd he take it?"

"He cried. Asked whether 'the boy' was alive: Jones."

Jewell was silent.

"You hear me?"

"I heard you. It was hard for Selma?"

"Yep. Yep. And now, we're going to go order a headstone for King."

"No rest for the wicked," Selma said, her voice flat, just controlled, necessary.

"What did she say?" Jewell asked.

"Nothing. We're gonna get his full name. King Charles Freeman Needham. Did you know that?"

"I guess I did." Jewell would put that full name into the letter she'd been writing for a month. She'd mail it now for Rayne's sake, finally.

———

In the late afternoon in August, when everyone said it was too hot to do a wedding in South Carolina, the wedding party drove up to Selma's old Methodist church in a rented Town Car, because Lillie wouldn't marry from the truck, followed by the Needham "Family Leadership," and a dozen and a half other family members. They pulled up the driveway to the old church that King had helped build with his ten-dollar donation and the thousand feet of seasoned lumber. It was a simple old wooden building set up off the green grass with yellow bricks.

Afternoon sun passed directly through three large windows in front and seemed almost to pass through the back windows, sun and breeze moving through, to refresh tired sharecroppers whose short, hard lives brimmed with brutal losses. The signs said that the building had been built in 1925 and used as a church and school until the 1980s. Behind it sat a squat new Methodist church, air-conditioned, made of whitewashed concrete blocks.

Rayne and Lillie had been adamant about no pre-wedding parties or attendants or frills. Lillie had just taken her nursing exams, and Rayne was now working out a schedule that would allow him to do jobs in Philadelphia until December, then live in the old house in Gunnerson and begin construction on the family-run bed-and-breakfast during the winter. They'd had no time to plan, and refused to spend big wedding money with new travel costs. Exhausted, they invited Khalil to tell them what kind of wedding he'd like. He reminded them that it would be hot, and that everyone had told him about a great swimming hole down the hill from Selma's old church, the site of church picnics and baptisms. He wanted a swimming-hole wedding.

Accordingly, the bride and groom and guests were instructed to wear bathing suits under their clothes. In the trunk of the Town Car was a huge basket of fried chicken, and ice chests with champagne that Jewell and Jack had sent and lemonade and watermelon.

Ivy conducted the service with a reverent verve and dispatch. After fifteen minutes, in which everyone but the bride and groom fanned themselves, Rayne and Lillie were married, and the party began the walk down the hill toward the swimming hole, including Selma, who bounced in the wheelchair as long as she could, and then made her way with her walker. Lillie walked next to her, still wearing her off-white veil, attached by a headband to the slick short hair she'd just cut.

"It didn't used to be this far," Selma said several times.

Lillie gave her hand to Jones, who seemed almost apologetic to be stronger than Selma despite being several years older.

At the pond, the dark water lapped just the slightest bit. A few families had spread picnic tables with cloths. This was not the stunning seacoast or a man-made lake with paddleboats and cabanas. This swimming hole served local people, most of them white and working class. A few black families sat in little clumps, and a few black children joined the white children in the water, doing handstands, and swimming underwater while holding their noses shut. The sun was big and low in the west, burnished dark brass at the end of the day. Bronze light had begun to spill onto the river.

"A wedding!"

Others on the dirt beach moved their blankets to make room for the wedding party, who spread out, took drinks, and removed outer clothing self-consciously. Selma took off her shoes and knee-high stockings and placed them carefully on one corner of the blanket Lillie had spread for her. Then she folded carefully her pearl-gray dress. Underneath was a thin housedress. No way was Selma walking out of a wedding and straight into a bathing suit. Instead, she inched the walker to the water's edge, then called Khalil to run her housedress back to her blanket and then come into the water with her.

The wedding party watched the two at the water's edge, with puddles of orange-gold light splashing through the Spanish moss on overhanging trees. The sun backlit the boy's long, taut torso as he cartwheeled next to the great-great-grandmother. Her thin body sagged over the walker, and the skin on her thighs, which had once pulled 150-pound sacks of cotton, draped slightly toward her knees.

"Khalil!" Rayne called. "Watch Nana!"

"Look," Khalil shouted back. "She's taking her thing into the water."

Selma reached out and pinched him. "It's galvanized," Selma said. "It don't rust, and if it do, I'll get another one."

"You swim?" Khalil asked.

"I been swimmin since time began," she said. "One day I'm gonna swim back to Africa. Come on; show me something new."

"Okay, Dad," Khalil said loudly, and publicly, for the first time. He made a thumbs-up, and then did his own handstand next to her.

Selma called back that she would have to watch *him*.

Rayne and Lillie told the family that they were going back to the Town Car. Binky volunteered her niece and nephew to run the newlyweds' errands, but Rayne and Lillie waved them off. In the Town Car's air-conditioning they marveled at what they'd just done. Their bodies took in the luxury of the cool air. And time.

"You just want to get me pregnant, don't you?" she asked. "I felt it. I've been feeling it." She was partly joking.

"So what?" He smiled, seriously, almost relieved.

"And you're thinking that you might want to come live down here sometime?" she asked. "Come on, we're married. Talk to me now." These ideas had never occurred to her before, but when she said them, it was as if she'd always known.

"I might. Like standing in that church he built. So simple, but look at how the light comes through. I could build things here for a lot less."

Lillie wished her mother were alive. Then she kissed her new husband in the delicious newness of his commitment and twirled on his thick finger the gold ring that had been King's.

"Well, good thing about nursing," she said airily, "they got hospitals everywhere." She opened the car door to the hot and humid evening to return to their guests.

At the swimming hole, their family had taken over the two picnic tables. The burnt-orange wafer of a sun was dipping down over the rim of the world. Its rays glanced off Selma's galvanized walker, planted where she'd waded in. Rayne and Lillie breathed a single, sharp, fearful breath.

Then they saw her forty feet out in the pond, brown like the pond water, catching lavender-orange droplets of light as she laid her arm out along the water and her face toward the sky. Near her, Khalil broke the surface, laughing and proud, to gulp down all the air he could hold before diving back under.

Acknowledgments

I acknowledge gratefully the lavish resources and gifts of the mind and spirit that helped me write this book.

For space and time:
    Pew Fellowships in the Arts
    Yaddo
    Civitella Ranieri
    David and Rebecca Pepper Sinkler
    Helen Cunningham and Ted Newbold

For tough minds, generous hearts, and patience:
    Jane Dystel
    Miriam Goderich

For encouragement and strategy:
    Malaika Adero
    Todd Hunter

For careful attention:
Sybil Pincus
Martha P. Trachtenberg

For reading, listening, advising:
Rebecca Alpert, Sasha Anawalt, Houston A. Baker Jr.,
Beth Feldman Brandt, Tarana Burke, Carole Cary, Veronica
Chambers, Melissa Cotton, Helen Cunningham, Nancy
Hickman, Lorene Jackson, Debora Kodish, Hannibal
Lokumbe, Walter and Beverly Lomax, Isaac Miller, Biany
Perez, Susan Sherman, Laura Hagans Smith, R. C. Smith,
and Tina Smith-Brown

For courage:
Jenny Dietrich
John Hough

For hope and love,
Laura, Zoë, Ora and Sinayya, Samantha, Zachary, Joshua,
and Coleman